The
Suicide Note

J. McGregor Colt

J. McGregor Colt

2

Acknowledgments

I would like to thank Angie Jabine for her precise editing skills. She corrected my spelling, removed some commas and put them where they were more appropriate. And Cathey Flickinger, not only for her skills in graphic design, but, also for tolerating my lack of basic computer skills. Both these women are in Portland, Oregon and I recommend them highly.

I would also like to thank my good friend Suny Simon, my brother, Boyd Colt and my significant other, Jan Erickson, who all read an early version of this book and encouraged me not to give up. Thanks guys, without your input I would have just gone outside and pulled weeds or something.

J. McGregor Colt

Chapter
One

He maneuvers his pickup truck down a gravel road past the marina with sailboat masts towering overhead bobbing from side to side slowly in the gentle breeze. When he reaches the grassy shore with the rolling waters of the Columbia he parks head in, turns off the engine and just sits there. He waits alone there for about half an hour before the steel blue smoky sky erupts in an explosion of deep orange highlighting the scattered clouds above with a crimson red and the horizon below in a golden yellow. A teal blue ribbon cuts through the middle, separating the fury of violence and illuminating the rolling hills on either side of this majestic watershed. These hillsides, like bookends holding in the mighty waters, fade in the distance from a dark rich purple to a light lavender gray. Maxfield Parrish could not have defined a more spectacular sight. Windsurfers are out in abundance catching the last wind on what has been an ideal day for the sport.

5

J. McGregor Colt

He does not feel the dampness in the autumn air nor the chill that has permeated the interior from sitting so long without the engine running. Occasionally someone will pass in front and not notice him sitting behind the wheel, a jogger, an old lady walking her dog, windsurfers loading up their gear after a session on the water. He just sits there, eyes fixed on his house, or what used to be his house, across the river. He can see lights on and can make out the shape of a person occasionally passing in front of the massive living room windows but cannot make out if the person is child or adult, male or female…the house now has several of both.

While he sits in silence his mind dances around in the past. He revels in his successes, regrets his failures and imagines how things could have been if he had only done this or not done that. Had he taken those piano lessons his mother forced on him as a child seriously he could have been Elton John maybe or maybe Billy Joel; he fantasizes about being Billy Joel and being married to a beautiful fashion model and living in New York City and performing for thousands of admiring fans. He regrets not taking his studies more seriously and not being admitted to Harvard and not being Bill Gates's mentor and not investing in Microsoft or in Apple or in Intel and in all those high tech things that he knows absolutely nothing about but boy if he did he would be admired and respected by all. He sits there for a long time just imagining what it would be like to go back to his sixteen-year-old self with the knowledge he has at this moment. Of course he would not abuse these time-machine revelations he would have but what a powerful person he would be.

The Suicide Note

Another light comes on at the far end of the house. He knew it is the light in the master bedroom. His thoughts drift to the various things that have taken place in that bedroom over the past couple of years. He had participated in some pretty heated arguments with his wife and some pretty heated sexual experiences, also with his wife, in that end of the house and he wonders what might be going on in there at that moment. He fantasizes that his ex-wife is having a heated sexual experience at that very moment. He envisions her with her legs in the air and spread wide for another man and can hear her screams of pleasure. It tears him up, he is emotionally obliterated with the vision that has trespassed over the boundary of his already discontented mind.

A young, attractive woman jogs by and he is diverted by the loveliness of her tiny rear end squeezed inside her tight-fitting stretch pants. His eyes follow her bottom until she disappears into the darkness. He has had a very active libido and begins reminiscing about his sexual exploits, his former girlfriends and the wonderful sexual experiences he has had over the course of his fifty years. He remembers what it was like to hold a naked woman next to him, to feel her firm breasts and to gently rub his hands over her round bottom. He remembers all of those things, including the pleasure he got from his ex-wife. She is the most beautiful, the most sensual and the most willing of all the other women he had experienced. He thinks about satisfying himself but refrains.

His mind drifts back to his childhood, to all the various places he had lived as a child. He wonders what things could have been like had he confronted his stepfather about his alcoholism; if he had been able to talk his stepfather into a life

7

J. McGregor Colt

of sobriety, how things might have been different. He wonders what his biological father might have been like. He fantasizes about a life of luxury with a loving father who would have taken him fishing, would have played catch with a ball, taught him how to ski and how to play golf. He regrets not having that kind of a father. He imagines growing up wealthy, what that might have been like. He imagines growing up loved, what that would have been like.

An odd thing that he has carried with him in the back of his mind all his adult life is a type-written note that someone had thumbtacked to the bulletin board hung in the hallway outside the headmaster's office. He had spent a lot of time in his high school years in the headmaster's office so he was very familiar with the bulletin board. It displayed classroom changes, football game schedules, general announcements and the occasional words of wisdom. The particular note that he has always remembered read, "The rebels of today will be the leaders of tomorrow." He does not know who wrote it but he took it to heart. Now he is thinking that perhaps it was bad advice.

The longer he sits there in the pickup the more disappointments in himself he musters. Why had he not stayed with his first girlfriend, the one from high school; she loved him, adored him and would have done anything for him. He disappointed her and disappoints himself at the thought. Why had he dropped everything and run off to Europe with a floozy? She used him, cheated on him and he is very disappointed in his poor judgment. What, he wondered, ever became of that Australian girl he lived with in Switzerland? Why had he squandered away years on heavy drinking and cocaine use? He knows that he could have been much

8

The Suicide Note

further ahead in the game had he not done that and he is disappointed in himself for his own weakness.

He can make out some activity in the house across the river, lights on and off, people walking around inside. His thoughts turn to how hard he had worked to get such a nice house with a pool and a view of the river and the bridge and how prestigious it is to own such a house. He reminds himself of the extravagant parties at the house, the pool parties for the kids, the friends that would come over and just hang out. There are many nice things he is capable of remembering but these niceties do not last very long because the ugly things overwhelm. The bad always seems to overwhelm the good, he thinks.

Tears fill his eyes as he thinks about his siblings. He has a brother and a sister to whom he is not close. His brother lives far away but his sister is not that far. She has tried to stay in touch with him over the years but he always pushes her away. He wonders if he has done that because he wants nothing to do with any part of his long-dead stepfather. He regrets the way he has treated his siblings in their adult years and tries to remember good things about his childhood with them. He cannot.

Once again his mind returns to his most recent past. He angers at how he has been treated, at how he has been treated by his friends, by his family, by his ex-wife and by the court in the State of Washington. During the course of his divorce proceedings he had been accused of being a wife-beater, a child-molester and a drug addict. He is none of those things but the court ruled against him and he lost eighty percent of his net worth. At fifty years old he has been sentenced to start all over again. This he feels he cannot do and with a trembling hand he reaches over and grips the handle of the

9

J. McGregor Colt

object resting on the passenger seat next to him. As he reaches over and looks down he doesn't recognize his own hand, he isn't even sure who he has become or how he even got to where he is. At that moment he has lost contact with his own essence.

10

Chapter
TWO

Benjamin always had a lot of friends; he was friendly to most people and well liked as a result. There were very few people he encountered throughout the duration of his multifarious and arcane life that did not take a liking to him because he made it easy for them. He attracted people to him without putting out much of an effort. He was charming and he was good-looking. Being good-looking helped with getting the door open but it was his charm on which he glided freely into recesses of the willing person's mind.

I never really had any true friends.

The first significant day in the life of Benjamin B. Mathews—other than the day his mother gave birth to him in the back seat of his grandmother's one-week-old Coronet

11

J. McGregor Colt

Blue 1949 Packard Super Eight, or the day he and his, usually cold and unengaged, father stood out in the backyard on an evening after dinner by the clothesline and looked up into the clear, star-sprinkled sky together in search of the passing Russian Sputnik, or the day he got caught shoplifting a pack of chewing gum in the drugstore next to the school bus stop and was taken downtown to the police station and waited in terror for his, this time, hot and outraged father, to pick him up—is the damp and gray Pacific Northwest day in mid-January that he is placed by his concerned parents in a private college prep school for boys in a brand new town on the opposite end of the country and three thousand miles away from anyone he knew other than his parents and his two insignificant, at this stage in his life, siblings.

It is now the middle of his ninth grade year in school, he is fifteen years old and at a point of uncertainty in his life, a point of transition where he senses something of importance is impending. He hasn't yet nailed down what is going to happen but he senses that something is supposed to happen and he knows that whatever it is had better happen pretty quickly or he is going to have to take matters into his own hands. There is a feeling of uneasiness or an anxiety that consumes most teenage boys at this fragile time in their lives and Benjamin is not immune, he too is stricken by angst.

He has just passed that irritating and often-times even painful hash mark in the sand of time known, universally, as puberty, has survived the threat of nuclear destruction by the evil empire of the United Soviet Socialist Republic, has endured the wrenching heartbreak shared by the world of the Kennedy assassination, and has been filled with delight and a

12

The Suicide Note

tad bit of envy by the Beatles' introduction to North America on The Ed Sullivan Show. He is frightened, sad and excited all at the same time and just when there seemed to be a lull in the action he is transplanted from suburban Hampton, Virginia where his father had been stationed at Langley Air Force Base, to a base outside suburban Tacoma in the State of Washington, a place so remote and foreign to him that he had to look it up on a map and still isn't really sure of where he has landed.

Everyone at The Puget Academy had grown up together. Their parents are well off; doctors, lawyers and Indian chiefs, not real Indian chiefs of course but rather dentists and chiropractors who made a great deal of money and figured themselves to be superior in some way to the common folk and therefore chiefs of their own egos. It was with an assumption of superiority that these parents joined together the previous decade to form a private boys' day school so their little darlings would not have to endure the crass proletariat masses populating the public school environment in their sheltered suburban community of Ponder Point; it offered them yet one more thing in the array of successes each were consumed with to brag about to one another in their own pretentious ways at the Ponder Point Golf & Country Club on Saturday night after the husbands played a round of golf and after the wives had attended to their children's various sporting activities, completed the grocery shopping, had their hair done and their nails properly manicured. Now they were being introduced to a newcomer and had, not likely, ever been introduced to a newcomer before and certainly no one as unlikely as Benjamin.

13

J. McGregor Colt

Benjamin is an unassuming boy of medium build, a good height-weight ratio as they say, with straight dark shiny chocolate hair, cropped such that it covers his forehead and tickles the top of his ears. In contrast to his dark hair he has fair skin and striking, bright cerulean blue eyes. It is these eyes that mesmerize most people upon first encounter. Benjamin is an attractive young man with a bright smile and a commanding presence but on this day he stands awkwardly and appears very much out of his element in a sports coat and tie. The coat he is wearing is too large and hangs loosely off his shoulders as he is escorted into the assembly room by Mr. Edgar T. Pelegrini, the headmaster, and shown where he is to sit. Mr. Pelegrini always wears a bow tie. There is truly nothing masculine about a bow tie and the fact that he wears such a thing contributes to the nickname "Pelegrini the Weenie." The students at The Puget Academy are required to wear a coat and tie and as Benjamin did not own such things he is wearing one of his father's sports coats and a clip-on tie, which he will soon learn is gauche, tacky, base, unacceptable by these new standard bearers to whom he will now need to adjust, his mother bought the day before so he had something for the occasion.

Mr. Pelegrini soon announces that Benjamin's father is a sergeant in the United States Air Force and has just been transferred to the base down the freeway. As The Weenie drones on Benjamin shrugs humbly and looks back across a room of a little over a hundred of his fellow students, about a dozen teachers and an assortment of other staff now stretching and turning to get a glimpse of him. Benjamin's preconceived disdain for the circumstances he is being forced

14

The Suicide Note

to endure and any defiance he may have envisioned wanes quickly as a crimson glow overtakes his face, revealing not only embarrassment but also the fact that he isn't so tough as he wants to appear. The community, especially the families at The Puget Academy, rarely mixed with anyone from the Air Force Base. The Air Force people keep to themselves, consumed with family activities and community centers on base, and the local community keep to themselves as well. The general feeling in town is that military people are inferior in some way. They have their own schools, their own stores, movie theaters and recreational facilities and never had any reason to come in to Ponder Point. The enlisted men would frequent the bars and nightclubs in the more questionable areas out by the Interstate and there would be stories of trouble and fights and arrests and such but The Puget Academy families are well insulated from all that.

The Puget Academy families are the upper crust of Tacoma, Washington in the 1960s. The Ponder Point area of Tacoma, especially Ponder Point Farms with the towering Douglas firs lining serpentine driveways leading to mansions on the lake built by timber barons, brain surgeons, law firm partners and orthodontists, Ponder Point Golf and Country Club with its sprawling links, well-manicured greens and Gatsbyesque clubhouse on the shores of Ponder Lake, is the stomping ground for all the pampered boys and the likes of Benjamin Mathews are simply not welcome. They do not suffer newcomers well and certainly not some GI's kid.

Ponder Lake is a large, peanut-shaped natural lake about four miles long and about a half a mile wide at its narrowest point. It is popular in the region for boating and fishing and

15

J. McGregor Colt

accommodates two public parks with boat ramps for the locals to enjoy its abundance. On one end of the lake is Ponder Point Golf & Country Club and the upscale neighborhood of Ponder Point Farms where most of The Puget Academy families live and on the other end is the Air Force Base where Benjamin and his family live.

Immediately following the morning assembly, having survived the usual faculty announcements, a sermon from the school chaplain and a lecture on ethics and morals from the headmaster, the newcomer is introduced. Benjamin stands up in front of his chair and blushes his acknowledgment. He remains standing in manifest discomfort as Mr. Pelegrini tells his brief history and asks that all make him feel welcome. Afterwards they scuffle on to various classrooms and all is quickly forgotten regarding Benjamin Mathews.

Puget Academy includes students from kindergarten through twelfth grade separated into two areas of a 200-acre campus bordered by thick forest to the north, a crashing creek to the east, small farms to the west and a middle-class housing development to the south. Several of the faculty members and their families live *Leave It to Beaver* style in that neighborhood.

The Upper and Middle School share one building and the Lower School another and about in the middle of both is the gym. Almost everyone turns out for sports. There are only a few who do not... the "sports dodgers." These less-athletic types are not so much picked on or ridiculed for being sports dodgers as they are revered because they are mostly of exceptionally high IQ. The only thing more respected than

16

The Suicide Note

being a star athlete at Puget Academy is being an Honor Roll student. The boys are taught to perform on the sports field and in the classroom as well. They are being groomed for the Ivy League, for Stanford, for prestigious institutions of higher learning and certainly not for some community college or trade school. They are being groomed for success and for leadership. Unfortunately what comes with all this grooming is the predisposition to being an incorrigible snob. Their parents are snobs, the children are little brat snobs and Benjamin catches on to that rather quickly.

That first day, as everyone leaves the assembly to head for class, Benjamin is shunned. He is escorted to class by the headmaster, introduced to Mr. Hartley, a hard-nosed history teaching football coach or hard-nosed football coaching history teacher, depending on one's perspective, and sits down in a fog of confusion. It is quickly apparent the moment Benjamin joins this new world that everything is way over his head. The classroom lessons are over his head and the general social structure of things is way over his head. He is ignored throughout the morning classes, sits alone at lunch and ignored some more in the afternoon. No one even hears him speak until Sports.

Football is now over and basketball season is just beginning. At Puget Academy there are no choices. A student plays football in the fall, basketball in the winter and baseball in the spring. There are no choices except one... "The Play." If you are in the school play you are excused from sports, actually; if you are in The Play you are excused from pretty much everything. The play is not just a haven for the Sports Dodgers because some of the better athletes are also in the

17

J. McGregor Colt

school play. The play is highly respected and acting roles are highly sought after by all who attend The Puget Academy. The school produces one play a year and it takes over half the year to rehearse and build sets. At the end, the performance sells out the Ponder Point Theater in town year after year. The Puget Academy play is a major social event and fundraiser for the school.

Benjamin emerges from the locker room in the gym for Middle School basketball practice dressed in brand spanking new and crisp school-color-green gym shorts, which hang like a ballerina's tutu from his waist. The T-shirt he had been wearing under his clothes all day, colored socks with, coach-borrowed, gym shoes are the only accessories to the gym shorts. Not being aware of the proper procedure he had not brought any of his own gym gear. He stays close to the coach during practice, does what he is asked, albeit, poorly as Benjamin is clearly not an athlete, and never says anything. Whispered ridicule of him becomes more vociferous by the end of the drills and quite excruciating by the end of scrimmage.

There is a ten- or fifteen-minute free time after practice to play a little ball before retreating to the locker room to shower, dress and get ready for home. Several students start shooting baskets at the end of the court away from the Upper School players as Benjamin lingers nearby as an observer. Shortly Dan Spence, the requisite bully, starts picking on and taking the ball away from Robby Beasley, the requisite nerd. Benjamin is experienced with bullies. He reflects on past encounters he has with his own bullies and wonders what makes bullies bully. Was it some sense of inferiority

18

The Suicide Note

the bully had about himself? Was it a result of being bullied by an older sibling or a father? As he thinks this through the scene unfolds. Dan evolves from innocent teasing to taunting ridicule to worse as Robby whines.

At one point Dan flings the ball into Robby's face, drawing a little blood from his nose and bouncing the ball in Benjamin's direction. Benjamin grabs the ball in commanding fashion and dribbles off slowly and deliberately in the opposite direction away from the bully and his prey.

"Hey, new geek, how 'bout the ball?" Dan insists and Benjamin keeps dribbling.

Dan looks to the sidelines for approval or for the acknowledgment that he is not going completely crazy and that there are other witnesses to the disrespect being displayed by this person of unknown origin.

"The ball, the ball, you idiot!" Dan repeats with no response.

Dan is committed at this point and has to follow up. He couldn't just let Benjamin dribble away with the ball. The onlookers all stand in silent anticipation of Dan's rage as he runs up to the newcomer and grabs him on the shoulder from behind. Benjamin turns and throws the ball, smack, full force into the face of his attacker. Dan falls to the floor and there is another bloodied nose. What happens next is quite possibly the main event that places Benjamin in an elevated position in his new little society.

"How do you like it, asshole?" Benjamin challenges.

Dan lunges at Benjamin's feet and drags him down to the floor where an awkward wrestling type of encounter proceeds. Benjamin had never been in a fight before and

J. McGregor Colt

really doesn't know what to do other than to avoid getting punched. He doesn't have the desire nor the ability to inflict pain on another human and has never learned how to do so. Whenever he tries to punch there is something inside him that holds back his arm and his punches go nowhere. It is very fortunate for him that this attack is short-lived.

Just a few moments before the assault a few of the Upper School basketball players drift down to their end of the gym and are able to separate the brawling underclassmen before too much physical damage is endured by either participant but Dan wants to keep going. He is being held back as he is yelling and promising retaliation and it is John Clements, the Captain of the Varsity basketball team and Junior Class President who steps up in Benjamin's defense. John gets right up close in Dan's face and tells him that if there is going to be any more of this nonsense that it will be he whom he would be fighting.

All the boys are stunned at this. John is the idol of all the kids in Middle school. John is a Junior who has everything going for him. He is remarkably handsome, has a great wit, is the star of all athletic endeavors and has already been accepted to Yale, which gives him the respect of all. John has stepped in on the side of the newcomer and a whole new light is shining on the situation.

Slowly the varsity team reassembles to the other end of the court and the underclassmen retreat to the locker room in silence, get dressed, and disappear into the awaiting vehicle of a parent or chauffeur. So ends the most significant day in the life of Benjamin Brian Mathews... or at least one of them.

20

Chapter
Three

Benjamin's mother, Gloria Newton Mathews, is from a wealthy New York family... at least they were wealthy before the Great Depression. Gloria grew up with privilege and money until she was about ten or eleven years old. Her father owned the only silk importing business in North America and was very successful but when the Depression hit, one of the first thing people learned to live without was silk. J. Raymond Newton Importers had been a thriving business for two and a half decades. The Newtons owned a very large waterfront estate on Long Island, had a summer place at the Jersey Shore and their children wanted for nothing. Eventually

21

J. McGregor Colt

J. Ray, as he was commonly known, had to close down his once lucrative business and tighten his belt a bit. For a little while he was able to carry on the appearance; he had stashed aside a wad of money and everything continued on as usual for about two years but eventually the money dried up and the Newtons had to start giving up on some of their luxuries.

They sold the place at the Jersey Shore first. Then they began selling off artwork and then furniture in the home place. Gloria and her sisters did not really understand the significance of what they had grown accustomed to. They did not understand why they could not continue living the way they had been. It was very hard on them but not nearly as hard as it was when they found their father hanging by a rope in the carriage house. J. Ray Newton committed suicide and had left a note blaming himself for failing his family and apologizing to his daughters. His daughters never forgave him.

After the Long Island estate was sold at auction Gloria's mother took her three daughters and moved to Harrisburg, Pennsylvania where she had a sister who was able to put them up. It was a drastic lifestyle change for all of them. They went from a pampered life with servants to a rural life on a farm where they grew their own vegetables and slaughtered their own chickens. The Great Depression had also hit Pennsylvania farmers.

Gloria was eighteen when World War II broke out in Europe and by that time was well fed up with farm living. She lasted about two years on the farm on the outskirts of Harrisburg and now had an avenue out. She had been taking nursing classes in town and once she got certified she joined the Army Medical Corps and shipped off to France.

22

The Suicide Note

During the war Gloria spent most of her time at temporary combat zone medical hospitals moving from place to place as needed. She saw the worst of war, young men blown to pieces physically and emotionally, covered in blood and dying. Limbs were being amputated without proper anesthesia and these boys were crying out for their mothers. Gloria comforted them the best she could as many died in her arms. She remained strong and steadfast in her resolve to serve her country in such a way and felt it her duty to comfort the wounded soldiers.

Johnny Blake was one such wounded soldier. Johnny was a young First Lieutenant who had taken some shrapnel in his leg. It was a minor wound but while he was in the field hospital he had become attracted to his young nurse. He discovered that she was from his hometown of Harrisburg and that he actually knew her aunt and uncle. He was relentless in his pursuit of her but never got anywhere. Gloria deflected Johnny's advances and eventually he was shipped back to his unit and the entire incident forgotten as Gloria had many more soldiers to attend.

After the war Gloria returned home to Harrisburg. By this time her mother, who was a very attractive woman herself, had fallen in love and was about to marry one of Harrisburg's most prominent citizens. Howard L. Monaghan was President of Harrisburg Bank & Trust and quite possibly the largest landowner in the area. He owned all the land on three sides of Gloria's aunt and uncle's place and his bank held the note on their place as well. Soon Gloria would be living, once again, a life of luxury. But she was lonely and without male companionship.

23

J. McGregor Colt

She attended her mother's wedding unescorted. Her two younger sisters were there along with their boyfriends. Her sisters knew everyone in attendance but Gloria had been away for a couple of years and didn't know anyone. After the ceremony a glamorous reception was held in the clubhouse of the prestigious Town & Country Club of Harrisburg. All of the high-you-mucky-mucks of Harrisburg were in attendance including First Lieutenant Johnny Blake and his parents.

Johnny was looking very dapper in his dress blues. He had served out the rest of his term, had returned stateside and was awaiting a discharge from duty. Gloria noticed him across the room right off. He was very handsome, something that she had not really focused on while on duty at the field hospital in France. Once Johnny noticed her he immediately crossed the room and said, "I have been very eager to meet up with you again."

Gloria blushed.

The two enjoyed a great deal of one another for the next couple of weeks. Johnny spent time with Gloria's mother and new stepfather and Gloria got to know Johnny's family. The Blakes were another prominent Harrisburg family who did very well financially during the war. Johnny's father was the CEO of Pennsylvania Pharmaceuticals, Inc. PPI had the government contract to supply pharmaceuticals to the United States Military during the war. It was very lucrative and made the Blakes millions. Gloria soon fell in love with Johnny. He was not only attractive to her physically but was also very charming and, apparently, also quite wealthy. Not yet having served out his entire obligation to the United States Army eventually Johnny had to return to duty at Fort Bragg

24

The Suicide Note

in North Carolina to await a discharge. He had not been at Bragg long when he was informed that he did not yet have enough "points" to be discharged and was going to be shipped out to the war in the Pacific.

At the end of the war in Europe soldiers were placed in one of four categories. The Category I soldiers remained in Europe as part of the occupying force. Category II soldiers were immediately redeployed to fight Japan. Category III soldiers were assigned to bases stateside and retrained before a reclassification to a Category I or II. Category IV soldiers were returned home and released from further duty. The whole thing was based on a complex point system. Johnny thought he had earned enough points to be placed into Category IV but the Army thought otherwise. Before he could say a proper goodbye to Gloria he was on a troop carrier crossing the Pacific.

Johnny was gone and Gloria was lonely once again. She had her own suite in the estate of her new stepfather but needed an outlet. The Monaghan estate was not the least bit modest. The five-story Victorian home boasted 17,000 square feet of luxury with too many bedrooms to count, a ballroom and a separate structure for accommodating quarters for servants, of which there were many. A short walk from the main house was the massive hay barn and sprawling horse stables. The Monaghans also bred their own foxhounds and there was a large kennel structure not too far but removed from the stables. Gloria quickly found a diversion from her loneliness and post war trauma at the stables.

She had learned to ride during the summers spent at the Jersey Shore as a child. Although she had not been on a

J. McGregor Colt

horse in many years the skill required quickly returned and she spent most days riding and caring for the horses. Her stepfather gave her a horse of her own and it was this horse that dominated her time for several months. There had been no word from Johnny and she cherished her time in the stable.

At the stable one morning she encountered a young stable hand about her age. Joe Mathews had served in the Pacific as an enlisted man in the Air Force and returned a decorated veteran. He had been awarded a Distinguished Flying Cross, the Bronze Star, a Purple Heart and was discharged as a Corporal. His family background was a bit sketchy; he had been a major juvenile delinquent as a teenager but when he returned to Harrisburg after the war as a hero Howard Monaghan gave him a chance and hired him to work in his stables.

Gloria held absolutely no romantic interest in Joe but spent the major part of her days with him and the horses. They got to know each other very well. He opened up to her and shared stories of his challenges overseas and she did likewise. They were good for one another in that they could vent regarding the adjustments with which they were struggling after the war. It was a very healthy friendship and soon they were both comfortable with themselves and were no longer holding the pent-up rage that had slowly grown in them over the atrocities of the war they had witnessed up close. This bond between them continued on for most of the summer of 1945 and in August the war in Japan came to an abrupt halt.

At the end of the war in the Pacific Johnny did not immediately return to Harrisburg but soon Gloria received a letter from him postmarked San Francisco. This was the first

26

The Suicide Note

letter she had received from him since he had been shipped off at the end of May. It was dated September 5, 1945, and held apologies for not writing, explanations of where he was and what he was doing, and professed his love for her. Johnny was apologetic and loving, Gloria was smitten and by Thanksgiving Johnny and his parents joined the Monaghan family in Harrisburg for a magnificent welcome-home, the-war-is-over feast. It was assumed that the young couple would now be married and start a family of their own.

The following year went by quickly. Johnny and Gloria spent a great deal of time with one another but not all the time. Gloria still spent time at the stables with her horse and visiting with Joe Mathews, whom she considered to be her best friend. She had no girlfriends and did not bond with Johnny as she could with Joe. On occasion Johnny would come down to the stables and they would go for a ride but Joe and Johnny kept their distance from one another. Joe did not like Johnny, thinking him to be just another overly privileged rich kid with no redeeming qualities. Gloria was an overly privileged rich kid but at least she had some redeeming qualities, including being very nice to look at. Johnny paid Joe no attention.

One day down at the stables Joe shared with Gloria his distrust of Johnny.

"He's a phony. I don't trust people who aren't themselves." Joe said.

"Oh, Joe, we're all phonies, don't you think?"

"I'm not. What you see is what you get. I am being myself."

"I think that the only time that we are ourselves is when we are by ourselves," Gloria proposed.

27

J. McGregor Colt

"That's ridiculous," Joe retorted as he threw a pitch of hay into one of the stables.

"The moment someone else walks into a room with us, we make certain adjustments. The moment we realize we are not alone we adjust to that reality."

The conversation was quickly spiraling over Joe's level of cognitive abilities.

"Oh, I don't know about all that," he uttered almost to himself.

"Yes, and the moment that we open our mouths to speak we are no longer being ourselves. We adjust our speaking, we adjust the manner of our speaking based on who we are speaking to…that's being phony. We are being ourselves inside our heads. Our thoughts are being ourselves but the moment we speak them it's phony. Everyone is phony. The only time we are not phony is when we are completely alone with our own thoughts."

"Wow, I don't know about that one, Gloria. I'm gonna have to give it some thought."

Joe had work to attend to and Gloria returned to the house. The two enjoyed each other's company and always ended their encounters feeling good about themselves.

It was a pre-Christmas dinner at the Blakes' house where Johnny and Gloria announced that they were engaged to be married. Gloria's mother was thrilled, Johnny's parents were thrilled and Howard Monaghan asked for another Scotch. Howard didn't really care too much for Johnny. He had not been impressed with him as a child running around the Country Club, he had not been impressed with him as a young adult before he shipped off to war, and he

28

The Suicide Note

was not impressed with the way he treated his stepdaughter. Howard Monaghan was very observant. He noticed that Johnny was a spoiled and pampered child and he noticed that it had carried on into his young adulthood. He noticed that Gloria did not receive a single letter from him while he was overseas. This is not someone Howard felt he could rely on and he did not think Johnny was someone that Gloria should rely on either but he remained silent on the subject and wished for them the best.

Now that they were engaged Gloria let her defenses down. Johnny had been trying to get her into bed with him but she repeatedly resisted his advancements. Gloria stood her ground; she was a virgin and was dedicated to remain so until marriage. They had planned a June wedding but Johnny was relentless in his pursuit of having his way with her well before that. He was familiar with the pleasures of the flesh and wanted Gloria's badly. On an evening in early spring they consummated their love. It was not the least bit romantic and was, in fact, awkward. Gloria found no pleasure in it and Johnny was abrupt in his exit from the premises after it was over.

For the next couple of days Johnny was absent. When he finally did come around he was either cold or irritable. The couple quietly bickered over silly things and when it got to planning the wedding they bickered loudly over that. They didn't really feel comfortable around one another anymore and did not have sex again. Johnny drifted away. He was tormented with something.

By the beginning of May, still six weeks from the impending nuptials, Gloria learned that she was pregnant.

29

J. McGregor Colt

She was devastated. In the 1940s unwed women did not get pregnant; at least not proper women as she most certainly was brought up to believe that she was. Johnny had, once again, been absent for several days and she had nobody in which to confide, nobody with whom to share her situation. She walked down to the stables, the only place she could find solace, and came upon Joe Mathews.

Joe was packing some personal belongings into a duffel bag. When she inquired what he was up to he informed her that he was planning on rejoining the Air Force. He confided that he had not really been happy as a civilian and that he had found comfort and self-worth by being part of a military unit. She encouraged him, tried to compose an understanding demeanor but eventually broke down in tears. Joe was uneasy about offering comfort but Gloria broke and wrapped her arms around Joe's neck and collapsed into him. He held her in his arms and let her cry it out. He wasn't sure what she was crying about but he was pretty sure it wasn't because he was going off to the Air Force.

When she regained her composure she confided in her best friend that she was pregnant, didn't want to be pregnant and wasn't really sure she even wanted to marry Johnny Blake. It was all very dramatic and quite cathartic. Joe wasn't sure what to do with this new information or what else to do to comfort Gloria but he knew he had to get going or he would miss the bus to Wichita Falls, Texas to report for duty at Sheppard Air Force Base. When they said goodbye to one another they kissed. It wasn't a peck on the cheek, best-friend sort of a kiss, it was a long full on the lips, I've always loved you kiss. When they separated they both knew what the other needed.

30

The Suicide Note

After that day in the stable several more days passed before Johnny showed up again. When he did, he was drunk. He had been drunk a lot that spring and the wedding was rapidly approaching. Johnny was suffering from what now is called Post Traumatic Stress Disorder. He seemed to always be drinking, was being abusive and Gloria had not yet told him she was pregnant. It all came to a head one day three weeks before the scheduled wedding.

Gloria caught Johnny at a rare sober moment and told him that she was expecting. At first Johnny was furious. He accused her of sleeping with the stable boy. He let her know that he had observed how they were around one another and that she was not fooling anybody. She broke down in tears and assured him that she had never before or after slept with a man other that the one and only night that they had been together. Johnny calmed down but left. He was very agitated.

Again Johnny went missing. Several more days passed and one afternoon the Dauphin County Sheriff came to the Monaghan Estate and met privately with Howard Monaghan. When the two emerged from Howard's private study they looked very somber. After the sheriff left it was Howard's job to inform his stepdaughter that her fiancé had committed suicide. After he informed her of the devastating news he handed her an envelope and left her to herself. The envelope contained a letter from Johnny blaming himself and apologizing to their unborn child. It was rubbish, she thought and mirrored the letter that her own father had written several years prior. She was more disgusted than upset.

As time progressed it was getting more difficult for Gloria to hide the fact that she was pregnant. She finally told her

31

J. McGregor Colt

sisters and then her mother. All kept the secret but eventually something needed to be done. In those days the unwed mother-to-be was sent away somewhere. While all the options were being discussed Joe Mathews returned from Air Force mechanic training camp. It was Howard who mentioned one night at the dinner table that he had seen Joe in town dressed in his uniform. Gloria's attention was piqued and the next day she drove herself into town and looked him up.

Joe's parents did not live in one of the nicer neighborhoods of Harrisburg and Gloria's car did not go unnoticed by the poorly clad neighbors sitting on their front stoops. Gloria parked in front Joe's parents' house and as she exited the car four or five neighborhood hoodlums approached her in an intimidating manner with cat calls and "hey babies." Within seconds Joe came out of his house and got in the middle. It was obvious that the boys were afraid of Joe and immediately respected his request to vamoose.

Gloria and Joe sat on the door stoop and talked for a couple of hours. She told him about Johnny. Joe told her he was being stationed to Langley Air Force Base near Hampton, Virginia to further train as a jet engine mechanic and that he had been promoted to Staff Sergeant. They had a great talk and agreed to stay in touch. While Joe was at Langley he wrote to Gloria every day and whenever he had a three-day pass he would catch a bus to Harrisburg and spend time with her.

By the end of his advanced training Gloria was eight and a half months pregnant and not even making an attempt to hide it anymore. She lived at the Monaghan Estate and never went out. When Joe was home on short leaves they would spend time together walking around the estate. Howard

32

The Suicide Note

liked Joe and welcomed his presence. Not so much with Gloria's mother but eventually she came around realizing that her daughter had very little chance landing a man with a baby in tow.

One afternoon while on a walk with Joe, Gloria's water broke. They were about a half-mile away from the house and Gloria could hardly walk. Joe picked her up and carried her back to the house. Her screams could be heard from the house and when Gloria's mother saw what the situation was she yelled at Joe to take her car. Joe gently placed Gloria into the back seat of a brand new V-8 Packard and roared on down the driveway towards town and the nearest hospital. Gloria was in a great deal of pain and could not hold back the crowning baby trying to escape her womb. By the time the Packard screeched into the circular driveway of the emergency entrance to Harrisburg General Hospital she was giving birth. Joe ran in and got a nurse to come out and assist. Gloria gave birth to a baby boy in the back seat of her mother's car at 3:27 p.m. on December 2, 1948. It was a Thursday.

What happened next was complicated. Since Joe had been the one to bring Gloria to the hospital the nursing staff needed his information. Joe provided his full name and date of birth as requested. When Gloria was asked for the first name and middle name of the baby she replied Benjamin and Brian. Both Joe and Gloria had their minds elsewhere and did not give much thought to the questions they were being asked by the nursing staff. The next day a nurse came into the room while Joe was sitting on the bed watching Gloria holding her new baby and asked them to sign the birth certificate. The certificate read Benjamin Brian Mathews and listed Joseph

33

J. McGregor Colt

Ryan Mathews as the father. Before Joe could say anything Gloria asked the nurse if they could have some privacy. Once the nurse cleared the room Gloria whispered into Joe's ear. "Well, I guess you gotta marry me now, Sarge."

A week later they were married at the courthouse in Harrisburg and the next day hopped on a bus to Moody Air Force Base in Georgia. Benjamin was not aware of any of this until many years later on the ride home with his father from the Okaloosa County, Florida Sheriff's office after having stolen a pack of gum from the drug store by the bus stop outside the main gate at Eglin AFB. Sergeant Joe Mathews, fed up and outraged with his son's attitude, chose that moment to tell Benjamin that he was not actually his son but, rather, his stepson. He explained to Benjamin that he had adopted him, raised him out of the kindness of his heart and that he and his mother could have easily given him up for adoption as was the custom of the time. It was at that moment that Benjamin started to understand why his father, or stepfather as he now understood it to be, treated him differently than he treated his younger brother and sister.

34

Chapter
Four

For the remainder of his first year at The Puget Academy Benjamin keeps to himself and the rest of the boys keep to themselves except for the occasional opportunity they have to make fun of him. It is David Clements who is the instigator and the one who makes fun of him more than anyone else. It is a jealousy sort of a thing with David. The rest of the boys make fun of him because David does. David is the de facto leader, the commander of attention and will not allow anything but total domination of any situation.

Benjamin, on the other hand, is charming. The faculty like him although he is neither a particularly good student nor a

35

J. McGregor Colt

notable athlete but he is enthusiastic and personable. The parents like him as he is amusing to most, respectful to all and always seems to be of good cheer. The moment that Benjamin does not have a smile on his face is rare. Girls ask about him. David hates that the most. They want to know who he is and go on about how "cute" he is. This is all very annoying to David who, up till now, has always been the center of attention among his peer group.

David does all he can to discredit Benjamin and, for the most part, has the majority of his classmates on board. He goes out of his way to draw attention to Benjamin's lack of social qualifications. Benjamin lacks polish, he lives on a military base and his father drives a beat-up old Ford. These factors are totally and completely inferior in all ways to the requirements of their social hierarchy. Nonetheless, Benjamin burrows his way into the hearts of the many he encounters.

David Clements' father is a nationally respected heart surgeon and had developed a special plastic heart valve used to replace failed versions of the valve we are all born with. This brought him fame and money but is not the only source of the Clements' wealth. Mrs. Rose Wyrich Clements is a Wyrich and that alone is enough to give the family a very prominent place in the social order of the entire Pacific Northwest if not the entire country. Rose is the granddaughter of Wolfgang Otto Wyrich.

Wolfgang Otto Wyrich was a German immigrant who migrated west and formed what eventually became the largest timber company in the world. Wyrich slowly bought out competing companies and made huge purchases from

36

The Suicide Note

the railroads to assemble what became the largest privately owned land holding in the nation. He eventually settled in Tacoma and started a family after marrying the daughter of the second-largest privately owned landowner in the country. Rose Clements' brother is the President and CEO of The Wyrich Company at this moment.

On one occasion at David's family dining table his mother asks who this Benjamin Mathews is. She seems genuinely interested in knowing him. Before David is able to malign, big brother John praises.

"He's a great kid, lives on the Air Force Base; his dad is a sergeant or something. He's a real nice guy. Dave and his brat buddies pick on him all the time."

"David, why?" his mother queries, "why do you find it necessary to belittle yourself so? You must learn to be more tolerant and find compassion for those less fortunate than yourself. I happen to know that the Mathews family have sacrificed a great deal to send Benjamin to Puget and you do not need to make matters any harder for them." ...

David is devastated. Both his mother and his older brother have landed on the side of his nemesis and he is being reprimanded at the dinner table in front of the servants. Even his father is raising an eyebrow in his direction; what humiliation he endures.

For the remainder of the year David stays away from Benjamin and stifles all ridicule. Benjamin simply becomes a non-issue with David and, if mentioned, he figures a way to draw the attention elsewhere.

That summer David's days are filled water-skiing with his brothers, lounging around the pool at the country club,

37

J. McGregor Colt

chasing the young, vivacious Sally Hobbs and Jiffy Sorenson around in their bikinis, and playing tennis with his friends. There are no Benjamin Mathews sightings and not too soon into the summer not even a mention. It is an out of sight, out of mind kind of a deal.

Benjamin makes the acquaintance, that summer, of another kid from the air base, Robert "Woody" Garwood. Woody is the son of Lt. Col. Archer Garwood, a well respected C-17 cargo jet pilot. These are the jets that Benjamin's father is trained to keep in the air. Usually the officers' kids do not socialize with the enlisted men's kids but Benjamin is an exception to this.

The two boys meet at the Teen Club on base which is open to both officers' and enlisted men's children. On Benjamin's first visit Robert Garwood introduces himself to Benjamin as Bob. Benjamin initially finds Bob to be a very talented fellow both in wit and athletic prowess, much more so than himself. This offers Benjamin somewhat of a challenge. Where Benjamin has been considered to be charming and good-looking perhaps Bob is considered to be even more so by the parents and peers with whom he encounters that summer. At The Puget Academy Benjamin had impressed many without exerting much effort but now he has some competition for attention and is often left in the shadow by Bob's presence. He does not, however, display any concern and this, in a way, only adds to his own charm. Bob and Benjamin make a good team and those with whom they come into contact share comfortably in the camaraderie.

Benjamin stays on base the whole summer and hangs out on the opposite end of the lake at the Officer's Beach Club. His relationship to Col. Garwood's son gains him access so

38

The Suicide Note

long as he is accompanied by an officer's dependent. It is there at the beach where he makes many new acquaintances and adds to his growing gaggle of admirers. And it is there that he meets Anna Kerr.

The young, nubile Anna is endowed with a classic beauty. She is a tall, svelte blond with the round face of a cherub, large oval sky-blue eyes, and has a freshness of nature about her. Her Scandinavian heritage is obvious as she stands far ahead of anything else nature has to offer yet there is an innocence that comes with the package. Anna is not aware of her head-turning, double-taking beauty and does not use it against her admirers or to her advantage in any way like many others might. She is truly a vision of innocent beauty and Benjamin is completely enamored with her the moment she comes into his field of view.

Benjamin also spends a great deal of time over at the Garwood quarters on base. Col. Garwood knows Sergeant Mathews as a diligent and respected jet engine technician who works on the planes he flies. He welcomes Benjamin into his home and treats him with respect. A male adult treating him with respect is something completely foreign to Benjamin and he begins to gain some self-worth as a result.

Bob has two older brothers who refer to him as "Woody." Benjamin picks up on the name quickly, assuming it is a nickname for Garwood. Bob doesn't much like being called Woody, it seems, but the name stuck and is used exclusively by everyone but Bob's parents. As Benjamin eventually learned, Woody is not a nickname for Garwood but, in fact, a name given to Bob by his older brothers because he always seems to have a bit of an erection.

39

J. McGregor Colt

Woody is a very horny guy and becomes sexually aroused at the slightest suggestion. At school he gets an erection while sitting at his desk and when the bell rings to announce that it is time to get up and go to the next class he has to gently maneuver out of his seat and place his books in front of his crotch to hide the bulge. It could be, at times, excruciatingly embarrassing for him. The nickname Woody is very appropriate and widely used despite any annoyances he may suffer.

Woody and Benjamin jostle for Anna Kerr's attention and in the end it is Benjamin who wins the prize. Woody is more demanding and has a possessive nature about him that Benjamin lacks. Benjamin is less self-confident and expects less from people. That makes him a wimp in the eyes of Woody but endears him to Anna. Demanding something of somebody or defending a position on a subject is where Benjamin falls short. He is unassuming in many ways and apparently Anna prefers this to the somewhat overbearing Woody.

Anna is, likely, the only thing Benjamin wins that summer. Woody is bigger, stronger, better-looking and more entertaining and his father outranks Benjamin's father by a significant amount. The fact is, when Woody is around Benjamin seems shy. If Benjamin will be coming out of his shell he is not going to be coming out soon with Woody around. Any shell cracking will have to come later but Benjamin, Woody and Anna hang out together all summer. Anna lines Woody up with a variety of girls she knows and they will double-date to the drive-in or to a teen dance. The highlight of the summer is taking the train to Seattle for the KJR Radio Summer Teen Spectacular where they see

40

The Suicide Note

Herman's Hermits and a variety of other popular groups. Anna cries when Peter Noone takes the stage and Benjamin realizes right then that he needs to be able to extract that kind of emotion from people, he needs to be that attractive to the masses. That desire festers deep in Benjamin for the rest of his life. He needs rock star acclaim.

When summer is over Benjamin returns to Puget Academy and Woody and Anna go to the local public high school in Ponder Point. When David Clements first sees Benjamin after summer break he realizes that he is in trouble. Benjamin has matured noticeably over the summer. He had been a good-looking kid already but now his baby fat has turned to muscle, he has gotten a bit taller and he now, at least, looks like an athlete. Others at the school greet him with good cheer and right off the bat he begins making alliances with David's friends. David is going to have a rough time shunning him.

The Puget Academy is demanding on its students; complex academics are taught and intricate academics are expected to be learned in return. The boys at Puget do not dawdle in the trivia of Hemingway or Crane as they do in the public school but, rather, dive deep into the complexities of Homer, of Dostoevsky, of Faulkner. Their time is not wasted in rote memorialization of the United States presidents order of succession or the names of the capitols of each state but is spent on understanding the meaning of such things and how they play out in the history of the country. Latin is taught, Greek mythology is studied and every student is expected to learn to speak French. There is also a strong focus placed on the arts. By graduation every student can hear the difference

41

J. McGregor Colt

between Classical music, Romantic music and Neo-Classical and most could identify the composer and name the piece. Impressionism, Cubism, Surrealism, and, of course, the Masters are all studied in depth. Parents make a large financial commitment to assure that their children will enter adult life a considerable step ahead of the pack. Athleticism is also emphasized.

Benjamin does not turn out for football but is friendly with all the football players. Being on the football team and attending the after-school practices required would put an undue burden on the transportation between the base and the school. Football is, therefore, neither practical nor is it encouraged by his parents. Being accepted and even sought out by the football players is, however, not normal. Usual and standard practice is that football players hang out with football players and sports dodgers hang out with sports dodgers. He is breaking the rules. But it all comes crystal clear on the Friday night of the first football game. Benjamin's connection with the girls at the Ponder Point High School has been something David Clements has completely overlooked.

Benjamin arrives to watch the Junior Varsity home field football game in a spectator capacity with an entourage of unknown faces in Anna and Woody and Woody's date, Leslie. The two girls' beauty is so distracting that the Puget players are falling over one another on the field. They lose the game and don't even care. They just want to get it over with, get back to the locker room, change and hang out with Benjamin and his entourage. After that, David immediately implements a plan to befriend Benjamin; he waves a white flag.

42

The Suicide Note

For the next several weeks David goes out of his way to hang out with Benjamin. They study together, become lab partners in biology and are general after-school chums. David invites Benjamin over to his house for a weekend and his parents love him. Big brother John starts stopping off at the base to pick him up for school so he doesn't have to take the bus with all the geeks. Benjamin quickly becomes a part of the Clements family and David is able to slowly pry him away from Woody. Now Anna is setting David up with her friends.

Woody and Benjamin still do things together and David gets left out only to hear of their adventures on a Monday morning. This is not working for David so whenever he can he needs to dangle a bigger carrot. David has a lot more carrots and a lot more to offer Benjamin than does Woody. He has a nicer house, a swimming pool, a ski boat and much greater privilege. After a time with this tug of war nonsense David relinquishes and starts including Woody in their activities.

By their junior year David's house is the hangout and Benjamin, Woody and David are an inseparable trio. David lives in a mansion on the lake inside the country club, all very hoity-toity and all very exclusive. The greatest thing, however, is that his parents travel a lot and don't keep track of the beer. Many weekends there will be half a dozen friends from The Puget Academy and Woody at the house for drunken orgies. Throughout their high school years at least a dozen Ponder Point High School girls lose their virginity at David's house.

Sex and beer is what drives them and Benjamin and Woody are the prime movers. They have all the girls at the public schools dying to be with the rich kids from The Puget

43

J. McGregor Colt

Academy and Benjamin is also able to get GIs on base to buy beer for them. It is a beautiful set-up. If one of them doesn't have a date for Friday night Benjamin or Anna will make a call and most any girl will break a date to be with one of them. They really have it made. Sex and beer keep them happy throughout their Junior year in school. Things are going very well for these young teenage boys.

On one occasion while driving back to the base from the Clements' house Woody turns to Benjamin while he is driving.

"Benjamin, I want you to start calling me Bob."

"What? Why? Everybody calls you Woody. Most people don't even know your name is Bob."

"Yeah, that's just it, my name is Bob. It's not Woody; my name isn't Woody. My asshole brothers started calling me that as a joke and now everyone is." He is starting to get agitated.

"I fucking hate that name, it's embarrassing."

This is the first time that Benjamin has seen this side of Woody. It is a weaker, vulnerable side and is not very becoming.

"So, look, Benjamin... if you would just start calling me Bob everyone will start calling me Bob. People respect you. They'll do what you do."

"Gee, I don't know, Woody, yer askin' an awful lot here." Benjamin says playfully. "Are you offering any money? I mean, what's in it for me?"

At this point Woody is very upset but they reach their destination and his two older brothers are sitting in the front yard so he has to be cool.

"How about I don't kick your fucking ass? That's what's in it for you." Woody replies in a low voice as he gets out of the car.

44

The Suicide Note

Benjamin never does refer to Woody as Bob but always loves telling the story as they get older. Eventually Woody just accepts his name and eventually he even comes to introduce himself as such.

Spring break of their junior year David's parents go to Hawaii with his younger brother and leave him behind. John is away at college so Benjamin, Woody and David have the whole house to themselves. Benjamin is still with Anna; he is a one-woman kind of a guy. Woody and David also have steady girls but one night they are all dateless and decide to go up to the Lake Hills Roller Rink in Bellevue for a teen dance. Their first stop is the Air Force Base for the requisite GI Beer where they buy two cases. They always buy massive quantities because they always drink entirely too much and they start drinking as soon as they get in the car.

They had taken Benjamin's mother's station wagon but David is driving with Woody riding up front and Benjamin in the back seat. Benjamin is the only guy who never found it necessary to sit up front, in fact, he preferred sitting in the back. There were great wrestling matches over the years to see who made it to the prized shotgun position and when they were over and the dust settled and the breathing got longer there would be Benjamin sitting quietly in the back waiting.

About half way up I-5 Woody and David get into a row about his driving. Woody is criticizing David's abilities as a driver and complaining that he is not capable of negotiating the vehicle within a single lane of traffic. This goes on for several minutes and when the comments become shrieks David pulls over to the shoulder and tells Woody to drive the car himself. Benjamin is sitting in the back in

45

J. McGregor Colt

silence through this whole exchange, drinking his beer and minding his own business. One would think that when David relinquishes the wheel to his critic that things would calm down and they would simply continue on their venture. The only problem is that David has pulled over on the left side of the freeway, the fast lane side of the freeway. Apparently this is illegal in the State of Washington.

As soon as Woody merges them back onto the freeway they are accosted by flashing red lights in the rear view. They, that is to say, Woody and David, are still arguing when the lights come on and after a moment of silent review of their situation, beer in the back, minors in possession... panic sets in. Woody does not pull over right away, however. Woody has a plan. They have a quick discussion about his plan and immediately take action. When Woody gets over to the right shoulder they bolt from the car, scurry up a hill, straddle a fence and disappear into the dark. David loses both Woody and Benjamin in the confusion and eventually makes it back to Ponder Point and to his house about two o'clock in the morning through his efforts hitchhiking.

The next day David doesn't hear one word from Woody or from Benjamin. He stays around the house alone all day, cleans and reorganizes his room, plays pool, watches television. He is a nervous wreck not knowing how things turned out for the other guys but he is afraid to call them. The following day is Sunday; his parents return and for a day he sort of forgets about the whole ordeal. When school starts up again on Monday David looks all over for Benjamin before Assembly. Nobody has seen him so he thinks maybe he is sick or something. Assembly starts and bow tie-clad Mr. Pelegrini gets up and makes a very grim announcement.

The Suicide Note

"Benjamin Mathews was arrested Friday night and thrown in jail, where he remains at this moment. He was arrested for possession of alcohol by a minor. There were two other boys with Benjamin Friday night who eluded the Washington State Patrol. Benjamin has not told the authorities who these two other boys are but I have assured them that it was no one from The Puget Academy. We know that Benjamin is of a somewhat lesser station in life and we were willing to take a chance with him. He has let us all down and we will not be seeing him here at Puget again."

The students are aghast at this announcement and a murmur swells in the room before the headmaster taps the podium with his signet ring.

"If you have the occasion to see Benjamin off campus I strongly urge you to give him a wide berth for he is no one with whom you should be associating."

At this point David's heart is racing. He does not know what Benjamin would say about his involvement. He does not know how he got arrested. Of course it was Benjamin's mother's car so he really doesn't know what or how to think. David's thoughts are of panic, fear overcomes him. After assembly all his friends come up to him and smother him with questions. David has to get out of there. They all know he was with Benjamin Friday night and David figures the idiots are going to give him away.

"Get the fuck away from me," he growls and rushes down the hall to his first class.

The day is an unpleasant mixture of anxiety and stealth. David is scared but can't show it without the risk of falling under suspicion. He tells everyone that Benjamin never

47

J. McGregor Colt

showed up at his house Friday night and that he did not know anything about what he did or who he did it with. Most buy off on that but he knows that he is not out of the woods yet.

Several days go by, David's parents quiz him intensely on the subject but he remains steadfast in his denial of all knowledge in the situation. Finally Woody calls. When Woody and David bolted up the hill Benjamin had stayed behind.

"The son-of-a-bitch went down with the ship." Woody proclaims.

Woody's story is similar to David's on how he had made it home and how he had handled his parents' inquisition but he had not yet talked to Benjamin. Neither of them know how strong Benjamin's resolve is to keep them out of it or if he has any resolve at all for that matter. Their conversation includes all the what-ifs and whys and ends without closure. Neither of them sleep well that night.

The next day Benjamin is enrolled at Ponder Point High. He is the big man on campus there. The hoods are in awe of him, the preppies are jealous of him and the girls marvel in him. He has them all eating from his hand. Big shot private-school-elitist-goes-bad and they love it. Benjamin doesn't feel so good about it, however. His parents took away all privileges, which include the air outside his house. Anna's parents forbid her to see him and Woody ridicules him for being stupid enough to stay in the car. Woody does not take into consideration that it was the car of Benjamin's mother and a little hard to explain how the car got to the side of the freeway filled with two cases of beer.

Benjamin never divulges to anyone who his partners were that night. Everyone at Ponder Point High suspects Woody's

48

The Suicide Note

involvement because Woody wants them to. He recognizes the attention it is bringing to Benjamin and he wants in on some of that. They are all isolated from Benjamin for the rest of the school year and neither David nor Woody have any socializing with him until early that summer.

While under house arrest, Benjamin endures the brunt of Sergeant Joseph Mathews' wrath and abuse. Over the years, as Joe was transferred from base to base, and as he advanced in rank, he became a hardened, no-nonsense man at home and gave in to the foibles of alcohol. Although his peers loved him and found him to be a fun-loving person to be around, his wife and children began to fear him and did everything they could to avoid anything that might set him off. Now that Benjamin is stuck at home it is difficult to avoid his stepfather's anger and abuse.

Joe would come home from work in the evenings, take off his coat, go directly to the kitchen, fill a large tumbler with ice and fill in the air spaces left in the tumbler with bourbon. At the first sound of the ice cube tray cracking in the kitchen Benjamin and his brother and sister would make themselves scarce. By suppertime Joe would have polished off two tumblers of bourbon, be in a very foul mood and looking for something or someone to take it out on. That outlet is usually Benjamin.

The Mathews family always has dinner together around the dining room table. From a distance it looks like a wholesome Norman Rockwell scene but in reality it is far from it. Joe is seated at one end of the table, eyes glassed over, the kids keeping their heads down, remaining silent and praying that they are not called on or singled out for some infraction. Benjamin's mother sits at the other end and

49

J. McGregor Colt

attempts to keep things calm by talking about the weather or the neighbor's cat or some innocent nonsense. Sometimes that would work but mostly it does not. Joe has become an angry and abusive alcoholic and Benjamin's home life a living hell.

Joe had not always been this way. It seemed to Benjamin that the anger and the abuse really kicked into gear after they moved to Virginia and Joe was promoted to Command Chief Master Sergeant. A rank of E-9 in the Air Force brings with it much more stress and responsibilities than Joe was used to. It was now Joe's job to report the goings-on of all the enlisted men in his Wing Unit to the officers in charge. No longer was he considered one of the boys. In Virginia Joe's job held more responsibilities and his peer group dwindled due to his advanced rank and job responsibilities. He was no longer just one of the boys griping about the bosses, he was one of the bosses. Prior to that time Benjamin remembers his parents as fun and party-loving people. There seemed to always be other adults over at the house and they were all enjoying each other's company. Most of the time the other adults would bring their kids along so Benjamin and his siblings had other kids to play with. The gatherings were loud and boisterous but not contentious. The contentious part grew in direct correlation to Joe's responsibilities.

By the time the Mathews moved to Ponder Point Joe was a full-blown, angry and abusive alcoholic and all his kids were terrified of him. When Joe barked out an order the kids obeyed and when they didn't do things to meet with Joe's expectations they were severely punished both mentally and, in Benjamin's case, physically. Benjamin has suffered beatings on numerous occasions but he shrugs it off as just a part of

50

The Suicide Note

life. Benjamin just figures that all kids go through what he was going through. He figures that all parents are degrading and abusive to their kids. It's all Benjamin knew until he started hanging out with some of the other Puget Academy families.

51

Chapter
Five

The summer between their junior and senior year in high school is the best time of Benjamin's life. His restrictions are lifted and he is welcomed back into David's house by David's parents. By this time the incident surrounding his arrest is forgiven and everyone has come to realize that Benjamin's father is an abusive alcoholic.

The only time I can remember ever enjoying life was the summer between my junior and senior year in high school.

David's mother takes Benjamin on as her own little rescue project. She forgives him his past indiscretions and makes a point of including him in all the Clements' family outings that summer. Benjamin cruises the San Juan Islands in David's grandparents' yacht, goes to Eastern Washington with

52

The Suicide Note

David, John and their father to go fly fishing, and joins the Clements family for dinner at fancy restaurants in Seattle on a few occasions. Benjamin has never done any of these things with his own family. He enjoys himself immensely and isn't afraid to show his appreciation. He is entertaining, a constant source of jokes and interesting conversations. Benjamin is really happy.

Anna's parents are a different story, however. They are still forbidding their daughter to associate with a criminal. It isn't so much that they are afraid Benjamin will steer their daughter down the wrong path, as it is they want her to associate more with David Clements. Anna's parents are big-time social climbers. Her dad is retired from the military and they are living off-base now and acclimating to civilian life. They think that a wealthy surgeon's kid would be a good catch for their darling Anna.

The boys easily find a way around the Benjamin blockade at the Kerr house. Whenever they have dates Benjamin and David pick up Anna first. Benjamin gets out of the car around the corner and David goes up to the Kerr house as if he were her date. Anna and David leave together, pick up Benjamin and then go get David's date. David gets to know Mr. and Mrs. Kerr pretty well and they get along very well. It is a good arrangement. There are a couple of occasions that they leave Benjamin hanging on the corner a little too long while hobnobbing with the parents and he is fuming by the time they pick him up but, other than that, it works out pretty well for him. He has a very good deal going. He gets to go out with the prettiest girl in town and doesn't have to play the insincere sycophant with her socially aspiring parents.

J. McGregor Colt

Benjamin and David don't see much of old Woody that summer. He is hanging out with the public school crowd. He has new friends and a new attitude. Woody is a tough guy and has a huge inferiority complex that makes him short on the ability to handle criticism or, at least, what he perceives to be criticism. He is always looking for a fight it seems. The three drift apart but Benjamin alway stays in touch with him. David really doesn't understand the attraction Benjamin holds for Woody except to note that Benjamin always feels it is necessary for everyone to like him and that would include Woody, he assumes.

That summer Benjamin's father retires from the Air Force and the mental abuse bestowed from father to son magnifies. The Mathews family moves off base into a home they purchase in town. It is a nice home in a middle-class neighborhood. The house is not something Joe could have purchased on his own military retirement. Mrs. Mathews, who was still close to her family back in Harrisburg, plays a major role in its purchase and it is relatively close to Ponder Point Farms, the upscale neighborhood where The Puget Academy families live.

Knowing that he cannot provide adequate housing for his family, coupled with his inability to blend in with a civilian life-style, make The Sarge, as he has come to be known, drink even more. He would get drunk and make Benjamin stand at attention in front of him as he barraged insults.

"You will never amount to anything."

"What is wrong with you?"

"Are you stupid?"

"Your little brother is twice the man you will ever be."

54

The Suicide Note

"You're a loser."

This is pretty hard on Benjamin but he never talks about it.

He sees the great relationship the rest of his friends have with their fathers and he is too embarrassed to let on that his is not the same.

The only thing that is truly important to Benjamin and his friends is getting laid. Few of them had been and the ones that claim they have are probably lying about it. They devise all sorts of schemes to accomplish this feat. Nothing will deter them and nothing is beneath them in their endeavors. If they would have had access to the "date rape drug" they certainly would have tried it on their girlfriends, who were just as determined to remain virgins as they were to not. A case of Sunday morning blue balls becomes fashionable.

Billy Reece's grandparents have a beach place on Lawrence Island that they hardly ever use anymore because they have moved to Arizona. Lawrence Island in the Puget Sound is accessible by bridge and close enough to Ponder Point that they can go there, party, and still be back in time to deliver their girlfriends to the protective custody of their parents by midnight. The Reeces' beach place soon becomes known as the Lawrence Island Pleasure Palace or LIPP. The LIPP has an abundance of bedrooms with doors that shut and is completely isolated from any neighbors.

One by one, new young nubile prey lose their virginity at the LIPP... with the exception of one. Benjamin is not successful in his endeavors with Anna. It is either because he respects her more than the others respect their victims or because he does not have the killer instinct, the drive.

55

J. McGregor Colt

Eventually he gives up with her and starts going out with Melissa Stewart.

Melissa is not as attractive as Anna but she has one overshadowing attractive attribute—she is a willing sexual partner. The choice is simple. Benjamin and Melissa have sex almost every weekend out there and the whisper of a LIPPster becomes their mantra. When the LIPP is not available they find other locales; cars, boats, lawns. They spend the better part of the summer exploring each others body parts and discovering mutually satisfying sexual pleasures. Melissa would much rather spend an evening with Benjamin in the back seat of his mother's station wagon than attend a movie or a dance with him.

It is about midsummer when all hell breaks loose over at Benjamin's around the dinner table. He and his friends have plans for a big party over at the Sharps' house for that night. Ted Sharp's parents are in Europe and the boys have lined up a bunch of beer and girls and are going to have an orgy, or at least that's what they envision. The girls, surely, have something of a lesser thing in mind. At the dinner table Benjamin's by then drunk and abusive father informs him that he is not going anywhere that night and demands that he hand over the car keys. A little bickering back and forth and Benjamin, who has never stood up to his father before, screams out: "You're a drunk and you're always wrecking everything for me. Why don't you just leave me alone?"

As they both rise to their feet The Sarge responds, "Yeah and what the hell are you going to do about it, boy?"

Benjamin turns, goes to the kitchen, reaches in the liquor cabinet, grabs the first bottle he sees and pours it down the sink.

56

The Suicide Note

"This is what I am going to do about it!"

Benjamin is trembling in fear at this point. The Sarge comes up behind him and whacks him hard across the side of his head and right ear with an open hand.

"You idiot, I don't even drink vodka."

Benjamin pushes by him and runs out the front door. The rest of the family is shaken. His mother is screaming, "Now look what you've done, Joe."

"Leave him alone, Daddy," from his sister.

His little brother is frozen in fear. Benjamin gets the hell out fast and hitches a ride to the Sharps.'

He doesn't let on to any of his friends that anything is wrong until late into the night. The girls have gone home, there was no orgy. They just all got drunk and are passing out. Benjamin confides to Ted Sharp and to David that he can't go home and relays the sordid details. He stays at the Sharps' for a couple of days before David finally breaks down and confides the event Benjamin had shared to his mother. Rose Clements is horrified and immediately puts David in her car and drives over to the Sharps.' When they get to the end of their driveway in front of their house she lays on the horn. It is early in the morning and Ted and Benjamin are still in bed. Benjamin hears the horn and pops his head out the third floor bedroom window.

Rose demands, "Benjamin Mathews, you get down here right this second!"

Moments later Benjamin appears at the front door and is ordered into the car. As they drive off Mrs. Clements dominates the conversation.

"How dare you not come to me? How dare you? Don't you know that I will always look out for you?" She is crying.

J. McGregor Colt

When they get home she calls over to Benjamin's house and tells his mother that Benjamin is with her and that she will be over to pick up some clothes and things for him. She also makes it known that The Sarge had better not be there when she arrives. Rose Clements is not somebody that you want to take lightly and pretty much everybody knew it.

Benjamin moves in to a spare bedroom and quickly becomes another member of the Clements family. It is great for him. He has a brother his own age and he is in hog heaven. He has never been a part of such luxury. Maids to pick up his room and do his laundry, a cook who is always making tasty treats and a loving family environment around the dinner table each night.

Mrs. Clements immediately goes on a personal crusade to make Benjamin whole. She takes long walks with him and lets him know that he is someone very special, that he has a certain talent that others do not possess. She tells him that he does not realize it now but as he gets older he will realize that he has a charm about him that will carry him to wherever he wants to go in life.

"Doors will open easily for you, Benjamin."

Included in all this is her campaign to get Benjamin back into The Puget Academy for his senior year. The headmaster tells her that it is not possible, it will send the wrong message to the other Puget families and that Benjamin is not the type of person he wants attending his school. Mrs. Clements is insistent and under the assumption that Benjamin must have been on some sort of a tuition scholarship program she even offers to pay his full tuition.

58

The Suicide Note

"That's not the issue, Mrs. Clements. Benjamin's tuition has always been paid, in full, and on time by Howard Monaghan of the Harrisburg Bank & Trust in Pennsylvania."

"What is that all about?" She is perplexed.

"Certainly the Air Force does not pay their enlisted men enough money to afford the luxury of an education at Puget. Benjamin's mother is from a family of substantial means. It is her family who is paying for his education."

Mr. Pelegrini is being somewhat snooty about the whole thing and Rose is getting a bit irritated with him. She wants to grab his ridiculous bow tie and strangle him with it but she restrains herself.

Rose is not deterred, lobbies several of her friends, and together they threaten to withdraw their children from the school if Benjamin Mathews is not readmitted. Well, it works. Benjamin rides to school the first day with David and his little brother and is an instant icon. He has been the first person to get thrown out of The Puget Academy and the only one to ever get back in.

A couple of weeks after the school year begins Benjamin moves back in with his family. Secret negotiations between The Sarge and Dr. Clements nets Benjamin a place back in his own house with a promise that his father would stop drinking. David still goes by and picks him up for school and everything seems calm at the Mathews house. Mrs. Mathews is always cheerful and The Sarge is always gone by the time David would get there.

That year Benjamin and David decide to get involved with the school play. David is ineligible to play football due to his failure to pass the physical. An ingrown toe nail has

59

J. McGregor Colt

left him limping around for a couple of months that fall but if there is anything more prestigious than playing Puget football it is being in The Puget Academy play. This is not just any school play; it is a major production. Tryouts start early in the year and by mid fall they are into full on rehearsals, set production and lighting scenarios. All this spans the time of four months and the performances take place just before spring break.

Mr. Edmonds, the drama/art teacher at Puget, takes the play very seriously and makes sure that every detail is perfect. He was involved in Broadway productions in his youth and brings this experience, in a very serious way, to the boys at Puget. If you do not take him seriously, you were out. From the angle of the spot flood to the placement of a scenery partition to the timing of a walk-on, everything has to be perfect and gone over and rehearsed to perfection. In the end the play will be attended by not only the who's who of the Puget Sound region but by drama critics from afar. Okay, maybe that last part is a slight exaggeration but it is a very big deal nonetheless.

This year's production is Melville's *Billy Budd*. Benjamin and David both try out for the lead. David secretly prepares very hard for the tryouts. He doesn't let on to Benjamin that he is taking any of it seriously; in fact he plays the whole thing down and makes out as if he doesn't really care about getting the part. Benjamin seems generally uninterested as well and doesn't practice for the auditions at all. David wants the part badly and gives what he thinks to be the performance of his life when it is his turn to audition.

David views from the back of the room during Benjamin's audition performance and knows immediately that he doesn't

The Suicide Note

have the chance of a snowball in hell of beating Benjamin out for the leading role. Benjamin is a natural-born actor. He becomes Billy Budd in such a convincing way that the room stills and all eyes go to Mr. Edmonds in anticipation of his response. Benjamin is brilliant and smooth. He doesn't seem the least bit uncomfortable in front of an audience and articulates the lines with such fluidity and confidence that one would think he had played the part on Broadway.

Benjamin wins the lead hands down and David is crushed. David has out-performed Benjamin in every aspect of their young lives to this point. David gets better grades, David is a better athlete, David is from a wealthy family and, most importantly to all their friends, David got laid first. But Benjamin is a born performer and can get anyone to eat from the palm of his hand in the process. Although David is offered a lesser role he declines in favor of Production Manager. It is a prestigious position and it does not carry the risk of being thought inferior to Benjamin. Benjamin is spared the humiliation of having to apologize to David.

It works out well for both of them and their friendship is made stronger. Benjamin gets the leading role and David gets to boss everybody around. He is in charge of everything. He oversees the building of the sets, sets up the lighting, makes sure everyone has their scripts and memorizes their lines. Mr. Edmonds directs and puts a lot of pressure on David, Benjamin and the entire company. David suffers many sleepless nights of tossing and turning trying to remember if he did this or did that. Later in life David reflects that this is when he first started losing his hair.

While all this is going on the boys still have world history, chemistry, calculus, advanced placement French and

61

J. McGregor Colt

are expected to do well in all. They sit for their SATs, apply to colleges and still find time to drink beer and romance their girlfriends.

In the spring Benjamin puts on the best performance that anyone has ever witnessed of a high school performer. After the first night's production the newspaper gives him such high praise that they have people standing in the back of the theater to see him the second night. Mr. Edmonds is beaming and Benjamin's acclaim is spread throughout the region fast. Benjamin's light is beaming brightly in this fifteen minutes of fame. For at least a short period of time this attention being paid him goes to his head. He is off Melissa and back to Anna. He figures that now she will lie down with him for sure. Benjamin has always been deeply in love with Anna and even though he feels for Melissa he has always dreamed of Anna. He wants Anna above all else but still his hormones call for release and Melissa has been a willing participant.

The come-back is short lived. Anna will still not succumb to his advances and it frustrates Benjamin so much that he actually becomes verbally abusive towards her. They again break up and Benjamin slithers back to Melissa who is hurt but willing to take him back. Melissa loves Benjamin as much or more than Benjamin loves Anna. Melissa will do anything for Benjamin; she idolizes him and will put up with any transgression. To Benjamin, however, Melissa is always his second choice and he thinks a little less of himself for being with her.

After spring break college acceptance/rejection letters start coming in. David is fortunate in that his father had gone to Stanford and it is a foregone conclusion that David

The Suicide Note

will be going to Stanford as well. David has talked Benjamin into making an application in hopes, out of some miracle, some strings will be pulled and he will be coming with him. No such luck. Benjamin receives a very polite rejection letter from all of the colleges for which he applied. He has low SATs and medium grades and only applies to Ivy League or Little Ivy schools. For some Mr. Pelegrini will make a phone call and the bar can be lowered but not for Benjamin. The Weenie still begrudges Benjamin for what Rose Clements had forced his hand to do and he is not going to extend him any extra effort.

In the wake of all the rejection letters Benjamin decides that he wants to attend UCLA and major in drama. He fills out an application, gets a letter of recommendation from Mr. Edmonds and includes clippings from the newspaper about his performance in *Billy Budd*. No one has ever seen Benjamin try for something any harder. He is consumed and after about a month a letter comes from UCLA saying that he has been accepted. Benjamin is ecstatic. This means more to him than the night he lost his virginity with Melissa. He has visions of becoming a movie star. This is finally a way for him to escape from under the threat of his stepfather's downward thrust. He leaves school that day on a cloud.

The next day, however, is somewhat different. The Sarge has put the kibosh on the whole nonsense. It has been pointed out to Benjamin that the tuition for UCLA, for a nonresident student, will be beyond the Mathews family budget and he will need to attend a school in Washington. As high as he had flown the previous day he has fallen the next. Yet another in a long list of disappointments for Benjamin Mathews.

63

J. McGregor Colt

With a month left to graduation the boys are all set to head off the following fall to schools around the country. The Puget Academy prides itself in its ability to get the privileged kids to the privileged schools. David is going to Stanford, Billy Reece to Yale, Ted Sharp to Williams and the rest all to good schools. Benjamin is listed as "Undecided" in the graduation program.

Shortly after graduation Benjamin and David drift apart. Benjamin finally registers at the University of Washington. Woody Garwood will be attending there in the fall as well and he and Benjamin start making trips together up to Seattle to check things out and get involved in all the fraternity house nonsense. None of that is interesting to David so the trio just stop hanging out together.

64

Chapter
Six

P alo Alto, California in the fall of 1968 is still in the throes of the "Summer of Love." The campus is alive with young inspired overachievers in tie-dye T-shirts and bell-bottom pants. Hippie beads are required accessories and the platinum vibrations of Jimi Hendrix's guitar or the gravel howl of Janis Joplin echo through the halls of the coed dormitories at Stanford University. Marijuana, wine and mescaline are omnipresent. David Clements is free, he is what's happening and he is on a mission.

Although the weekdays are filled with the regimen of higher learning the weekends are filled with keggers and trips into San Francisco, "The City," for shows at the Fillmore

J. McGregor Colt

Auditorium, the Avalon Ballroom and Wonderland. The groups he sees he almost takes for granted—the Grateful Dead, Jefferson Airplane, Crosby, Stills and Nash and Janis are always playing somewhere and David is there. The ongoing Vietnam War protest is large and consuming at Stanford but he never really gets involved in any of that. He is against the war just like most of the other students but David is more involved in the freedom of the moment. Wine, women and song, to coin a phrase, is a tad bit higher on his priority list than "bringing the boys home." David is selfish and quite willing to admit it.

Benjamin, on the other hand, falls head first into the antiwar movement up in Seattle. David hears stories of Benjamin's escapades through Anna; she too is at the University of Washington and communicates with David regularly. Benjamin drifts away from the fraternity/sorority scene and gets involved instead with the much less social and more serious campus political scene. He helps organize protests and marches and is very involved in the closing of the I-5 Freeway protest. This involvement, this commitment is either because of the deep feelings he has about the military injustice of the war or because of the sincere hatred he has for his military stepfather, but Benjamin's feelings are deep and sincere. He passes out pamphlets, writes articles, gives speeches and throws rocks. He is against the war and doesn't seem all that interested in sex, drugs or rock and roll like most other wholesome all-American college students.

Anna and even Woody are involved in the fraternity/ sorority scene. Woody has pledged a house and is a pretty popular guy with the jocks. He runs track, plays intramural

66

The Suicide Note

sports and is an all-around party animal on weekends. Anna pledges a sorority and soon becomes a sweetheart of all the fraternity parties. Neither socialize with Benjamin although both try. He just isn't interested in their thing and as time passes the space between them grows.

Over the Christmas break Anna and David get together. They fall in love with one another and in the vacant parents bedroom at the Clements house they have sex. It is her first time but she is ready and a very willing participant. She is a vision with her long silky blond hair falling halfway down her naked back to expose her firm well-shaped hips and bottom as she gets up from the bed and walks away after it is all over. David never really gets that vision out of his head and clones the situation many times in his mind over the years. He never does completely stop being in love with Anna.

Their love-making continues throughout the short vacation as a marathon, it seems. Anna can't get enough of her new-found amusement and only one week after David's arrival back in Palo Alto she goes down for a visit. She only stays a weekend and the two never leave the dorm room. When she gets back to Seattle she run into Benjamin on campus and tells him of her relationship with David. He is deeply hurt and years pass before Benjamin and David speak again.

My so called best friend fucked my high school sweetheart when I could not.

By their senior year in college Anna and David are no longer seeing one another. She is dating others and so is David. The distance between their campuses make it difficult. Benjamin has rekindled his relationship with Melissa Stewart at some point that year and she has moved into his

67

J. McGregor Colt

off-campus apartment with him. Benjamin doesn't have any other girlfriends during his college days. Benjamin has always wanted Anna, fails to see why he can't have her, and fails with any other women he tries to lure. Benjamin is awkward with women. He can handle a crowded room, he can be very entertaining but when it comes to one on one with a member of the opposite sex, especially a beautiful one, he clams up and becomes uncomfortable to the point of making the woman uncomfortable as well. Benjamin wants to be with a woman who displays physical beauty; it makes him feel good about himself, it makes other men admire him, envy him, and he likes the way that feels, but beautiful woman make him feel uncomfortable. Eventually Benjamin settles.

Melissa is the only one with whom he feels relaxed and at ease. She is the only one with whom he has ever made love. He has found someone with whom he feels comfort and with whom he can have sex and he latches on to her. They get married a week after graduation and on their wedding day Benjamin discovers in Melissa something that he has never seen before. He had never seen her in make-up. She is plain-looking in comparison to the other women in his circle because she never paints up her face the way they do. On their wedding day she has her hair and make-up done by a professional and she looks stark raving gorgeous. The transformation is incredible and Benjamin feels very good about himself that day. Melissa never wears make-up again after that but Benjamin's memory of what she could look like if she wanted to weighs heavily with him.

For a honeymoon they drive south down the Washington, Oregon and California coastline, camping along the way.

68

The Suicide Note

When they get to Palo Alto they pay David Clements a surprise visit. David is not only surprised by the visit, he is stupefied. David thinks it is pretty stupid of Benjamin to get married so young but he keeps his opinion to himself. He is glad to see Benjamin and delighted that the Anna thing between them is over. They are old buds again and it feels good to both of them. David remembers that Benjamin is always fun to be around. By now Benjamin has dropped all the antiwar crap and just wants to party. The three of them cruise down the coast to Monterey and go to the Laguna Seca races together. The night before the event, in their shared motel room, they get into a discussion about the races. Melissa thinks that the races are formula cars and Benjamin informs her that they are not formula cars but sports cars that they will be seeing in the morning. She does not know whether to believe him or not so she turns to David and asked what he thinks. At this Benjamin is agitated.

"Don't you dare question my intelligence. What are you asking him for," he screams. "I'm your husband and you had better take my fucking word for it." He flies out the door slamming it behind him.

Melissa and David look at each other in momentary shock but take out after him. The whole husband/wife loyalty thing continues at a loud pitch in the parking lot for a while before they are able to settle him down and Melissa is able to convince him that she does respect him and does believe that they are, in fact, sports cars and not formula cars. This whole incident is a reminder to David how insecure Benjamin really is with himself and how much damage The Sarge had really caused to the person down deep inside.

69

J. McGregor Colt

Benjamin demands loyalty and is deeply hurt when the people he relies on for such loyalty fails him. It is no more apparent than it is this night in Monterey that his demand for unconditional loyalty will burden Benjamin for the rest of his life. Benjamin did not benefit from a father who championed him. He had been ridiculed and belittled all his life by his stepfather. The Sarge never attended nor showed interest in any sporting events he participated in early in life so later Benjamin just didn't bother trying. His father never took an interest in his grades in school so he never tried very hard to get good ones. Benjamin was never encouraged and was, in fact, discouraged whenever he tried to succeed at anything. Benjamin had become a very insecure young adult.

The three travel in tandem up I-5 together, camping for a couple of days at Lake Shasta and David basically shares the second half of Melissa and Benjamin's honeymoon with them. When they get home Melissa and Benjamin rent a house in Ponder Point and David moves back in with his parents. The summer is spent doing all the things they have always done. Melissa has a job but Benjamin and David cruise the lake, drink beer and smoke pot all summer. By fall Melissa is pretty fed up with all this nonsense and demands that Benjamin do something with his life.

His parents are pretty disgusted with his lack of responsibility as well. The Sarge is very ill by this time and is self-confined to his bed. The alcohol and cigarettes had gotten the better of him and this, coupled with his loss of purpose after retirement, renders him a sloth. The good news is that Benjamin does not have to listen to him anymore. If there is any criticism coming from The Sarge it falls on deaf

70

The Suicide Note

ears because Benjamin would never go upstairs at his parent's house to say hello to him. This bothers his mother some but Benjamin doesn't care. The damage has been done and the opportunity to mend wounds is not going to be given by Benjamin.

Woody Garwood has a job selling real estate and is doing pretty well with a new car, fancy clothes and he is styling in his white belt and white shoes. This intrigues Benjamin and soon he is down at Woody's office peddling real estate right along with his old buddy. Quickly, Benjamin finds his niche. Woody and Benjamin don't sell houses; they are "land brokers." They work for a company that specializes in ranches, farms and acreage and are traveling across the state to Eastern Washington to do so. They find a large ranch, persuade the rancher to sell and then sell it to one of their investors. The investor will subdivide the ranch into twenty-acre tracts and give it back to them at twice or three times the price he pays per acre. They make a bundle doing that. There is a big get-back-to-nature thing going on in the mid-1970s and Woody and Benjamin are cashing in on it big time.

David is still floundering around not doing much of anything with his degree in Environmental Science from Stanford. He tries freelance photography for a while and works in one of his grandfather's mills as an office clerk. David is bored as hell and Woody and Benjamin are having a ball playing cowboys in Eastern Washington. One night drinking beer at Melissa and Benjamin's, Woody talks David into joining them down at the Pioneer Land Company. David doesn't really like Woody all that much but it sounds fun and easy and Benjamin is there so he does it.

71

J. McGregor Colt

Shortly after David joins them Benjamin falls into the big one. He had sent a letter of inquiry to a big cattle rancher in Goldendale, in the south-central part of the state. The rolling, timber-covered wilderness, bisected by crashing mountain streams with pockets of lush meadows north of this small cowboy town, is more beautiful than Benjamin has ever seen and George Smithson owns 22,712 acres of it. Mr. Smithson is getting old and his kids have all moved to the city and have no interest in being cattlemen. When Benjamin goes down for a visit he and Smithson hit it off instantly. The old cowboy loves Benjamin for his youthful enthusiasm and entrepreneurial attitude. Benjamin shows him that he can get three times the amount of money for his land if he subdivides. Large tracts of ranch land selling to other cattle ranchers are only bringing about $75 to $100 per acre but twenty-acre tracts are being purchased by city slickers for recreational purposes for $300 to $400 per acre. Most of the cattle ranchers are pretty pissed off about the large acreages disappearing but old Smithson doesn't care one bit. He wants the money.

Benjamin makes about half a dozen trips down to Goldendale over the next couple of months and always stays out at the Smithson Ranch. He helps out around the ranch during the day and stays up at night with the old man, talking. George Smithson has a million stories about the ranch and ranching in general and Benjamin is genuinely interested in hearing them all. The old man is the father that Benjamin has always wanted and, to the old man, Benjamin is what he wished his own sons would have been. They are a good match, treat one another with mutual respect, and Benjamin makes

72

The Suicide Note

a deal with Smithson to sell. He lays out the whole project on paper, hires a surveyor and a road builder and persuades the old man to do some selective logging to pay for all the costs involved in development. Benjamin has some fantastic marketing ideas and he is really brilliant when it comes to getting a piece of property to the market place.

Once he has the listing contract signed and everything organized he presents the whole package at his office meeting back in Ponder Point and gets a mixed response. Pioneer Land Company has been concentrating its efforts up in Okanogan County at the northern border with Canada. They have several large projects up in Okanogan in which many of the agents have their investors involved and it is their responsibility to get that property sold. Nobody wants to travel down to Goldendale to sell Benjamin's project except Woody and David. The first time Benjamin takes them down there they too fall in love with the area and the project. They realize that Benjamin has really stumbled on to the big one. They have nearly $7 million worth of real estate to sell all in one place.

The boys get to work right away but it goes pretty slowly. Benjamin places ads in the Portland *Oregonian*, the *Yakima Herald* and in the *Tri-City Herald* and the response is weak. They write good ads. The same ads in the *Seattle Times* and *Tacoma News Tribune* for land in Okanogan are ringing the phones off the hook. A couple of months pass and Mr. Smithson is getting a little nervous. He has sunk a great deal of time and money into building roads and paying for surveys and is not seeing any return. One day his wife and he drive the four hours to the Pioneer office in Ponder Point and visit with Benjamin and his broker. The meeting does not go well.

73

J. McGregor Colt

Glen Davis, the broker at Pioneer Land Company, is a good guy but he can be abrasive and undiplomatic at the most inopportune times. Glen basically tells George Smithson that all Pioneer's efforts are being concentrated up in Okanogan and that people don't really want to buy twenty-acre tracts in the Goldendale area. Of course Glen has never been to Goldendale and has no idea what the hell he is talking about but the damage is done. Two days later Benjamin receives a letter from Smithson thanking him for his time and efforts but letting him know that his services are no longer required. Benjamin leaves for Goldendale immediately.

By the time Benjamin returns home from his emergency Goldendale run he will do the best selling job he has ever done. He has persuaded Smithson to stick with him for six more months under the following conditions: Benjamin will leave Pioneer, form his own company and hire his own selling crew to work exclusively on the Smithson Ranch. That is not the best selling job he has ever done. The best selling job he has ever done is persuading Woody and David to join him. David has just passed his broker's exam and Benjamin needs a broker. Woody is one of Pioneer's top agents and the three of them work and play well together. Leaving an established company with an established clientele is a tough decision for both Woody and David but Benjamin has painted a pretty rosy picture of fame and fortune in Goldendale for them.

They come in as equal partners. Benjamin could have kept it all for himself but he is always very generous and needs to have the security of knowing that they won't bail out on him so he makes them equal partners. Mathews, Garwood & Clements, Inc. is formed in the winter of 1976. Benjamin

74

The Suicide Note

thinks that using their names, law firm style, will give them a sense of class and credibility. It works. By the spring the Smithson Ranch is selling like hot cakes. Benjamin had been right. Their advertising is finally reaching the right market and they are in Goldendale every weekend greeting carload after carload of prospective buyers. Smithson loves them, Goldendale loves them and they are rolling in the dough.

While Benjamin is winning the struggle a young man must overcome when he first starts out, he is losing the struggle a marriage must overcome when it first starts out. Melissa does not share the struggle. When a young woman and a young man are starting out together it is a struggle. They struggle to pay bills, to eat, to live with one another, they struggle to find themselves, to find their niche and to find it together. Building each other up, supporting each other emotionally, is another struggle unto itself. If these challenges are not shared the relationship will fail. If the challenges are not agreed upon the relationship will fail. Melissa does not share Benjamin's struggle and, in fact, belittles him for having one. She wants him to get a job with a regular paycheck, health insurance, a pension and that is not something that Benjamin can bring himself to do.

Melissa does not like the idea of not having a husband home on the weekends to share her life and so she leaves him. At first Benjamin says terrible things about her. He tells his partners that she is cheating on him...she is not. He tells them that she is a horrible bitch who does not support him and that she thinks that what they do for a living is wrong and immoral. In fact all Melissa really wants is to be closer to Benjamin and have him home to do things with her. Benjamin

75

J. McGregor Colt

sees this as a display of disloyalty and lack of support and after four years of marriage they get a divorce. In the end, the failed marriage is Benjamin's fault. His inability to share in Melissa's emotional struggle is what really brings everything tumbling down. Benjamin is incapable of sharing his feelings. Everything he has he needs for himself, for his own survival.

Chapter
Seven

Immediately following the divorce Benjamin buys a brand new shiny red Mercedes 450 SL sports car and moves to an apartment on Lake Washington in Seattle. The Mathews, Garwood & Clements office is in a freestanding office building owned by Wyrich Timber Company alongside the freeway in Federal Way. The building is highly visible from the traffic along I-5 and located halfway between Seattle and Ponder Point so his commute is the same either way. Woody and David start seeing less of him at the office right off the bat.

While Benjamin was married, Woody and David were single. While Benjamin went through his divorce Woody and David get married. When they used to travel to Goldendale during the Melissa era Woody and David would chase all

77

J. McGregor Colt

the women they could and Benjamin would just sit there and watch. He was always faithful to Melissa even when they were out of town and being big shots in the quiet little towns of Eastern Washington where there seemed to be an abundance of bored and desperate women. Now that the roles are reversed Benjamin makes up for lost time and starts drinking heavily. Of course they are all drinking heavily in Goldendale on the weekends but Benjamin is now drinking heavily up in Seattle during the week and going out to discotheques almost every night. He eventually discovers cocaine. He has the fancy car, the luxury apartment on the lake and the cocaine. Benjamin becomes very popular up in Seattle with a whole new group of hangers-on.

By 1977 Seattle had become more of a big city than a big town. Major League baseball, football and basketball franchises had located there, restaurants and bars flourished with beautiful women and the discotheques stayed open until the wee hours of the morning. Benjamin goes for it in a big way. He has season tickets to the Seattle Supersonics, memberships in private nightclubs and hangs out with the local celebrities. He and his partners all still go down to Goldendale together on weekends but Woody and David don't see him on a very regular basis at the office during the week. If it weren't for their success with the Smithson Ranch sales and Benjamin's relationship with old man Smithson, Woody and David would have a problem with it. As two married guys who had settled down into their married-guy lives they enjoy hearing Benjamin tell them about his exploits in Seattle, the night life and the women.

78

The Suicide Note

Benjamin has finally overcome his problem with women. He has found a confidence that he never had before. The car gives him the look of importance, the apartment gives him the appearance of credibility but it is the cocaine that gives him the confidence. He always carries cocaine and it is the bait with which he gets the women. Beautiful women fight over him, they call the office constantly looking for him and he is getting laid more than anyone Woody and David have ever known.

After a couple of years of this high living coupled with ever-increasing financial advancements, Benjamin meets Carly Winterberg at one of Seattle's raving discotheques one night and falls in love with her blindly. Carly is young, pretty and, like Benjamin, very charming and witty. She isn't just another of the coke whores he was hanging out with. She is very sophisticated and from a good Seattle family in The Highlands. Her father is a newspaper publisher. Carly outclasses old Benjamin Mathews and Woody and David figure that out immediately. Carly is much younger than they all are and would have still been in college had she not dropped out. She doesn't work so she is always coming with Benjamin to the office for his brief appearances there. The whole thing is starting to wear on Woody and David like a John-and-Yoko kind of a thing. Carly's presence in the office is a distraction. The three partners cannot bond, cannot strategize without interruption, and this becomes a bone of contention between them.

The Smithson Ranch is just about sold out by the end of 1979 and Mathews, Garwood & Clements, Inc. has invested their huge commissions wisely into some land of their own. They have projects all up and down the east slopes of the

79

J. McGregor Colt

Cascade Mountain Range, Lake Chelan, the Methow Valley and one 6,000-acre tract in the Ellensburg area. They have made it big in the land business and are well known and respected throughout the state. Instead of simply collecting commissions for selling someone else's land they now have about $3 million in real estate contract collections coming in and another $5 or $6 million in land for sale in their own names. By the time they are 30 years old they are self-made millionaires and love to brag about it to one another whenever the opportunity arises.

Woody and David are happily married and having kids. Benjamin is head over heels for Carly and spending money like a ten-year-old with a pocket full of quarters at the penny arcade to keep her happy. They all get together with their wives and do things. Benjamin and Carly are great fun to be with; they know everybody in Seattle, it seems. Professional basketball players, football stars, political figures, restaurant owners and famous hair dressers all greet Benjamin and Carly wherever they go and are always at their house for parties.

Benjamin had bought a beautiful home in a plush neighborhood outside Seattle and Carly has moved in and taken over. She goes on a spending spree with Benjamin's credit cards to buy furniture, wall hangings, window treatments and everything else needed to furnish a home. Benjamin never complains about her spending to her for fear she would dump him but Woody and David hear about it. Benjamin keeps urging them to sell contracts so he can get more cash and they refuse. This infuriates him.

"Look, I'm not working my ass off for nothing. I need more money," he would say.

The Suicide Note

He is already being paid $10,000 a month in salary by the corporation but is going through it like water and as far as working his ass off... not so much. By then they have hired twelve salespeople and those are the ones who are working their asses off. The boys are clipping coupons and Benjamin is hardly in the office at all anymore. Finally, one day Benjamin calls a meeting with Woody and David and tells them that he wants to sell out his interest in the company. He looks like hell, like he had been up for days on a cocaine binge. He has been looking like that more and more of late and Woody and David are more than eager to buy him out.

A fair price is determined by their accountants and they give Benjamin a combination of cash, contracts and land for his interest. Within a week Benjamin and Carly take the cash and move to Zermatt, Switzerland. Benjamin had already sold his beautiful house for a ridiculously low price and was barely able to pay off the mortgage. Just like that, Benjamin is gone and things get real quiet around the office. Business slows down but that is more a function of the economy than a function of Benjamin's absence. It is the Reagan years. It is hell for the small businessman and especially hell for real estate. Interest rates are over 16% and hardly anybody is buying recreational property in Eastern Washington but Woody and David are still trying. They sell their Mercedes and their BMWs and started driving Subarus and Hondas. They cut their salaries and even sell contracts to meet their financial obligations on properties they own.

Benjamin leaves the country with at least $250,000 in his pocket...at least that's what he gets from Mathews, Garwood & Clements. He leaves his contracts with them to

81

J. McGregor Colt

collect for him and he leaves the land. They hear from him just about every month with a letter and a couple of times he even calls. He seems happy. He is being a ski bum. He and Carly are renting a chalet at one of Europe's most luxurious ski resorts. Zermatt, Switzerland is right on the border with Italy in the shadow of the Matterhorn. It is very picturesque and a romantic spot for two lovers to hang out. There are no motorized vehicles allowed in town so transportation and deliveries are restricted to horse-drawn sleighs and people pulling sleds. The only way in or out is a half-hour, steep hill climb or descent by train. That whole winter Benjamin only leaves once.

There is one bar in town where the English-speaking people hang out and it happens to be owned by an expatriate from Seattle. The Brown Cow is a short walk from the various ski trams, trains and gondolas and Carly and Benjamin are seen in there most everyday après-ski and well into the night. They make friends with a group of Australians, New Zealanders, a couple from South Africa and a handful of Americans who all live there and have various jobs in various hotels. Neither Benjamin nor Carly work. They ski all day and party all night and there is always a fresh group of people to party with. Every couple of weeks a new group of tourists, ready to party, arrives and an old group leaves to return to their normal and somewhat boring lives. Benjamin's and Carly's lives are far from boring.

Benjamin is getting to be a fairly good skier and starting to look pretty buff. He has some muscle tone and has lost the weight he had put on over the last several years of sitting around on his ass nursing a hangover in Seattle. There is no

82

The Suicide Note

cocaine in Zermatt and the people he is hanging out with are way too health-minded to want to have anything to do with it. This is all good for Benjamin but he is still needing to feed Carly's compulsion for the material...fur coats, expensive ski outfits, jewelry and dinner in restaurants. Carly does not cook.

Word gets around town that the Super Bowl is being broadcast live on a cable television station in Italy. Five American guys and a couple of Canadians talk Benjamin into joining them on a trip into Italy to watch the game. They plan out their trip over the period of a couple of evenings at The Brown Cow and figure the best spot will be in Stressa, Italy. One of the Americans in the group speaks pretty good Italian and calls ahead to make sure they can get rooms in a hotel that has a television that gets the station they want. It is all set; Benjamin will be going on a road trip with the guys.

On the morning they leave Carly walks Benjamin to the train station and kisses him good-bye. At the last minute one of the American guys bails out and stays behind. Bakersfield Bart is a tall good-looking guy whose father is the largest table-grape grower in America and is from Bakersfield, California. This is Bart's third winter in Zermatt and he is pretty much your typical trust fund playboy born with the proverbial silver spoon in his mouth. He probably never really worked a day in his life but he is attractive and would be considered a good score for someone of Carly's ilk.

No sooner had the train left the station than Bart had Carly up to his apartment with her clothes off and her legs spread wide. The boys are gone for two days and Carly and Bart fuck the entire time, not leaving the apartment once. Upon his return Benjamin is none the wiser. Carly greets him

83

J. McGregor Colt

with a big smile and a kiss and tells him how much she has missed him. That night she makes love to him as if she had not had sex in weeks. Carly is quite a girl.

By late spring Benjamin calls his old office, asks how much money they have collected on his contracts and wants it wired over right away. Could it be possible that he has blown through a quarter of a million dollars in only seven months? It appears so. They had put only about $30,000 into his account and send it all to him by wire the next day. He is spending money like crazy and buys a used Volkswagen camper bus from an Australian who had bought it new and traveled through Europe in it for two years. Around the first of May Benjamin and Carly pack up their camper and head for Spain to meet up with three girls from Connecticut they had met skiing. The girls have rented a villa for a month on the beach in Almunecar, Spain and invite them down.

The villa is four bedrooms and two baths in an open-air kind of an arrangement. There is no glass in the windows, only shutters that you close if you get cold. It seems that most of the houses in the area are much the same. The villa is beautiful, with tile floors and fountains and handmade leather furniture. The girls share one bathroom and give Benjamin and Carly the other. It is a very comfortable situation and Benjamin feels good about himself being surrounded by four young and beautiful women. They all do everything together, a day at the beach, shopping in town and nightclubbing, all as a group. Benjamin gets to play the big shot with the locals who all think that the girls are his bimbos. It is still pre-season on the southern coast of Spain so most of the people they encounter on the beach or in the clubs are locals. None of

84

The Suicide Note

the girls are very attracted to the locals so they all stick pretty close to Benjamin. He loves it.

One day Benjamin is down on the beach reading a book by himself and the girls are all hanging out at the villa. Benjamin returns but is not heard coming in the door. The girls are in the kitchen talking and the subject of Bakersfield Bart comes up. One of them had slept with him and is telling the others how great he is in bed. As Carly could not be outdone she confides her Bart adventure to them as well. The whole thing is overheard in full detail by the devastated eavesdropper. Benjamin leaves in shock and goes back down to the beach to wrestle with the matter in his mind. He had, yet again, been betrayed. In his mind he is the buffoon, a laughing stock. How many others know of his girlfriend's infidelity? He has never experienced such pain in his heart. He is a shattered mess of different emotions. He feels anger towards Carly and then anger towards himself. What had he done wrong? He wants to cry but he can't and he doesn't want anyone to see that he has been so hurt. He is alone in this and there is no one to talk to, no one to scream at. If he goes back up to the villa and confronts Carly he would feel the humiliation in front of an all-female audience. This is something his fragile ego will not endure. Overwhelmed with a panic attack and in a fury he goes back to the villa, packs his bag, throws it in the camper and starts backing out into the road. The bag packing had been witnessed and by the time he is in the driver's seat all four women are asking him what is wrong and what he is doing.

"I heard your fucking Bart story, you flaming fucking cunt. Go fuck yourself."

85

J. McGregor Colt

Those words are the last words ever spoken to Carly by Benjamin and he doesn't even see her again until years later. It's not clear how she gets from there back to Seattle, her father probably bailed her out, but she does give David Clements a call upon her return. She calls and asks if he had heard from Benjamin or if he has seen him. David's only response is that he thought he was with her. Neither David nor Woody have heard from Benjamin and knew nothing of the story other than what Carly has told them. He had gotten mad at her and left her stranded in Spain for no apparent reason. It is another month before they hear from Benjamin. He is out of money and needs them to sell a contract for him. David asks about Carly but never really gets Benjamin's side of the story.

"She's a cunt. No, she's not *a* cunt she *is* cunt." Benjamin speaks defiantly.

David doesn't know what he means by that statement but it sounds funny to say, he laughs and repeats it over the years on numerous occasions.

Women react very violently about the use of the C-word. They can call men assholes, cocks and even cocksuckers without hesitation and know, in their frustration, that the man will not be as offended by these words as a woman will be to be called a cunt. Asshole and cock are both derogatory terms for a part of the anatomy and are used freely and openly in all sorts of venues but one mention of the word cunt and the room is all aghast and the speaker shunned. Pussy is an acceptable term for the same body part and could be considered a compliment in certain context but cunt is a very large no-no with all women from all social backgrounds.

86

The Suicide Note

Men know this and that is why the word is employed when appropriate. There is no single word a woman could say to a man that would have the same effect. A woman needs to add an adjective such as "little"..."you have a little cock," before coming close to having the same effect. The man, however, will never complain that it was said for fear someone might believe it. There are certain words in polite society that are simply not utilized; the F-word, more so, the N-word, but most of all, the C-word. In the current circumstance it seemed an appropriate moniker for Carly.

Benjamin travels around Europe alone feeling sorry for himself for the rest of the summer. He lounges alone for a while on the beach at Cannes, travels through Italy and takes the ferry from Brindesi over to the island of Corfu in Greece. The boys get postcards.

On Corfu he meets up with three Australians he had known in Zermatt; Patrick and Fiona, husband and wife, and Fiona's sister Mary. Mary is an attractive brunette, very well tanned from a summer of windsurfing and hanging out on the beaches of Corfu. Mary and Benjamin get together right away. Mary is horny and she had already been attracted to Benjamin from the winter in Zermatt. She knows of Carly's infidelity, sympathizes with him and assures him that all women are not like Carly. He seems comforted by Mary and even though he had planned on returning home to Seattle in October he is talked into returning to Zermatt and staying another season with Mary and her sister and brother-in-law.

Patrick and Fiona and Mary have a plan. Wolfgang Meier owns the only photography business in Zermatt. Wolfgang hires young women every winter to photograph tourists on

J. McGregor Colt

the mountain. At the end of the day the photos would be displayed outside his shop and the tourists could buy them for $12 apiece as a souvenir of their ski trip to Switzerland. It is a pretty good little business Wolfgang had going until his wife realized that he was taking liberties with many of the young photographers. Mrs. Meier gave her husband a choice: give up the photo shop or give up the wife and he realizes if he was going to give up the wife he would probably lose the photo shop in the divorce anyway.

Wolfgang had made a deal to sell the photo shop to Patrick and Fiona and train them on the film processing and general operations of the shop. Mary is staying on to be one of the photo girls and excited about getting a free season pass in the deal. It seems that they were short a little on cash and are able to encourage Benjamin to be their partner. Benjamin has the boys sell another contract for him and the money is waiting in his bank account by the time the four of them get back to Zermatt.

Benjamin invests $10,000 in the photo shop with the understanding that he was not going to work there. He wants to be a silent partner and they seemed fine with that arrangement but the photo business turns out to be little more work than Patrick and Fiona had figured on. The photo girls are supposed to be dropping off film for development throughout the course of the day but would often get side tracked and go off skiing with their friends or some guy they met on the slopes. Oftentimes Patrick would have to close down the shop and go up on the mountain searching for them and some film to develop. Other times the girls would show up late in the day with 10 or 12 rolls of film all at once and no

88

The Suicide Note

time left to develop before the tourists came off the hill and headed into the bars.

It is turning into a real mess and the arguing between Patrick and Fiona eventually makes its way into Benjamin's camp. They explain the logistics problems they are having and tell Benjamin that they are also having a problem meeting the overhead. Benjamin agrees that he will go topside every day and keep the girls on task and deliver the film at regular interval throughout the course of the day.

This plan works out well. Benjamin has fun and it gives him something to do other than hanging out in the mountain huts drinking beer and schnapps all day. The photo shop begins to do a flourishing business and they will sell about 200 photos each day. The girls get paid $2 for each of their photos that sell and the house will pocket $10. Now they are bringing in about $7000 a week in tourist photos and more from the various other photo services and products they supply and for a while everything seems fine between Benjamin and Mary until one day up on the mountain while Benjamin is making his rounds he stops and observes Mary from a distance. She is talking to a group of young male skiers and laughing with them and having fun. At first he just figures them to be random tourists whose photograph she had taken but upon closer observation he realized that she is being a bit too friendly with one of them and when they all ski off Mary follows. Benjamin cannot resist the temptation to follow the group and see what is going on with them and his girlfriend. After a bit they stop in to one of the mountain houses and sit outside in the sun for a beer. They are all playing around and being a little frisky with Mary and she seems to be loving the

89

J. McGregor Colt

attention. Benjamin is fuming and a jealous rage overcomes him as he skis down to them.

"Why the fuck aren't you out taking pictures?" he screams loudly enough to alarm the crowded deck.

"Who the bloody hell are you?" in a British accent, says the fellow with whom Mary has been the most friendly.

There is a little bit of awkward pushing and shoving that follow but no punches are thrown and Mary gets her gear together and skis away with Benjamin down the mountain. He screams insults at her most of the way down and by the time they reached town Mary's face is covered with frozen tears. Mary moves out that night from the apartment she shares with him and, once again, Benjamin finds himself alone and blaming others for the failed relationship. He figures that Mary had been cheating on him and that she is shacked up with the English asshole at that very moment. He cannot get the image out of his mind and does not get to sleep until early the next morning as a result of this self-inflicted anguish. Mary was not cheating on him and probably never would have cheated on him. It is all just his own insecurities messing things up for him again.

Within a few days Benjamin makes arrangements with Patrick and Fiona to recover the $10,000 he had put into the photo shop and quit-claimed his interest back over to them. He then takes off in his camper bus for Brugge where he boards a large ferry and crosses the Straits of Dover to England. He never sees or hears from Mary again. She is heartbroken, devastated for a while, and is never really able to understand what had happened.

Once in England, Benjamin finds his way to Beckenham in South London to the flat of Roger Jameson. Roger is a

90

The Suicide Note

record producer with whom he had skied and partied for a couple of weeks in Zermatt earlier that winter. Roger's girlfriend is a very talented French singer and had just released her first album with Roger prior to their visit to Zermatt. By the time Benjamin reconnects with the couple Angie's album is selling very well in Europe. The two are in a very good mood when Benjamin knocks on their door and are most delighted to see him.

Roger and Angie insist that Benjamin stay with them for a while in their flat. Their place is party central for many in the music industry around London. For the next couple of weeks Benjamin hangs out with a very fast crowd. Roger is good friends with Peter Banks, the original lead guitar player for Yes and the two of them are planning to produce an album for Ginger Baker. Baker's band members and the crew hang out with Angie and Benjamin at Roger's place during the day while Roger is at work in London producing an album for an up-and-coming group in his studio. Most nights the whole group piles into Benjamin's camper bus, drives to London, and hooks up with Roger and anybody else hanging out at his studio and hit the pubs and discotheques. There is always cocaine and Benjamin dives right back in with both nostrils. Benjamin had gone sixteen months without the slightest mention of cocaine and now he is right back into it. The allure of cocaine renders Benjamin morally bankrupt and ethically reprehensible. Benjamin and his new rock star friends will party all night long with drugs and loose women and sleep most of the following days. Before he gets completely out of control, before he kills himself with overindulgence, he talks Peter Banks into buying his camper bus and he hops on a

91

J. McGregor Colt

flight back to Seattle. He has completely given up on himself at this point and has lost any hope of self-possession.

Chapter
Eight

When Benjamin arrives at Sea-Tac Airport Woody Garwood and David Clements are there to meet him. One of the first things out of his mouth back home is, "Where's the tootski?" They didn't have any "tootski" but within a couple of hours they are all snorting lines of cocaine together in the bathroom at Jacques'.

Jacques' Restaurant, at the base of Queen Anne Hill in Seattle, is one of Benjamin's favorite haunts. He knows all the staff, he and Jacques are good buddies and this is where he and Carly had hung out. He is hoping to run into her there so she can see how great he looks. He is in very good shape after having spent all that time skiing the slopes in the Swiss Alps and has a nice bronze tan from all the time at the beach in

93

J. McGregor Colt

Corfu. He looks good. Woody and David celebrate with him for a while but about 11 p.m. they leave him there and go home to their wives and kids.

They don't see or hear from Benjamin for about two weeks when one day he just shows up in the office. His initial good looks, bronze tan and great shape are already fading and he looks like he has been hitting it pretty hard since his return. He wants to come back to work. He confesses that he is flat broke and owes the IRS a bunch of money. Woody is reluctant to let him come back because he's afraid he will be too disruptive. They really didn't have much going on, most of the salesmen had quit by then and they are having a real hard time selling any of their properties. It is all very frustrating but David figures with Benjamin back maybe things will change. Benjamin had always been a great motivator and David thinks that motivation is precisely what they need at that moment.

Things do not change, in fact they get worse. Woody had been right, Benjamin is a distracting influence. Benjamin no longer has any ownership interest in the company even though his name is still on the logo, but he likes to play it up like he is still on top of things with the girls. He is hitting the bar scene and the cocaine pretty hard again and there will be times that they don't see him in the office for three or four days in a row. Benjamin will always have some nonsense story regarding his absences. One time he even claims to have had a mild heart attack and had been in the hospital. It is a complete and total fabrication... he had been out on a bender. He seems to always be on the verge of bringing in the big deal but nothing ever goes together for him, yet he always has just enough money to get by somehow. Pretty soon all his old,

94

The Suicide Note

big-shot, Seattle buddies figure out that he is nothing more than a has-been, a flake and start staying away from him.

The only companion he has left is a bar owner down in Pioneer Square, Joey Braza. Joey is also a flake and is also a coke addict...they fit nicely sharing an apartment downtown that becomes the hangout for all the losers, scum bags and derelicts they meet in bars. "The tattooed and the toothless" is how David refers to Benjamin's newfound friends. Benjamin may have not yet hit rock bottom but with a flash light he can see it from where he is standing.

Joey has a slutty girlfriend with whom he has a couple of kids he neglects. Her name is Diana and she has an equally slutty sister, Nadine, who also has a little girl out of wedlock with some local musician. When Benjamin meets Nadine he is instantly aroused. Nadine is not only slutty but she also has a sultry air about her that Benjamin finds attractive. She carries herself well through the downtown bars and the evening air, the neon lights reflect nicely off her painted face. She is not well educated and does not adhere too closely to any sort of social code but she displays well her curvaceous body pressing out against the material of skin-tight clothing in which she accessorizes herself. It is easy to overlook her lack of social graces and understandable why Benjamin is so enamored with her... he is usually high and horny. Benjamin loves Nadine's little daughter Chelsea and when sober he pays a great deal of attention to her. He takes her to the zoo and plays with her at the park. All the things that any good father would be doing with his own daughter, Benjamin does with Chelsea but it is never on a steady basis because Benjamin is first, above all else, a coke

95

J. McGregor Colt

addict and an alcoholic and will disappear and not show up as promised on numerous occasions.

Nadine works as a bartender at Braza's Bar and Benjamin will stay out until closing time to give her a ride home. She is usually the one who has to drive because he is usually smashed by closing time. The two of them have a very rough relationship. They fight a lot and are breaking up and getting back together on a fairly regular basis. During the reconciliation after one of their really big fights they decide to move in together and live like a regular family with Chelsea. They rent a little cottage down by the lake in the Madison Park area of Seattle and Benjamin starts going to work on a regular basis. He is putting deals together and making a decent living again but Nadine's job is taking its toll on their relationship. She will be out until 2 a.m. and sometimes not come home until 3 or 4 a.m. She likes to party too and this drives the jealous, controlling Benjamin right up the wall. Pretty soon the couple is right back at it again with the fighting.

During one of their many separations Benjamin goes down to Ponder Point to stay the weekend with Woody Garwood and his wife. The two old friends reflect on the old days and share some good stories of past accomplishments. Woody is somewhat familiar with Benjamin's drug and alcohol overindulgences and is also aware of the on again/off again relationship he is having with Nadine.

"Benjamin; it's like this. You have a 110 watt plug in your hand and you are trying to shove it in to a 220 watt receptacle. You shove it in and, WHAM, you get shocked. You recover from the blow and look at the plug and figure that maybe you

The Suicide Note

can turn it over and try it again but, WHAM, it knocks you back on your ass again." Benjamin listens and is amused by Woody's animation.

"The electrical current hurts but you don't give up. You figure that maybe if you modify the plug you can get it to work so you grab a pair of pliers, twist and turn the tines, adjusting them in hope of getting them to fit into the receptacle but when you try again you get the same result. WHAM. You are thrown across the room and your hair catches on fire. One day you just gotta give it up before you burn down the whole fucking house, man."

Woody is really trying to help Benjamin out but his analogy falls on deaf ears. After about three or four months Benjamin is up to his old tricks again and things start spiraling downward fast. A DUI arrest costs Benjamin his driver's license for thirty days and he is confined to the house with Chelsea. He can't go out without Nadine to drive him and he can't go out looking for her when she is not home. And, of course, he can't go to work either. He becomes very despondent and introspective during this period of time and begins questioning his purpose in life. He knows that all his problems stem from his drinking and cocaine use and he promises himself that he will quit. And, for the thirty days he is without a license, he does quit. And, for even a little while after that, but before too long he is right back at it and he and Nadine are right back at the fighting again as well. They split up again, and give up the cottage by the lake.

Benjamin moves in with a bouncer in a bar somewhere. Within a few months he gets another DUI and this time loses his license for six months. During this period Benjamin hits

J. McGregor Colt

what most would call rock bottom. He never seems to be sober and is always recovering from or looking for cocaine. He never really sees daylight. He will pass out at about 4 in the morning and get up again to start all over at about 6 in the evening. He will settle his nerves with a shot or two of tequila before heading out to one of the bars he frequents to meet up with his buddies who are just getting off work.

There is always someone who is in the mood to party with him and it is never anybody good. By ten in the evening someone will show up with cocaine and before he knows it he is over at someone's house for an all-night coke party with the bar staff and their sleazebag regulars. He himself has, in fact, become a sleazebag regular at a couple of dive bars and is always welcome. On one occasion he gets so drunk at one of these establishments that he wanders into the men's room around closing time and passes out on the urine-soaked floor. He is not discovered until the janitorial service shows up to clean early the next morning. They throw him out on the sidewalk and he is observed by normal people walking by on their way to work. He is pitiful.

Nothing is going in Benjamin's favor so he concludes that in order to get his life together he and Nadine need to get married. Benjamin convinces Nadine that if she marries him everything will change for them, they will be happy, and she agrees. The wedding is like a hobo convention. All of Seattle's sleaziest bar flies are in attendance and it becomes a big drunken brawl. Joey Braza and Diana get into a public display of non-affection. Punches are thrown among rivaling factions of ne'er do wells and Woody and David and their wives, who had driven up from Ponder Point, can't get out fast enough.

98

The Suicide Note

Benjamin and Nadine's logic-defying marriage lasts two and a half months. Why, specifically, they break up is no clearer than why, specifically, they got married in the first place. By this time Woody and David are trying to stay away. He is a complete mess and within weeks of his divorce decree he is back in court filing bankruptcy. Benjamin had been a self-made millionaire by the time he was thirty and now is a self-made, self-inflicted, victim of bankruptcy by the time he is forty. He had sold all his contracts, spent all his money, lost all his real estate holdings and he still owes the IRS about $60,000. He just gives up and finds a bottle in which to drown his sorrows.

By the spring of 1990 Benjamin has hit rock bottom. He can't hold on to a job or to a woman. He gets a job with a commercial real estate firm in Seattle based solely on his past reputation from the previous decade and he is found out pretty quickly to be a useless loser and is fired. He drives several women away who are attracted to him for his good looks and fun-loving attitude but they too realize that he is a dead end street and pack their bags. Not only is his world on to him, he is finally on to himself and after many failed attempts to get clean and sober he checks himself into a drug and alcohol treatment center.

The Burnside Recovery Center down in Portland, Oregon is the only place he can find that is willing to take him in on the easy payment program. He has no money and no health insurance so he is very fortunate to get admitted to any facility. Burnside is just like any of the other places except that there are a high percentage of court-ordered customers there. These are people who probably are not yet willing

99

J. McGregor Colt

to admit that they have a problem with drugs or alcohol and are bitter about being forced to go there. Benjamin is neither forced nor bitter. The fact is, he is thankful to have a roof over his head, to be fed three meals a day, and to be in hiding from all the people with whom he had chosen to surround himself for the past several years. After he has been in Burnside for a couple of weeks he calls Woody and tells him where he is. Woody is not shocked but is a bit hesitant regarding Benjamin's sincerity. Although Benjamin seems humbled he also seems a little too confident about his recovery.

Burnside is based on the twelve-step program of Alcoholics Anonymous coupled with group therapy and lectures. Every morning after breakfast the entire population goes to the lecture hall for a speech by a professional recovering alcoholic. Benjamin is intent on his own recovery and listens attentively. Following the morning lecture they will break into small groups and discuss their abuses with one another. The food served at Burnside contains no sugar or caffeine. It is believed that sugar and caffeine cause mood swings that could trigger a desire to use drugs or alcohol. This takes some getting use to. Benjamin is addicted to his morning cup of coffee as much as anything else and admits later that his withdrawal from the caffeine was worse than from the cocaine or alcohol. After lunch they will repeat the morning schedule of a lecture, then meet in their group for an hour and a half before some late afternoon/pre-dinner free time. After dinner they all attend a big in-house AA meeting together.

Benjamin makes alliances with some of the people in his group. He is smarter than most of the people in there, they

The Suicide Note

look up to him and seek his guidance when a counselor is not available. This gives Benjamin back some of the self-esteem he had lost and helps a great deal in his own recovery. Neither Woody nor David visit Benjamin at Burnside, feeling uncomfortable with the whole business and that it is Benjamin's deal to handle on his own.

I have never had anybody that really cared about my wellbeing. My best friends never even showed me any support when I checked myself in to a drug treatment center.

Before Benjamin is released he is required to do two things. He has to stand up at the evening AA meeting and tell his story and he has to write down what they call the First Step. The First Step is to be a personal accounting of everything in a person's life that led to his or her drug and alcohol abuse. The writer is to describe how the abuse dominated their lives, how it affected others in their lives and how it destroys their own life. Shortly after completing the program at Burnside Benjamin mails his First Step to Woody and David in an effort to make amends. Benjamin's story answers a lot of questions for them and fills in a lot of blank spaces. After reading Benjamin's story they are both drained and filled concurrently. The autobiography that Benjamin wrote drains them of the animosity they felt towards him and fills them with love and concern for his wellbeing.

Benjamin truly seems sincere in his recovery and he soon moves out of Seattle and gets a job selling land for the old Pioneer Land Company back in Ponder Point. Glen Davis welcomes Benjamin back and is thrilled to have an old master salesman back under his wing. For the next several months

J. McGregor Colt

Benjamin is able to prove that he still has it and is once again a top producer. He spends most weekends back down in the Goldendale area of Klickitat County, Washington. Listing, selling and reacquainting himself with all the right people in the county comes easy. Everything picks up for him right where it had left off over 10 years prior.

After about six months of success Benjamin proposes that Glen open a branch office in Willow Creek, Washington. Willow Creek is on the north end of a bridge spanning the Columbia River to River City, Oregon. It is the gateway between Klickitat County, Washington where all the land is and Portland, Oregon where all the people are. Benjamin knows that there are big-time opportunities in the Columbia River Gorge because of its proximity to Portland and because of its endless recreational opportunities.

The River City area of the Columbia River Gorge had become the epicenter for windsurfing, mountain biking, river rafting, hiking and skiing, and more and more people have a desire to be there. He sees the getting-back-to-nature deal of the early 1970s being reborn again in the early 1990s and this time he wants to be right in the middle of it. The hippies that were buying property from him in the '70s to get away from urban growth and living off the land eventually returned to the mainstream. They got jobs, got married, had kids and are now ready for some exercise. They owned their homes in Portland, Seattle, Spokane and are now successful enough to be buying property for second homes in the spectacular Columbia River Gorge so they can be close to the things they love to do.

There is a real estate boom in full force in the Gorge and Benjamin seizes the opportunity. Glen Davis is too insecure

102

The Suicide Note

about Benjamin's sincerity to agree to open up an office in Willow Creek. He knows Benjamin's history and is afraid that he will get left holding the bag if Benjamin relapses. Benjamin leaves the camaraderie of his friends in the Seattle/Tacoma area and the security of Pioneer Land Company and moves to small-town Willow Creek, Washington where he knew absolutely nobody.

I finally escaped from the assholes and back-stabbers who called themselves my friends and moved to Willow Creek.

After securing a lease on a storefront on the main street of town, getting properly licensed with the state and purchasing "For Sale" signs, office supplies, a copy machine, a fax machine, stationery and getting hooked up with a couple of telephone lines, Benjamin has $300 left in his bank account. He is fortunate enough to have enough people in the Gorge who believe in him so he does have some listings on a few pieces of property and places an ad in the *Oregonian*. The phone starts ringing in response to his ad as soon as it comes out. He sells two pieces of property the first weekend he is open for business and is an immediate success. He remains sober and is home every night and to bed early. Benjamin is in his office almost every day by 7 a.m. and works at least twelve hours a day. The people of Willow Creek, although leery of his intentions, are very impressed by his work ethic.

That first summer Benjamin is busier selling tracts of land in the Gorge than he had ever been in his life and the money starts rolling in again. He makes friends with the local windsurfers and business owners alike. Everybody takes an instant liking to him and soon any skepticism that may have preceded him fades. He is accepted and respected by the

103

J. McGregor Colt

community and gets so busy that he eventually realizes that he is going to need a sales staff to help him out. Benjamin had always been a great recruiter. He hired every agent they had ever had at Mathews, Garwood & Clements and he knows exactly who he wants and how to get them. He doesn't even consider hiring anybody already in the business because he really has no respect for residential real estate agents to begin with. He, like a lot of people, thinks most real estate agents are lazy and dishonest. Benjamin prefers to hire untrained, energetic and honest men in their 20s or 30s and he will train them to be land sales agents.

There is a distinct difference between a residential sales agent and a land sales agent. Benjamin feels that women should stick to selling houses and leave the ranches and farm acreage tracts to the guys. He is offended when a rancher lists his place with some woman in a Century 21 office wearing high heels and driving a Cadillac. He figures they don't have an understanding of the potential of large tracts of land, can't walk on it in their high heels and can't even get to most of it without a 4x4 vehicle. Land selling is for cowboys in blue jeans, not city girls in skirts. Benjamin is a chauvinist and goes on a mission to hire some agents. None of the guys he finds are from the Gorge originally. They all moved there because of the windsurfing but all are in great shape, energetic and well educated. He finds two guys from Vermont, one from North Carolina, one from Michigan, another from California and is also able to recruit one of his old buddies from Seattle. No more than two come on at the same time but within six months he has a great crew of six hungry men all in their late 30s.

The Suicide Note

Benjamin gets great enjoyment out of training these guys and is more excited at seeing them succeed than he is about the commission money they are generating for his company. He is more proud of himself for outselling all his competitors than he is of his quick financial advancement. To Benjamin it is the journey, not the destination. When he first got into the land business twenty years prior to this he made himself a promise. He knew that the top producers in the company he was working for were a little on the shady side but he wanted to prove that you do not have to be shady to be a success. He promised that he would outsell all the other agents and do it without cheating anybody else in the process. Benjamin is fair and honest with both buyers and sellers and with competing real estate agents as well. This philosophy he instills in his agents and he will not tolerate any diversion from this course.

They soon become the top company in the Gorge and all his agents are successful doing things Benjamin's way. For the next couple of years The Mathews Group thrives. Benjamin is once again back on top and is making a very good living but there is one thing missing. He has money, power, respect but he is alone and he has gone two years without getting laid. All Benjamin ever does while he is awake is work. He rarely even has time to eat. One of his favorite lines is; "Lunch is for wimps."

Attempts are made by his new friends, his new agents and their wives and girlfriends to get him to come out with them and meet some women, but Benjamin will always decline. None of these people know of his past and he is quite happy with their ignorance. He does not want to start

J. McGregor Colt

going out to bars or nightclubs in fear that he will start drinking again. He does not have enough confidence in himself with members of the opposite sex until he has a few cocktails so he just goes home at night and crawls in bed early and alone.

Benjamin had not yet bought a residence for himself and is living in a studio apartment above the garage of a beautiful estate overlooking the Columbia River owned by the local pharmacist and his wife. Brad and Jennifer Amanson own the drugstore in town and have another store across the bridge in River City. They are very successful and on occasion Benjamin will join them in the main house for dinner. Benjamin has confided in them that he is a recovering alcoholic and drug addict and knows that they will keep it a secret. The Amansons are not big drinkers in the first place and out of respect for Benjamin they never drink in front of him. They become close friends and Benjamin trusts them and respects them.

Brad and Jennifer eventually introduce Benjamin to a man from Southern California who is interested in opening up an Italian restaurant in the Gorge. Marco Centoni has two very successful restaurants in Southern California catering to the surfing crowd and is interested in taking advantage of the newfound windsurfing paradise of the Gorge. Marco is in his early 60s, has been in the restaurant business for thirty years in California and is very well known down in Orange County. Marco takes an instant liking to Benjamin and is very impressed with his real estate expertise and with his style. It is not long before Benjamin is able to put a deal together on a failing Mexican restaurant in River City and within a

The Suicide Note

couple of months is attending the grand opening for Centoni's Italian Cuisine.

Marco had completely gutted the old restaurant and was able to remodel the place to look like something you might see in Tuscany. Everyone in attendance at the grand opening is very impressed. Marco has a large family. His children, cousins, aunt, uncles, wives and grandchildren are in attendance up from California. Marco has three sons and a daughter, a beautiful 34-year-old daughter, Angelica, and the moment Benjamin lays eyes on her he falls in love.

Chapter
Nine

A ngelica is the most beautiful woman Benjamin had
ever seen.

*I fell madly in love with Angelica the moment I laid
my eyes on her and I have never felt love for anyone as intense as
the love I have for her.*

Benjamin got to know Marco's two oldest sons during
the restaurant renovation and has become good friends with
Antonio. Although Marco spoke with a noticeable Italian
accent all of his children are American-born and speak both
languages accent-free. On the evening of the restaurant
opening the predominant language being heard around the
room is Italian. Arms and hands are flailing and the sounds
emanating from the crowd are joyous and musical. Benjamin

The Suicide Note

ponders how the spoken Italian words sound like music, like opera. The chefs are Italian as is most of the staff. The members of the Centoni family are all there and have brought with them many friends and extended family from California. In the middle of all the singing and gesturing and dancing there is only one thing of interest to Benjamin.

It is Antonio who introduces Benjamin to his sister. Angelica stands about five feet five inches with long, straight, dark-brown, rich, silky hair she has combed back away from her face with no visible part. Her skin is flawless with an olive hue and appears soft to the touch. Her high cheekbones accent a most beautiful set of large dark brown eyes that mesmerize the admirer. Her eyes are her most outstanding characteristic but she is also very well put together physically and could never go unnoticed in any situation.

Benjamin meets her and spends the rest of the evening trying to impress her with his wit and charm. She is amused by the attention. Benjamin is her father's business associate and her older brother's sidekick. Benjamin is a dozen years older than she is and she is intrigued by the attention he is paying her. During the course of the evening Angelica laughs with Benjamin and lets him do all of the talking. She appears to be shy, polite and reserved. Her brothers get drunk, break things and she laughs and makes sure that everything is all right with the other guests. She is a very gracious hostess and a very doting daughter and sister. Benjamin is very impressed. The party continues on until past midnight and it is very well attended by all the right people from both River City and Willow Creek. It becomes obvious right off the bat that the restaurant has a bright future. Before saying

109

J. McGregor Colt

goodnight Angelica gives Benjamin her cell phone number and a promise to meet him in the morning for breakfast. As the two part there is a kiss and this kiss is truly the beginning of Benjamin's life.

"My life began when we kissed." It's something he will tell all who would listen.

The next morning is Sunday and Benjamin takes Angelica on a drive with him down the river towards Portland. On Sundays at the enormous Cascadia Lodge a magnificent brunch is served. The lodge was built about ten years prior to replicate the old lodges built by the Works Progress Administration during the FDR era. It sits on a hillside surrounded by tall timbers and a golf course and overlooks the Columbia River. The brunch served in the main dining room is buffet style and displays a very impressive assortment of epicurean delights from crab and oysters to flan and apple strudel. Salmon, baron of beef, German sausage, and, there are eggs too: Eggs Benedict, plain scrambled eggs, scrambled eggs with stuff, and customized omelets cooked to order.

On Sundays the Cascadia Lodge is simply a wonderful place to hang out, meet friends, and impress out-of-town visitors. Impressing Angelica is Benjamin's top priority at the moment. They dine and talk and get to know one another. After brunch they go for a hike in the forest surrounding the lodge. In a secluded corner they sit and kiss and things get quite intimate. It is obvious to Benjamin that Angelica is more than willing to take things further. By mid-afternoon there had been two calls placed to Angelica's cell phone. She looked at the caller ID and opted not to answer. Benjamin takes a men's room break back at the lodge and when he

The Suicide Note

returns to Angelica he finds her talking with someone on her cell phone. She seems slightly disturbed. When he asks her what is wrong he is told that Antonio is bugging her to come back to River City.

Antonio and his brother Giorgio are staying on in River City to run the new restaurant but Marco, his wife, the rest of the family and friends that had come up for the opening are all leaving in the morning and returning to Orange County. Angelica is to be leaving as well. Benjamin is not happy with this idea and lobbies for Angelica to stay a few more days. He says he will call Antonio and work it out. Angelica does not want Benjamin calling Antonio and it seems that maybe Angelica has not told her family that she is even with Benjamin.

Her cell phone rings again and this time she answers but walks off out of earshot of Benjamin and has a conversation in Italian with the caller. The conversation seemed heated to Benjamin but admittedly all the conversations the Italians were having over the past several days seemed heated. He just figures that is the way they communicate. When she returns her demeanor has changed and she is cheerful and energetic and as beautiful a person as Benjamin could have possibly envisioned himself being with. He is in love and blind and oblivious to any potential problems.

Benjamin is finally able to persuade Angelica to stay another two days. She calls the airlines and is successful in changing her flight to late morning that coming Wednesday. They go back to River City and she is successful in sneaking into her room at the River City Inn and retrieving her bag. She had only packed for a two-night stay so there is only

111

J. McGregor Colt

one suitcase and a make-up bag. Benjamin stays in the car while Angelica goes to her room and when she returns she is hurried and tells Benjamin to drive off. Once again Benjamin asks what is wrong and once again Angelica is not forthcoming with information.

"Did you tell anybody that you were planning on staying a couple more days?"

"Oh…um, I didn't run into anyone." she replies.

This seems odd to Benjamin but he does not dwell on it and defers to the spell ruling his thoughts at that moment. Angelica's beauty and charm have truly put a spell on him.

They drive back down the river rather than going to Benjamin's place just across and instead get a room at the Cascadia Lodge. The next two days and nights are spent naked in their room making love and talking and planning for a future. Benjamin is in heaven. He does not even check in with his office and since his cell phone is dash-mounted to his vehicle he does not communicate with anyone or listen to any messages for three days. Angelica has turned her phone off as well. They are in their own world of passion holed up in a room until Wednesday morning when Benjamin drives her to Portland International Airport.

Once the good-byes are over and Angelica boards her flight Benjamin returns to his car and listens to his phone messages. There are several from his office, a few from clients, a couple from friends and one very curious message from Antonio. Antonio's message is one of despair and concern for his sister. She is missing, her family is worried and her children are distraught.

"Her children?"

The Suicide Note

Angelica had made no mention of having children. During the course of the past several days between the passionate sessions of love making Benjamin and Angelica had shared stories of past relationships. Benjamin told of his past two marriages, his real estate successes in Seattle, his bouts with alcohol and drug abuse and his two-year sabbatical in Switzerland. Angelica mentioned a prior marriage to an abusive husband and shared stories of her family and many trips to the old country and their family home near Florence. There was never a mention of children nor of the desire to have children. All Benjamin knew was that Angelica was thirty-two, had been married for a period of time and had been divorced for the past six years. She mentioned that her ex-husband was an abusive drunk and cocaine addict and had beaten her on several occasions and that finally her brothers stepped in and saved her life by removing him from the scene. Benjamin did not question what removing him from the scene entailed but assumed that he is no longer involved in her life and left it at that. Now... he learns of children.

Benjamin's first call is Antonio. Benjamin has never been a liar. Antonio is a friend he respects and now he is in love with his friend's sister. Benjamin tells Antonio that Angelica had been with him and that he had just put her on a plane to the Orange County Airport only moments ago. Antonio is furious. He tells Benjamin that he should stay away from his sister and that she is trouble. He says that she had two small pre-school children who had been left in California in a questionable day care situation and that his parents are very upset with her. Benjamin tries to speak but is cut off by Antonio's tirade and is eventually hung up on.

113

J. McGregor Colt

"Dude, you should really direct your anger in a more productive way," he says out loud, in vain, after the connection had been broken.

Benjamin goes to the office and takes care of pressing business, gets caught up on overlooked transactions and other tasks such as advertising matters, signing checks and helping some of his agents work out kinks. His mind is not totally void of outside distractions. Throughout the course of the day he will take time out to place a call to Angelica's cell phone and will get no answer. He also tries Antonio's phone with the same result. By the end of the day he is a nervous mess of emotions and rather than go home he, instead, drives over the bridge to River City to find Antonio at Centoni's.

On an early Wednesday evening in mid-fall the new Centoni's Italian Cuisine is packed with patrons. This is Benjamin's first visit since the grand opening the previous Saturday night and the place is buzzing with activity. It feels good. He sees Antonio behind the bar as soon as he walks in and can hear brother Giorgio back in the kitchen singing out in Italian to the staff. It feels very good. Very good, that is, until Antonio makes eye contact with him.

The bar is full but Antonio has no problem screaming out, "What the fuck are you doing here? Haven't you caused enough trouble already?"

None of the patrons seem to pay much attention but Benjamin's face turns crimson as he is most embarrassed by the imagined attention being drawn to him. Benjamin likes Antonio but feels that he talks too loud, stands too close and touches too much. He makes bad social decisions and when Benjamin tries talking to him he is rebuffed.

114

The Suicide Note

"Fuck you. I'm busy. Go home."

Benjamin leaves and goes home. All night he places calls to Angelica's cell phone and there is never an answer. Finally her cell phone is turned off as the calls start going directly to voice mail without a ring. Benjamin gives up and goes to bed.

115

Chapter
Ten

There is a Centoni's Italian Cuisine in Laguna Beach, California which is at least three times the size of the River City operation. This is a stand-alone, one-and-a-half-story structure with a cobblestone-paved circular driveway around a large, beautifully tiled fountain. This restaurant is much nicer and caters to a significantly more affluent clientele than does the one in River City. The valet parking attendants are moving around Porsches, Ferraris and Mercedes to make way for the Bentley Continental with a surfboard protruding out the convertible top. Angelica is watching this scene out the window of the upstairs office where she sits totaling the lunch receipts, making new banks for the evening shift and contemplating her latest dilemma.

116

The Suicide Note

Angelica is not new to dilemmas. She has been a constant source of frustration for her parents and for her brothers. She has been in and out of many bad relationships and the cause always seemed to be her own poor choices. Angelica is indeed not the person she portrayed to Benjamin. She is not as charming at times nor, in fact, as beautiful. It seems that she too has had her bouts with alcoholism, drug abuse and questionable behavior when it came to men and to sex. She is not capable of feeling remorse. Guilt and fear elude her and it has become apparent to those that know her well that she has found a creative alternative to sanity.

Angelica is back working in the family business but is on probation and being closely watched. She has stolen money in the past, has disappeared for days, for weeks and will always return with something or someone else to blame. This time she has made another bad choice. Benjamin is not the bad choice; it is her deceptive behavior with her family, her lack of responsibility to the business and her temporary abandonment of her children. This is yet another cause for stress within the family and poor Benjamin is floating through it all totally in the dark.

Benjamin is never able to find a home telephone number for Angelica but finally gets up the nerve to call the Laguna Beach restaurant. He asks for her and is put on hold. Some minutes pass before he hears; "Yes; this is Angelica." He is flushed. He announces himself and asks if she is all right. She explains that she is working and can't talk.

"Angelica; I think that I am in love with you."

"That's so sweet but I really can't talk right now. Call me later." She hangs up the phone.

117

J. McGregor Colt

Later comes and goes and she still has not turned on her cell phone. Benjamin cannot concentrate at work, Antonio will not speak to him on the phone and Angelica is totally out of touch. Finally after a weekend of torment Benjamin returns to work, conducts his weekly staff meeting and announces that he will be taking the next ten days off.

Benjamin had not flown into Orange County in a number of years and notices that they have changed the name of the airport to John Wayne Airport. He thinks that's cool and also enjoys the fact that you get off the plane and exit directly on to the tarmac; also very cool in a Humphrey Bogart/*Casablanca* sort of way. Benjamin is on a mission and his arrival on a windy and rainy fall Southern California day is the perfect start for the movie playing in his mind. He makes it through the airport terminal and in short order is heading down the San Diego Freeway in a rental car towards Laguna Beach.

He had taken a matchbook from Centoni's in River City and on it is the restaurant's address in Laguna Beach. Benjamin is somewhat familiar with the area as he had spent some time down around Newport Beach and Balboa Island in some of his escapades as a youth. He had taken one memorable trip with David Clements in the summer between high school and college and he knew his way around fairly well. When he gets off the 405 he is still some distance to the beach and he starts recognizing things. Laguna Beach has not changed all that much but he is still not confident enough to not ask for directions to Centoni's at an AM/PM Mini Mart while buying a pack of cigarettes. The attendant knows the place and directs Benjamin over two blocks and down one.

The Suicide Note

Centoni's Italian Cuisine is very impressive to him and much larger than he had expected. He walks into the bar at around 3:15 in the afternoon. The lunch crowd has dwindled and the dinner crowd has not yet arrived. The bar only has four or five customers and behind the bar is another of Angelica's brothers, David. David greets Benjamin with surprise and welcome. It comes immediately apparent that he is not privy to what has transpired between Benjamin and his sister and is very friendly.

"So, what are you doing down here? Does my Dad know you are in town? Sit."

"No, I just got an urge to get out of the Gorge for a few days. The weather really sucks up there this time of year."

"Yeah; but it is really beautiful up there my friend. Hey, Angelica, look who's here."

At that Benjamin turns in his stool at the bar and is face to face with her. She has both hands covering her mouth and utters, "Oh my God; what are you doing here?"

"Angelica, can we go somewhere and talk?" As Benjamin speaks these words Marco comes from around the corner.

"Ange... up to the office!" Marco speaks softly but sternly and Angelica disappears.

"Mr. Mathews; why don't you and I take a walk?"

There are times when Marco speaks that one can barely hear an accent. This was not one of those times and his voice sounds like someone in an old Mafia movie speaking to someone about to get whacked. David is completely confused and simply goes to the other end of the bar to attend to customers as Marco escorts Benjamin out through the kitchen where prep cooks are getting things ready for the

119

evening crowd and singing and telling loud stories in Italian. It all looks very interesting to Benjamin until they get outside to the alley. The alley has four large metal dumpsters and an assortment of recycle bins all overfilled. Parked next to three or four motorcycles, a Vespa and a rack of bicycles is Marco's black SL 500 Mercedes.

"Get in; I got some errands to run." He sounds polite and non-threatening.

Benjamin is not afraid of Marco. They have been business associates and even friends for nearly two years now and Benjamin trusts him and Marco, in turn, trusts and respects Benjamin. Benjamin gets in the car and they drive off. Angelica watches from the upstairs office bathroom window. She is in tears.

Marco is a handsome man, thin yet muscular, and stands about the same height as Benjamin's 5 feet 10 inches. Today he is very sharp in a beige silk suit with a black shirt opened enough to expose dark chest hairs and some sort of gold medallion on a gold chain. Marco likes to wear jewelry and is proud of his gold Rolex, wristband and rings. He is very stylish for a man in his mid-sixties. Benjamin is wearing a pair of jeans, a flowered shirt and discolored Adidas. The two of them look out of place together.

"You look like shit, my friend." Marco says after a long silence.

"Well, I feel like shit, Marco."

"What the fuck are you doing with my daughter?"

"I am madly in love with your daughter."

"You are fucking crazy. First of all let me tell you that it is never a good idea to be madly in love with anybody and

120

The Suicide Note

secondly you don't even know Angelica. She is my daughter and I love her but she is not for you. She has many troubles, my friend...many troubles."

"Well, maybe I'm the one who can help her with her troubles," Benjamin fires back, unwavering in his resolve.

By now Marco is on the Pacific Coast Highway exceeding the speed limit by at least 10 miles per hour. Oil rigs are bobbing up and down like giant hammers out one side of the car and surfers are unloading or loading their boards from their vehicles on the other side. They continue on for a while in silence. At a major intersection, at what seems to be a desolate spot, Marco turns to the west and they are soon pulling into the parking lot of the Ritz Carlton at Laguna Niguel. After a valet takes Marco's keys a bellman greets them.

"Are you dining with us today, Mr. Centoni?"

"No, Richard, I am just going to have a coffee with my friend here."

Marco knows that Benjamin does not drink and would have much preferred that he did under the current circumstances. Richard escorts them to the main dining room and instructs the hostess to bring a pot of coffee. As the main room only serves dinner it is not yet open and the two sit alone and undisturbed.

"Benjamin, I like you. We have shared some good times together and you have shared with me some of your personal background and for that I respect you. You have treated me fairly in our business dealings. I have made you some money and you have given me what I hope is good advice so I too will make some money."

"Well, I think..."

121

J. McGregor Colt

"Please; you no think and no speak. I just want you to listen, *e chiaro?*"

Marco takes a sip of his coffee and Benjamin follows suit. Benjamin is not sure what he is in for but he knows when to shut up and listen; at least this is something that he has learned to do in his sobriety.

"Benjamin. You say you are in love with my daughter to me. You tell me this but all I can think is that you are an idiot. You don't even know Angelica. Angelica is a very troubled person and she has caused me and my wife a great deal of difficulty over the years. When she was just a little girl we knew that something was wrong or different about her. She does not know how to tell the truth. She is always lying about everything. We send her away to expensive private school. When she come back she just break our heart. Fucking *melanzana!* I like you Benjamin. You take my advice and hop back on the airplane and go home. This is no good for you. Angelica needs to take care of her business here. This is not a business for you. You stay out of it. I am giving you fair warning, my friend."

Marco had never spoken to Benjamin in this stern manner before and it is obvious to Benjamin that he is sincere and concerned. He knows Marco is giving him what he thinks to be good fatherly advice.

"With no offense intended to you, Mr. Centoni, I would ask that you do not block my access to Angelica before I leave. I will leave but I need to talk to her before I go."

"Block your access? I will do nothing. I have said my piece. You are a big boy. You do what you want and, *dio non voglia,* Angelica will do what she wants just as she always has. Now let's go. I will give you a ride to your car. You have a car?"

The Suicide Note

"Yeah!"

They get up and leave. Marco tries to pay for the coffee but the hostess will not take his money.

"No, please, Mr. Centoni, it has been taken care of."

Marco and Benjamin drive back up the coast and speak only of generalities; how the River City restaurant is doing, the beautiful area they are driving through, the incredible amount of money settling in Southern California. There is no more talk of Angelica and when they get back to the restaurant in Laguna Beach Benjamin gets out of the car and Marco drives off.

By now it is a little past five in the afternoon and the light has faded. There could have been a sunset but the sky is overcast and it is impossible to tell if the sun has passed the horizon or not. As Benjamin enters the bar he sees Angelica sitting with a group of people in front of a cocktail. The bar is beginning to fill with a Friday after-work crowd and when Angelica sees Benjamin approaching she stands to greet him. She is a bit nervous but introduces him to her friends and asks him to join them. Benjamin sits and orders a beer. This is the first alcoholic beverage he had ordered in over three years but the words flow easily from his lips.

"I'll have a Corona."

"So, you down here from Oregon, Benjamin?" asks a very attractive black woman sitting with them.

"Yeah, I guess I brought the weather with me?" Benjamin feels awkward and just wants to get Angelica alone so they can talk and sort things out. Angelica assures him that the weather has been like this all week and tells the group that it is probably nicer up in River City at the moment.

123

J. McGregor Colt

When the waitress comes around to bring Benjamin his beer and to check on things Angelica orders another rum and Coke. Benjamin whispers to her that he would like to go somewhere and talk but she insists that they have one more so Benjamin complies and takes a sip of his Corona. Within an hour the bar is packed and many people have come over to their table and are introduced to Benjamin. Soon more drinks are ordered and by the time David comes over to tell Angelica that she has a phone call, Benjamin has had two Coronas and a shot of tequila. The party is on. Benjamin has made several new friends and is being somewhat the life of the party.

When Angelica returns from her phone call she seems upset.

"Benjamin, I have to go and take care of something. Why don't you stay here and have fun?"

"Wait a minute!" he says quietly to her, "I came down here to see you, not party with these guys. I'll go with you."

"No, you can't. I'll call you later." And she turns to leave. As Benjamin stands up to follow her the beautiful black woman says, "Let it go, dude!"

Benjamin answers; "I can't" and follows Angelica out the door.

"You can't come with me, I have to go pick up my kids."

"Why didn't you tell me you have kids?"

"It's complicated, Benjamin."

"What's so fucking complicated?" Benjamin's voice gained several decibels and he has drawn the attention of the valet parking attendants.

"This dude bothering you, Angelica?" a large black guy in a valet uniform belts out as he approaches them.

124

The Suicide Note

"No, it's okay, Tyron; he's a friend of mine."

"Yeah, that's just it; I thought we were more than friends." Benjamin says to her calmly as he reaches down and grasps both of her hands gently.

"What we had at Cascadia meant a lot to me. I opened up my heart to you and I thought that you had opened up yours to me. I am in love with you, Angelica, and I don't care about your past, the fact that you have kids or any other bullshit you haven't told me about. I love you and can't stop thinking about you and I kinda got the impression that you felt the same way." He lets out a long sigh. "There. I guess I got that off my chest."

Angelica smiles and says, "Okay; come on, I gotta go pick up my kids."

By that time they are around the corner, and in the parking lot reserved for employees Benjamin turns her around, puts his arms around her firmly and they kiss long and hard. Angelica is in love too, he figures, and everything is going to be all right.

Angelica's car is a thirty-year-old white Mercury Comet four-door sedan that is faded by the sun and rusted around the edges by the salt air. Angelica refers to this mode of transportation as her "Vomit Comet." There is evidence of more than one fender bender and the passenger side rear door is red. This car is a true pile of junk but Benjamin climbs in the passenger seat and before Angelica can put the car in gear he locks her in another long and hard kiss.

"We gotta go now, I'm really late," she says gently and affectionately.

Benjamin has finally relaxed and they head out the driveway and south down the coast on the PCH. As they

125

J. McGregor Colt

drive down the coast Benjamin tries to let Angelica know that whatever her past is or whatever her reason is for not telling him about her past, it is all right. He tries to let her know that regardless of her past he is willing to start from right now.

"Listen, my angel; I too have a past. I too have done things that I am not exactly proud of or want to go around telling everybody about. It's all okay. If you have things that you don't think are any of my fucking business... it's all okay."

"It's not that, Benjamin. Look, I was married before, okay?"

"Yeah."

"And I got two kids, okay?"

She is a little upset, visibly getting stressed out and her voice is trembling a bit at this point. Benjamin senses her tension and tries to calm her nerves. He understands that this whole situation of him just showing up, putting her on the spot, busting her in a lie, is very stressful.

"Hey; it's all okay. Tell me about your kids. I love kids."

"Yeah, well, you may not love my kids."

"Wait a minute. If I love you I will be loving everything about you and everything of you. I want you and everything that comes with you. I can't just say, like okay, I love your left leg and your ass and the upper right side of your face and say but I don't love the rest of you. I love all of you and accept what all of you is... including your kids, okay?"

"Yeah; okay, Benji."

"Benji?"

"Yeah; Benji, that's what my brothers call you."

"Benji!" He repeats and ponders his new name with acceptance and the assumption that it is not meant to be

126

The Suicide Note

derogatory. He knows that her brothers like him. He knows Antonio is mad at him at the moment but he knows Antonio respects him. The conversation takes a turn to the lighter side as they turn off the PCH and head up the hills into San Juan Capistrano. Benjamin is unfamiliar with this area as he had never been any further south than Laguna.

"So where do the blackbirds hang out?" Benjamin makes a reference to the annual swallow migration for which the Mission San Juan Capistrano is known.

"Blackbirds? You'll be seeing some blackbirds here in a minute." She laughs.

"It's good to hear you laugh, Ange. You have a great laugh."

"Ange, huh! My dad's the only one who calls me that."

"Yeah, well, now we're even."

"Yeah, well... I hate that name." She is getting agitated so Benjamin drops it and changes the subject in hopes the mood direction shifts back to where it had been thirty seconds prior.

"What did you and my fucking father talk about anyway? I bet he had plenty of bullshit for you."

Just as that is said she swings The Vomit into a left turn and enters the Mission Trailer Park. They have entered into an entirely different world; almost an entirely different planet in comparison to the multi-million dollar palatial estates of Laguna that they had been passing earlier. The sky is completely dark now, it is a little past seven o'clock and as they drive through the serpentine Mission Trailer Park blacktop there is no sign of life other than a few dim lights and the occasional glow of television sets beckoning from within the transient hovels. Benjamin has really not had any time to contemplate his current surrounding or question why he

127

J. McGregor Colt

might have been placed there before Angelica stops the car in front of one of the more fatigued trailers.

"Stay here." She is obviously still agitated from the "Ange" liberty and/or the fact that Benjamin had had a conversation with her "fucking father."

As Benjamin sits there contemplating his surroundings, recapitulating the past six hours in his mind like a documentary or, perhaps, an episode of *Unsolved Mysteries*, the door to trailer number 14 swings open and displays Angelica and two others in an explosion of riotous expletives. Benjamin has no time to focus his eyes on the participants in this fatuity before he exits the car.

"Hey, what's going on?" he utters tenuously.

"Who the fuck is this asshole?" comes from a squat young woman of Hispanic descent.

"Yeah, who the fuck are you, asshole?" follows an obviously agitated young black man advancing toward Benjamin with malicious intent.

"Hold on, Robert, he don't know nothin'... he's not involved, yeah?"

Robert holds short of confrontation with Benjamin about six inches from his face. Benjamin does not waver nor flinch nor let on in any way that he has nearly shit his pants. Robert is only an inch or so taller than Benjamin but at least twenty years his junior and appears to be twenty times his strength. Robert works out and with his shirt off, as it is at this very instant, it is painfully apparent to Benjamin. Benjamin turns on the charm.

"It's cool! I just came along to meet Angelica's kids. Are they inside?"

128

The Suicide Note

"Yeah, Robert, lay off. This is Benjamin, he's a friend of my Dad's." Angelica words do not register to Benjamin but put a different spin on Robert's aggression as he backs off immediately.

"Okay, cool." Robert is much calmer and Benjamin takes advantage of the lull to take control of the situation.

"Robert, why don't you and I go inside and get the kids? Okay, friend?" Benjamin suggests as he palms Robert gently on the shoulder.

"Okay, cool" as Robert turns and leads Benjamin into trailer number 14.

Angelica and the other woman stay outside and their debate continues in undertones. This Hispanic woman is surprised to see Angelica's chaperone and with no evidence proving his involvement opts to continue the rest of her consternation out of this new intruder's earshot. Angelica prefers the privacy for the balance of the discussion more than is evident as well. Benjamin follows Robert through a door which leads immediately into the kitchen facility of the single-wide urban palace to witness a clutter of empty beer cans, wine bottles and several days of unwashed dishes. A garbage pyramid is under construction in the far corner and through an opening above the sink Benjamin can see a television screen displaying some cartoon show in the next room. Passing through the kitchen and into the next room takes three steps and displays the backs of two small children seated only inches from the screen.

"Hey, Mandrake, this is your mom's friend. Get your stuff, you guys are going home."

J. McGregor Colt

A young boy and a younger girl turn and look up at Benjamin. They are immediately excited and in their enthusiasm, leap at him.

"You a friend of my mom?" the boy queries.

"Yeah!" answers Benjamin with very friendly enthusiasm.

"Who are you?" the girl pipes in.

"Well, my name is Benjamin. What's your name?" He speaks slowly and cheerfully and ends his question on a higher pitch to show her he is harmless and caring.

"My name is Isabella but you can call me Izzy. I'm almost six."

"Wow, you are getting old. Why don't I help you get your stuff and we'll go put it in your mom's car outside? She's outside waiting for us. Where is your stuff?"

"I'll show you!" they both shout very excitedly as they run down the hall.

Halfway down the hall a collision occurs and both kids fall to the floor in tears. Robert has gone back outside and Benjamin is left alone to console the two crying siblings. Angelica's children are black. She has finally confided that she had been married and admitted to having children but had failed to display the "race card." Benjamin had never been racially judgmental and is even somewhat racially oblivious so he takes to this latest offering without hesitation. There are young kids on the floor crying and in need of comfort and Benjamin takes the mantle of nursemaid without question.

He kneels to the floor and holds each in an arm and they cling to him as if they had been starving for his affection. They soon calm and show him to a small, cluttered room

130

The Suicide Note

that appears to be where they had been sleeping. Izzy shows Benjamin a suitcase and together with Mandrake they fill it with much of the room's clutter. As they weave their way back and exit through the kitchen door to the poorly lit area where the car is parked, the conversation between Angelica, Robert and the Hispanic woman ends abruptly and Angelica gives her kids a big group hug.

"Okay, my sweeties, are you ready to go home?"

Angelica is very loving with her kids. She is easily capable of turning off the intensity of the anger in the adult conversation she had been having with a switch and turns to love and nurturing with the children with an execution worthy of award. Worthy of award in retrospect albeit not worthy of note in Benjamin's mind at the moment, as he is quite eager to exit this scene and get down the road.

"Okay, gang, why don't we get in the car and get out of here and leave these guys alone. Nice meeting you guys."

Benjamin lifts the young ones into the back seat. He is a bit hurried and Angelica follows without words and opens the driver's side door.

"Sorry Silvia, I'll call you later."

"It's okay, but you know what I'm talkin' about, girl. Bye, Benjamin, it was good to meet you too."

They pull out in silence and Benjamin turns to the back seat and helps the kids get on their seat belts. Benjamin decides to direct his attention to the back seat rather than involve himself in any conversation or attempt at explanation with the driver. He also is conscious of how incredibly cool and understanding he is being in doing so.

131

J. McGregor Colt

"So Izzy, you told me you were almost six. When is your birthday?"

"My birthday is August twenty-first." Mandrake pipes in.

"He asked me first."

"You're a poopie."

"Mandrake!" Mom scowls.

"Okay Izzy, when is your birthday?" Benjamin repeats

"October sixth."

"Wow, you are almost six. You're gonna be six on October sixth. That's comin' right up. So what do you want for your birthday?"

"I want a race car that you can really drive. A real one. Like at Walmart." Mandrake would be heard.

"He's talking to me. Mom! Drake won't let me talk."

"It's cool, Izzy. Mandrake wants a race car. What do you want?" Benjamin is being very diplomatic.

"I want..." and again she is cut off.

"She wants a poopie." Mandrake is having no part of the attention drawn off of himself.

"Drake, you stop that right now or I am stopping this car." Angelica is calm yet firm and Mandrake knows from experience that he has pressed the outside of his mother's patience envelope as much as he is going to on this occasion. Benjamin is somewhat relieved to hear Angelica call her son Drake as he feels the name Mandrake is a little over the top.

"Izzy; okay, what do you want for your birthday?" Benjamin pursues.

"Well, you know those things where you can cook. You know those cook things that have cookies and Barbie things..." she is having difficulty explaining.

132

The Suicide Note

"She wants Easy Bake." Drake pipes in.

"Mom! I wanted to tell him."

"Drake, let her tell him."

"Oh, I know what an Easy Bake Oven is. Do they still make those? My little sister had one of those when she was just about your age."

Benjamin is having fun talking with Angelica's kids and is doing a great job communicating with them on their level. Considering he hasn't spent all that much time around kids except for Nadine's daughter Chelsea, he seems to be a natural-born father or children's advocate. Or maybe the two beers and shot of tequila he had an hour prior have not yet worn off, but he is into it.

Angelica leaves San Juan Capistrano and heads back up the PCH towards Laguna Beach.

"So where do you live?" Benjamin asks.

"In Mission Viejo," she replies.

"Isn't that back that way?"

"Yeah, but you need to get your car and a room," she says bluntly. Then adds quietly just to him, "You really can't stay at my place. It wouldn't be right with the kids. You know. I don't work tomorrow so we can get together."

Benjamin buys off on that logic and accepts the fact that he will be getting a room and then getting together with Angelica in the morning. As luck would have it there is a motel just adjacent to the restaurant and he notices the vacancy sign is lit when they pull in next to where he had left his rental car.

"Okay, you guys, I guess I'll see you tomorrow." Benjamin announces as he leans over to try to kiss Angelica. His kiss

133

J. McGregor Colt

is deflected and he catches on that this too wouldn't be right with the kids.

"Bye, mister!" Izzy says sweetly.

"His name is Benjamin," Drake interjects.

"Yeah, good-bye kids. You take good care of your mom. Bye, Mom." And he closes the car door and stands there as they drive off in The Vomit.

The sounds of a lively bar crowd float through the damp night air as he grabs his bag from the car. He can see Tyron and two other valets horsing around at the valet stand as he crosses a small side street to the Santa Catalina Inn and his thoughts are dominated by the persistent passion he now carries for Angelica. She has latched or he has allowed her to latch herself onto his heart, obfuscating any sense of the reality he had just endured. This woman had come into his life only two weeks ago. They spent a glorious three days together of uninhibited sex. They had hiked together in the forest, laughed together in the rain and cuddled together in front of the television. He had opened up his soul to her and felt that she had done the same. Her brother tells him that she is a thief, her father tells him that she is troubled and he has just learned that she was married to a black guy and has two kids. None of the latter seems to have overcome the former in his mind and he is vertiginous with love.

Benjamin goes through the check-in process at the Best Western affiliated establishment, goes to his room, showers, shaves and is forthwith back to the bar. David is now entertaining at the original table Benjamin and his new friends had occupied and with him is the attractive black woman he had met earlier and who had warned him to "Let it go, dude."

134

The Suicide Note

"Hey, how you doin' D?" Benjamin asks as he places his hand on David's shoulder.

"Ben-jeee! Hey, you all know my good friend Benji?" David has let his alcohol consumption show a bit and everyone at the table lets Benjamin know that he is cool with them and makes room for him to sit down. His space is squeezed between David and the lovely black woman who, by now, is being very friendly and energetic in her acknowledgment of her acquaintance with the returning stranger.

"Hey, dude, you're Angelica's friend! This dude came all the way down from fucking Oh-ree-gone to see Jelli." She announces to the table and about half the rest of the bar.

Benjamin's new friends have a significant lead on him in the alcohol consumption department but he is not deterred. He orders a Corona and a shot of tequila. After explaining where River City is, what he does up there and his relationship to Marco, skirting the issue of his relationship or hoped-for relationship to Angelica, Benjamin's attention turns to the ebony beauty on his left.

"I'm sorry but I never got your name," he says in a flirtatious manner.

"Beverly!"

"Oh yeah? That's my mom's name" is his feeble response.

It is, in fact, not his mom's name but he says so in an attempt to show his acceptance of her. He wants to let her know, in this ridiculous manner, that he is not the least bit prejudiced regarding the color of her skin. He figures, for some reason, that if she thinks that she shares the same name with his mother that would do the trick. It's awkward for white people when they want to get across to a black

135

J. McGregor Colt

person that they are not a racist, that they are not insensitive. The dichotomy, of course, is that the color of the skin is even noticed in the first place. Benjamin figures that it would make things a lot easier on everyone if a law were passed making it mandatory for people wanting to have children to only have children with someone of a different color than oneself. By his calculations, in two generations everyone would be the same color. There would still be stupid people but at least their stupidity would not be seated in racism.

"Well, Benji; I'm not your mom," Beverly whispers in a very sexy voice into his ear as she gives the back of his neck a gentle squeeze.

Benjamin downs the shot of tequila that has just arrived and orders a round of shots for the whole table. It is apparent that his three years of sobriety have come to an abrupt end and that he is now swinging hard on the pendulum to the dark side of social conscience. Benjamin drank to relieve social anxiety and at the moment has a very relaxed take on the situation. As the night progresses Benjamin and Beverly become very friendly with one another. There is touching and whispering and this does not go unnoticed by the other members of their party.

"Hey, Bev, you gonna share this guy with the rest of us or you hogging him for yourself?" comes from another woman sitting across the table.

"Oh, no, I gotta get home." Beverly stands and shares good-bye hugs and kisses around the table.

"Yeah, I need to get goin' too." Benjamin adds with probably not the best timing. He forgoes the hugs and kisses but lets everyone know that it was nice to meet them and that

The Suicide Note

he would be around all week and would probably be running into them again.

"Thanks for the shot, dude," is offered by a young blonde surfer type who had been sitting at the table, and others add their gratitude as well.

Benjamin and Beverly walk out together and within moments Tyron appears from the shadows.

"Want your car, Bev?"

"Yeah, thanks, Tyron."

Benjamin stands in the courtyard with Beverly waiting for her car to be brought around and although he knows he is drunk he does not dwell on it long.

"So, I guess I will head across the street to my room." He says and realizes that what he had said may have been construed as a plea or an invitation for Beverly to join him. The booze running with his blood and into his brain will make it difficult for him to not take her back to his room. He does not; however, have time to explore the attainability of such a quest before Tyron wheels into the courtyard in a newer shiny black 740 IL BMW.

"Wow, nice ride, Beverly," he says pitifully.

"Yeah, I'm in real estate too. Maybe we should get together and talk about it sometime; you know... compare notes."

"Yeah," again pitifully.

Benjamin is very impressed with Beverly not only by her gorgeous appearance but also by the sophisticated way she carries herself. And now this...she is successful as well.

"Come on, get in, I'll give you a ride across the street. You probably shouldn't be walking in this neighborhood." And she gives Tyron a wink.

137

J. McGregor Colt

Benjamin climbs in the BMW and is driven across to the entrance of the motel.

"Benjamin, you seem to be a real nice guy. Be careful with Angelica. I mean be careful to not…"

"Hold on, Beverly. Everybody I have talked to today has told me to be careful. What is your relationship to her, anyway?"

"My brother is the father to her children."

There is a short silence as Benjamin collects his thoughts and registers this new information in his data bank. He is reminded that Angelica has kids and that she had not originally told him that she had kids. He is reminded that she had been married before and that she had not told him that she had been married before. And, now he is reminded that she has multiracial kids and that the father of these kids may still be in the picture.

"So where is your brother in all this?"

"You are going to have to get that answer from Jelli

"Yeah, I guess I need several questions answered from Jelli. Good night, Bev, and thanks for your company tonight. I had a real good time. You have some great friends. Maybe I can get a rain check on that comparing notes offer."

She leans over and gives him a peck on the cheek before he exits the car and the evening is over. Benjamin goes straight to his room, strips his cloths off, falls back spread eagle across the bed and is asleep within minutes. There is a lot for him to think about but his brain is full and it is numb.

138

Chapter
Eleven

The morning brings with it nausea, severe headache, diarrhea and irritation along with beautiful blue skies. Benjamin endures a serious hangover, the weather takes an about-face and he is overcome by both. He stands naked at the sliding door of his second floor lanai contemplating the expansive blue of the Gulf of Santa Catalina and ponders his current ill health. As he has had no recent experience with hangover and therefore carried no antidote, he utilizes a wet wash cloth and falls back in the bed with it over his face. He knows he must persevere, he knows that this day will require his strength and after only a few minutes he gets himself into the shower and begins his morning regimen.

J. McGregor Colt

Benjamin suffers under as hot a shower as his skin can tolerate until he acquiesces to a seated position and remains with his head down, letting the force of the water massage the back of his neck for a good ten minutes. When he finally turns off the water and exits the glass enclosure his skin is bright pink and the bathroom is congested with steam. As he shaves and brushes and continues with his basic body prep he feels revitalization and is more assured that survival is imminent. After his second cup of self-serve motel-room coffee he is dressed and ready to face the outside world. It is a little before eleven in the morning. Before he leaves the room to search for sustenance he makes a quick call to Angelica's cell phone and gets the one-ring to voice mail thing again meaning that her phone was, once again, turned off.

"Hey, Jelli; it's me. I'm going out to find some breakfast or lunch or whatever. Give me a call." He hangs up and ventures out.

About half a block down the avenue he makes out a sign that reads; "Sunshine Cafe. Breakfast All Day," and he sets out in that direction, noticing that the employees at Centoni's are setting up the patio seating for lunch. He goes unnoticed by David, thinks that is probably a good thing, and makes it to the Sunshine just as his cell phone rings. He overlooks the possibility that the call could have been anyone other than Angelica and answered the phone with a goofy "Helloooooo."

It's his secretary calling from his office in Willow Creek.

"Benjamin? Is that you?" Connie asks, somewhat perplexed.

"Yes," he replies, equally perplexed.

"Well, I'm sorry to bother you on your vacation but we have a problem."

140

The Suicide Note

"Oh?" Benjamin loves that word perhaps the best of all words in the English language. It's very functional in all sorts of occasions. It can be a question, a statement, an exclamation, it can be the answer and the question. In this case it was the question.

"Yes, Mr. Bagley is here and he is asking that his earnest money be refunded to him right now on the Willis transaction."

"Who is the agent involved in the Willis transaction?" Benjamin is somewhat disturbed that Connie would be bothering him with this at this time but knowing that Mr. Bagley is probably standing right in front of her he hides his feelings.

"Ron represents Mr. Bagley and T.C. represents Willis."

"And are either one of them there?"

"No, Ron is up in Goldendale showing property and T.C. is at a closing at the title company."

"Okay, let me speak to Mr. Bagley."

"Hello; this is Don Bagley. I am sorry to disturb you on your vacation, Mr. Mathews, but this deal has gotten ridiculous. The property is not how it was represented to me and my wife and I do not want to buy it. We like Ron but we think that T.C. is trying to pull a fast one with us." Mr. Bagley seems friendly but firm.

"Don, I assure you that you will not leave that office today until you are totally satisfied and everything is made right. You have me at a huge disadvantage. I'm out of town and don't have the benefit of your file in front of me nor the benefit of my agent's version of what has transpired. I would like to say that it would be most surprising to me to learn that

141

J. McGregor Colt

T.C. would be attempting to pull the wool over anyone's eyes, but the fact is you don't want to buy something after learning something that you feel was not disclosed to you.... is that correct?"

"Well, yes."

"And how much earnest money did you put down?"

"Five hundred dollars."

"Okay, listen; I am very sorry for your inconvenience and will sort all this out when I get back. If you will give the phone back to Connie I will get you your five hundred dollars right now."

"Thank you. That is the way to do business and I promise you that we like Ron and will continue working with him and your company until we find the right piece."

"Well, thank you, Mr. Bagley. Now if you would give the phone to Connie I will get this taken care of."

When Connie comes back on the phone she is humble and apologetic.

"Look, it's okay, Connie; just write him a check out of the operating account. Fill out a Release of Earnest Money form and have him sign it. When T.C. gets back, tell him to get Willis's signature on it right away and have the title company release the funds to us."

"Can they do that?"

"Write on the form that I have already returned Bagley's money and make a copy of the check you are writing and have Bagley initial and date the copy, have Willis initial and date the copy and attach it to the form so the title company knows what's up. It shouldn't be a problem. If it is I guess I just ate five hundred bucks but we don't have some guy out there thinking that we rip people off. Okay?"

142

The Suicide Note

"Okay."

"I'll call you later this afternoon and see what's going on up there. Bye-bye."

"Okay, bye."

After he hangs up and turns to face the Sunshine Cafe he realizes that he has an audience. Most of the patrons seated in the booths by the window look like tourists and Benjamin figures that they are staring at him trying to figure out if he is some important movie person putting some important movie deal together on his cell phone. Remember, it is 1993 and although cell phones are not unknown they are not carried by everyone and they are somewhat bulkier and more ostentatious than they eventually become.

Benjamin enters the restaurant embarrassed yet self-inflated at the same time. He discreetly turns his phone off and sits down for breakfast. It is now nearly noon but he orders his old hangover favorite, Huevos Rancheros, and contemplates what has just transpired over the last phone call. Benjamin is a good businessman when it comes to public relation issues and is more than willing to give up the farm to save the face. His theory is that if one person feels that they are being wronged, whether right or wrong, they will spread the word and others will believe, or, want to believe, and those others will spread the word and soon things will get so blown out of proportion that the word will be that Benjamin Mathews is a crook. It is far better, in the long run, to nip any negative vibes in the bud immediately by bending over backwards to satisfy the perceived injured party. In the Willis to Bagley case, if the seller is not willing to release the five hundred dollars being held in escrow by the title company

143

then all Benjamin suffers is that relatively small dollar amount, but he has retained a customer for life. The customer will always remember the way Benjamin handles the problem and will remain loyal and, hopefully, tell their friends. That is worth, potentially, one hundred times the amount of any potential loss. He will, however; take it out of his agent's hide if not reimbursed. He is fair, even generous, but he is not an idiot.

His thoughts on this are interrupted when breakfast comes and he quickly wishes he had ordered something else, and...ordered it somewhere else. The Sunshine Cafe offers very little sunshine in its service and the Huevos Rancheros look like it had been mixed in a blender and poured onto a plate. He eats what he can, pays his bill and gets out of there. When he gets back to his room he turns his phone back on to reveal no messages. He tries Angelica's number again and again gets her voice mail after one ring.

"Hey, where are you?" He leaves another message.

Benjamin examines his face in the mirror, carefully scrutinizing every line, wrinkle, and blemish. He paces the floor of the room, stays for a while on the lanai observing the beauty of the Southern California coast, turns on the television and plops down on the edge of the bed. He is bored. Where is Angelica? What is he even doing there, he begins to question. Soon he starts fantasizing about Beverly. The night before Beverly had been very friendly, even affectionate, he recalls. He becomes aroused at the thought of her, goes in to the bathroom, sits on the toilet and masturbates. It is Beverly he is visualizing as he strokes his penis...not Angelica. The process only takes him a few minutes and results in a feeling of relief but comes with severe guilt. The guilt is not so much

The Suicide Note

the guilt that comes with self-abuse but more so the guilt that comes from the thought of Beverly over Angelica. Angelica is the one whose love has consumed him yet Beverly is whom he lusts for in this latest sexual fantasy.

"What's up with that?" he says out loud.

Masturbation is a woman's term. Men call it beating off. "Beating" meaning abusive and "off" meaning over quickly. For a woman there is no guilt associated with the act of masturbation. For a woman masturbation is simply an act of necessity. For a man masturbation is oftentimes necessary but the necessity of it takes a second seat to the guilt and the feelings of shame. For a woman it is a drawn-out process of pleasure on multiple levels. For a man it is more of a quick let's-get-it-over-with-before-someone-sees-me oriented ordeal. A man will lock himself in the bathroom, double-check behind the shower curtain for observers and take great pains to hide any evidence of pornographic assistance when the deed is done. A woman will lay spread eagle on her bed with the bedroom door open, spend an hour in uninhibited ecstasy and when the session is over she will leave the night-stand drawer wide open exposing whatever aides of stimulation she may possess for all to view with absolutely no feeling of guilt whatsoever. A man is guilty, a woman is proud.

He thinks briefly about the concept of masturbation, the act itself, but his guilt subsides quickly, he cleans up and leaves the motel room. As he passes by the front desk on his way out the door it crosses his mind, only for a moment, that the lovely young blonde working the desk had been observing him on a hidden camera during his sin against nature and is standing in judgment of him. The thought passes as he

145

J. McGregor Colt

encounters the warm sun and sea air accosting him in the parking lot. He takes a serpentine course through the cars in the motel parking lot, crosses the alley and advanced through the circular drive to Centoni's while he places another unanswered call to Angelica.

The lunch scene at Centoni's is an engrossing one. The dining room is full, the bar is full and there are two or three different parties in the reception area waiting to be seated. Benjamin finds a single stool at the bar and sits in it. It is several minutes before he is able to get David's attention.

"Hey, David, how you doin'?" He wants to inquire of Angelica's whereabouts but holds off.

"Benji! Can I get you something to drink?" David is being very proprietary.

David is the youngest of the brothers and the closest in age to the yet younger Angelica and still ten years Benjamin's junior. Benjamin has never taken any of the chronology of all that into account as he only considers David a brother to the woman he loves and thus respects him with all that that relationship entails regardless of the difference in age.

"I'll have a Diet Pee!" That had been his answer to that question for the past three years, and; it easily spills from his mouth.

"Pepsi?"

"Yeah, diet!"

David stands in front of Benjamin as he shoots Diet Pepsi into a glass of ice from a gun.

"So, everything cool with you, Benji?"

"Well, I guess, although I haven't been able to get a hold of your sister today."

146

The Suicide Note

"She was in here just a while ago. I think she took her kids down to the beach, man."

"Oh yeah? What beach?"

"Just right down here." David indicates a direction right where Benjamin's motel is located.

"You mean in front of my motel next door?"

"Yeah, you stayin' at the 'Wish-I-had-a-lina Inn?'"

"Next door?"

"Yeah, she was just here with her kids. It's her day off. She said she was going down to the beach. Just take those stairs right in front of where you're stayin' and you'll probably run into her

"Oh yeah? Was she with anybody?"

"No, man; but she said something about meeting up with Bev. Hey, I gotta get to work. Be cool."

Benjamin is puzzled. Does Angelica not want him there? Is she trying to avoid him? He is puzzled, a tad bit embarrassed, depressed and pissed off all at just about the same time so he decides to take the walk down to the beach and confront Angelica. He is totally prepared to hop on the next available flight back to Portland if things do not go well.

The stairs to the beach are steep and many. On his way down he is already contemplating the walk back up with trepidation. Although Benjamin looks to be fit and healthy he is a smoker and gets very little physical exercise. It must be his high blood pressure and adrenaline that keep him looking fit but any physical challenge will leave Benjamin winded so he usually avoids such challenges. If the store that sold the cigarettes were a block away he would get in his car and drive. In many ways Benjamin is lazy. At the bottom of the stairs

147

J. McGregor Colt

and onto the sand he spots Angelica and her kids right away. As he walks towards them Izzy spots him.

"Hey, look Mom; there's that guy!"

Izzy is excited and runs toward Benjamin. When she gets to him she wraps her arms around his legs and gives him a squeeze. Benjamin bends down and picks her up and continues walking with Izzy in his arms towards Angelica and Drake who are sitting on a large coco mat spread out over the sand.

"So how you doin' today Izzy?"

"We're making a sam castle."

"No, I said; how you doin', not what you doin."

"Oh, I'm okay. But, we are making a sam castle. Want to help

"Sure!"

"Are you Mommy's boyfriend?"

"Well, I don't know. Why don't we ask her?"

At that moment they arrive at the coco mat and Izzy does not want to leave Benjamin's arms when he tries to put her down

"Let go of him, Iz!" Angelica proclaims.

"Izzy wants to know if I'm your boyfriend."

Angelica smiles flirtatiously at Benjamin yet avoids answering the question.

"Drake, why don't you and Izzy go get a soda!" Angelica takes a five dollar bill from her beach bag and hands it to Drake.

"I thought we were making a sam castle," Izzy protests.

"It's sand castle, you poopie!" Drake is still being antagonistic.

148

The Suicide Note

"Drake, knock it off. Go get a soda from Digger and when you get back we can make a sand castle. I just want to talk to Benji for a sec."

Angelica's tone is congenial but firm and the kids run off towards a beach hut called "Digger's" about fifty yards away. Benjamin watches the kids running and bumping into each other and he laughs.

"You got some great kids there, Angelica."

"Yeah, they like you; Benjamin. I guess we need to talk. There was some stuff I didn't tell you. Okay, I'm sorry." She begins to cry quietly.

"Angelica; it's okay. My feelings for you have not changed. I came all the way down here to get you. I want you to get out of here and move up to the Gorge with me. I'll take care of you and I will take care of your kids. You need to get out of here."

"That's nice but it's complicated."

"It is only as complicated as you want to make it. It's as complicated as you allow it to be. The complication is something that you control. You can make it complicated or you can make it simple. It's up to you. You are driving the car of complication. Come on Ange; I love you, I will make everything okay for you, you deserve me. I am the greatest thing that ever happened to you. Don't give up. Be with me, let it happen. I'll love you like you have never been loved before and I don't give a flying fuck about your past. In fact if you didn't have a past I wouldn't love you so much."

Benjamin is on a roll. He has on his best salesman's hat. He wants her and is fighting for the biggest sale of his life. In Benjamin's mind Angelica is the most beautiful woman alive

149

J. McGregor Colt

and he wants the trophy desperately. He has always been successful with women but he has never felt about any of the women in his past as he feels about her at this moment. Benjamin is willing to do anything and say anything for Angelica's love.

I remember loving Angelica so much at first that I debased myself and groveled for her acceptance.

He gets down on the coco mat with her and takes one of her hands in his.

"Come on, Angelica, why don't you pack up your kids and move up to Willow Creek with me?"

"I just can't pack up and leave. I have some things I gotta do."

"Okay, I'll help you do them. What are they?"

Benjamin is being very presumptuous and overly ambitious in his insistence that Angelica, a woman he barely knows, drop everything and pack up her life and move it in with him to parts unknown. Angelica had hinted that she would love to move to the Pacific Northwest. She had let on how impressed she was with beauty of the Columbia River Gorge, the tall timber, the waterfalls and the view to the snow-capped volcanoes and she also expressed a desire to get out of Southern California. He remembers her saying to him as they lay on their bed at the Cascadia Lodge in nakedness; "I gotta get out of that hell hole." And he is now conceptually willing and, even eager, to help her get out.

"Benjamin; you don't even know me."

Benjamin hears these words like a cliché. Benjamin fell in love with nearly every woman with whom he had ever had sex. He tells every one of them that he loves them and has

150

The Suicide Note

absolutely no understanding of casual sex. If a woman has sex with him a door opens. His emotional door opens and everything just pours out. He is capable of changing his mind but there is always the moment when he expresses to them his feeling of true love. He means what he is saying at the time because at the time he truly has the feeling. Unfortunately most of the woman take him much more seriously than he is being. Benjamin really has no idea what love actually is. It is Benjamin's dilemma. He falls in love quickly and out of love without a thought. Perhaps he sincerely thinks that he has the feeling of love but upon further inspection, or sobering up, or whatever, is able to say "OOPS!" or "Never mind" with total disregard for what effect his "I love you" may have on the receptacle of the moment. A prior generation would have called him a "cad." He is a lovable cad and sincerely never means to hurt anyone. At this moment he is sincerely and deeply in love with Angelica and is totally incapable of visualizing any alternative. Benjamin never learned not to let his heart believe what his eyes are seeing.

"Angelica; I know what I need to know about you and I know that I love you."

There is a period of silence. This is rare for Benjamin who tends to say too much, to oversell. For once he has the sense to just shut up and it pays off.

"I love you too, Benjamin. I haven't been able to get you out of my mind since I left Oregon." There are tears in her eyes as these words reach an elated Benjamin.

"Well, why would you want to get me out of your mind. I am the greatest thing that ever happened to you." He hugs her tight and she responds, laughing out her tears.

151

J. McGregor Colt

Benjamin is more than elated; he is overjoyed. Angelica has said it; she has told him that she loves him and he is exuberant with emotion. The most beautiful woman in the world has just told him the most encouraging words he has ever heard and he is in with both feet, body and mind.

"I want to move you and your kids up to Willow Creek right away. I know this is sudden but you already said you wanted out of here. I don't see anything good for you here and only things that are good for you are with me."

"Okay; but what do I tell my Dad? What about my job?"

"Maybe you can work at the River City restaurant. Maybe you just let me support you and you stay home with your kids"

"My kids!"

"I see them. They're right over there playing with some other kids. You have great kids and I can't wait to get to know them and show them some fun."

"Oh, Benji, you're so sweet. I love you." They embrace again and kiss for a long time with total disregard for anyone who may have been watching.

"Well... hello, young lovers," comes a voice approaching. It's Bev.

"OOPS; hey, Bev." Angelica responds and wipes a bit of saliva from her lips.

"What are you two up to?" Bev drops her beach bag on the coco mat, removes a sarong exposing a curvaceous ebony body as Benjamin averts his eyes and is reminded of his escapades in the bathroom only moments ago.

"Looks like I'm moving up to Oregon." Angelica blurts it out as an announcement to Bev, Benjamin and the world.

The Suicide Note

"Girl? You are mad. Do your parents know? Did you tell your brothers?"

"No Bev, nobody knows. I just now decided."

Benjamin thinks it might be a good time to let the two women talk.

"I'm gonna go check on Drake and Izzy." And he walks away in the direction of where the kids are playing.

"What's all this about, Jelli? You just met this guy. Does he know about James?" Bev is displaying a deep concern.

"I have been hearing about him from my Dad and brothers for over a year. When I finally met him I guess I already knew him. He's really a great guy and the kids like him."

"Do you think you love him?"

"You should see him with the kids." Angelica avoids the question and Bev is on to it.

"Angelica, you told him you loved him didn't you?"

"Well, I do," she says with not the best of confidence.

"Jelli! You best be careful, girl."

"What do you mean?"

"You know what I mean. You been here before. Did you tell him about James? About Nathan and James?"

"No, just shut up about all that. I will. You just let me handle it."

"Yeah, well, you better 'handle' it." Bev lifts both hands and gives the quotation mark indication with her fingers.

"Look, Bev, this is my business. This is going to be good for me; for Drake and Izzy. I need to get out of here. Just stay out of it. Please don't mess this up for me."

"Okay; it's your life. When you leavin'?"

"I don't know."

153

J. McGregor Colt

Just at that moment Benjamin returns with Drake on his shoulders and Izzy supported in his arms across his chest. It is quite a sight and seems as if he has been a loving father to these two kids all their lives. The kids have attached themselves to Benjamin physically, emotionally, and quickly. They hunger for attention from their mother and starve for the attention of any father figure and it is never more than obvious than it is at this moment. As Benjamin tries to put them down they resist, the mass of bodies fall to the sand and Benjamin tickles the kids as they scream and squeal with joy.

Angelica and Bev are entertained as they watch Benjamin play with the kids and the heavy conversation between them is soon forgotten. As Bev watches Benjamin with the kids she soon speculates that maybe this thing that Angelica is doing will be good for her and for her niece and nephew. They spend several hours at the beach playing and talking and becoming more comfortable with one another. By the time it is time to leave they all feel very close to Benjamin and Bev especially is surprised in herself at how quickly she opens up to him with her trust and admiration. It is agreed that Angelica is going to take the kids home and return to Benjamin's room with them so they can all go out to dinner. Beverly leaves and wishes them all good luck.

154

Chapter
Twelve

A ngelica had chosen a restaurant up the coast to Newport Beach. The Reuben E. Lee is a decommissioned riverboat at the Balboa Marina. It is a restaurant Benjamin had seen on numerous occasions while vacationing in Southern California but had never visited. It is a big tourist attraction, is always busy, is hardly ever frequented by locals and thus Angelica felt it would be safe from being spotted by any of her friends, family or spies.

They arrive a little before seven o'clock and are seated almost immediately. Dinner goes well, the kids are fairly well behaved and Angelica and Benjamin share a bottle of wine. The scene is that of a simple American family vacationing with their two children and enjoying an evening out together. There is the question, in

J. McGregor Colt

Benjamin's struggle with hipness, of multiracial children accompanying two Caucasian parents but that could always be explained through adoption, he figures, and thus the parents could be perceived as being all the more loving and accepting.

After dinner the foursome take a stroll around the marina and admire all the million-dollar yachts and the beautiful people sitting on their aft decks enjoying the evening air. Izzy and Drake are having a great time with Benjamin. He tells them stories, makes them laugh and pays attention to them. They love him. Shortly into the car ride back to Laguna the two kids fall asleep in the back seat. It is after ten and they have had a long fun-filled day. The sleeping kids give Benjamin and Angelica an opportunity to talk.

"Okay, my Jelli; how are we gonna do this?"

"Do what, my Benji?" Angelica is being fun and playful as she slides her hand between his legs.

Benjamin becomes instantly aroused.

"Oh, so you want to get frisky." He says in a low voice encouraging her moves.

"Oh yeah, baby." She snuggles closer and kisses his neck

"Why don't you and the kids stay in my room tonight? There's a separate bedroom and the couch folds out into a bed for the kids."

"Okay, Benji; that sounds good."

"Okay; so how are we going to get you moved up to the Gorge?"

"Yeah; well I've been thinking about that. You should probably go back and give me a couple of weeks to get things settled up here and, you know, work it all out with my family and, you know..."

156

The Suicide Note

"Yeah; it's the 'you know' part I'm worried about."

"Don't worry, Benji. I am ready to get out of here and now that I've seen you with my kids I know that I am doing what's right. I am really sorry I didn't tell you about them. I was scared. I was scared you wouldn't like me or like them or didn't like kids. My kids have been the most important things in my life. They come first."

"And they should," Benjamin confirmed.

Angelica is being very affectionate and saying all the right things. Benjamin has a rock-hard erection that she is slowly stroking as she talks to him.

"You know, when you get home you need to start looking for a bigger place to live. Your studio isn't going to work out with two kids."

Benjamin had also thought of this and knows it's true. Brad and Jennifer probably would not be real happy if Benjamin showed up with a woman with two kids in tow taking over their garage studio. It was the Amansons who introduced Benjamin to Marco and in turn to Angelica but he is a little leery of their reaction to all this, and, the suddenness of all this. He knows he will need new digs.

"Okay, so I'll go home, find us a new place, you wrap things up down here and then you'll move up and we'll all live happily ever after."

"Sounds grrrreat!" She teases him and playfully sticks her tongue in his ear

He is overly aroused and reaches down and pulls her hand out of his crotch.

"Oh-eu!" She pouts.

157

J. McGregor Colt

"We're here and I won't be able to walk," he explains as they pull into the parking lot of his motel.

"Well, wait a second," she protests. "Do you have any wine?"

"No, I don't have anything in there."

"We should go to the store," she proclaims.

"Yeah, maybe we need to get some food for the kids too. There is a refrigerator in there."

"Okay, turn around and take a left at that second light

Mid-block after the left at the light is a giant lighted Grocery/Liquor sign announcing that it is open 24 hours. Benjamin pulls into the nearly empty parking lot and asks Angelica what she wants.

"Just get us some wine and the kids some cereal and milk for the morning. And; maybe some fruit... bananas. Maybe you should get two bottles of wine."

Benjamin agrees, gives her a peck on the cheek and has her lock the car door after he exits. He isn't long in the store and when he returns Angelica is just hanging up from a call on her cell phone. She seems startled and a tad bit nervous.

"Anything wrong?" he inquires.

"No; that was just Bev. I was suppose to do something with her in the morning and I was letting her know that I wasn't going to be able to make it." She says this very smoothly.

It all seems plausible to Benjamin and they drive back to the motel. Benjamin carries Izzy in his arms and Drake, who has woken up, follows behind. Angelica walks beside Benjamin carrying two bags from the Grocery/Liquor. In the room Angelica folds out the sofa into a bed and Benjamin places the still sleeping Izzy on top. Drake is wide awake by

158

The Suicide Note

now and wants to watch television. After a weak protest from Angelica it is agreed that he can watch television if he crawls into bed and keeps the volume down low. While all this is going on Benjamin puts away all the things he had just purchased and opens up a bottle of wine. His room has a little kitchenette complete with refrigerator, two-burner stove, microwave, coffee maker, dishwasher and a sink. The cupboards supply all the cooking, eating and drinking implements required for a party of four.

Angelica and Benjamin say good night to Drake and retire to the bedroom with the bottle of wine and two glasses. Beside the bed is a small table and two chairs. Benjamin places the two glasses on the table and fills them with red wine while Angelica retrieves a nightie from her oversized purse and disappears into the bathroom. Benjamin sits in silence for a few moments and takes a sip from his wine.

Angelica is in the bathroom longer than he had hoped and he eventually walks back out to the front room. The television is on but the two kids are sound asleep. He smiles, turns off the television and covers up both the kids. When he returns to the bedroom Angelica is posed on her side on the bed in a very sexy red nightie, holding a glass of wine in her hand. She has washed all the make-up from her face and has let her hair down which had been pulled back away from her face with a couple of hair pins earlier in the evening. Her skin is sparkling with a thin layer of moisturizer; she looks fresh and marvelous and very sexy. It is not long, not long at all, that they are embraced in passion on the middle of the king-size bed.

As things move from hot to heavy Angelica stops.

"Wait a minute."

J. McGregor Colt

She gets up, locks the bedroom door and when she returns to the bed she reaches down and unbuckles Benjamin's pants. Benjamin stands and cooperates while she removes them completely. He is already aroused with a substantial erection. Angelica kneels down and cups his genitals in her palm as she places her mouth around his penis. Benjamin slowly sits back on the bed and reclines, leaving his feet dangling over the side, overcome with ecstasy. Angelica knows her way well to a man's heart and this man is squirming in joy as he ejaculates into her mouth while she milks him for all he has with her hand gently squeezing his gonads. When he is completely spent Angelica gives out a little giggle and goes into the bathroom. Benjamin cannot move. He just lies there and is still lying there when she returns.

"You like?" she whispers in his ear as she washes him off with a warm wet washcloth.

"Oh yeah, baby, I like."

Benjamin has now convinced himself that that was the best orgasm he had ever experienced in his life and he is in love with Angelica even more now than he had been. She is actually cleaning him up with a warm wet washcloth and he is lost in jubilation. Benjamin sits up, slips on his boxers and retrieves his glass of wine from the table. He really hadn't been all that interested in his wine and his glass is still over half full as Angelica pours herself another glass. She takes a graceful gulp and places the bottle on the nightstand next to where she is sitting on the side of the bed. Benjamin notices that Angelica's eyes are a bit glassy and then observes that the bottle of wine only has about an inch left in the bottom.

160

The Suicide Note

"Wow, easy on the wine; Jelli." he says to her as he leans in and kisses her on the neck.

"Well, you got another bottle didn't you?" she whispers as she places her hand around his neck and pulls him on top of her on the bed.

Benjamin's concern for the amount of wine she has consumed passes quickly. Angelica is being very amorous, libidinous. Maybe it is the wine, maybe it is an attraction she holds uniquely for Benjamin. After they writhe around with one another on the bed for a while Angelica stands, guzzles the rest of her wine, strips out of her nightie and displays her fully naked body in front of Benjamin lying on the bed.

"Jesus, you have a fantastic body."

Angelica's skin must have high elasticity because there is no sign that she had ever given birth to two children. Her skin is taut, her muscle tone superb and her breasts high. She is gorgeous.

"Want to see my snake dance?" she asks as she raises her arms up over her head rotating her hips.

"You're killing me, Jelli."

"Why don't you get that other bottle of wine?"

"Yes, my princess," he replies and starts for the door.

"Oh, I'm not a princess, I'm the queen." Benjamin smiles and is back with the wine and the corkscrew in a flash.

Angelica has not stopped her dance in the time it takes Benjamin to open the bottle and pour her a glass. He never takes his eyes off her during the entire procedure and is once again lying on the bed and pulling her down to him. For a moment she resists as she quickly gulps from her wine glass.

161

J. McGregor Colt

The details of their love-making will be left to the reader's imagination but suffice it to say that it is lustful, long in duration, and climaxes in mutual satisfaction. Benjamin performs well and feels very good, maybe even a bit arrogant, about his performance. This time it is Benjamin who goes to the bathroom and returns with a warm, wet washcloth. Upon his return he notices that Angelica has finished off her glass of wine and is attempting to pour another one. She is very drunk and knocks over her glass, spilling wine all over the edge of the bed and on to the floor.

"OOPS!" she slurs and makes a failed attempt to get up.

"It's okay, lie down, I'll get it."

Benjamin goes out to the kitchen, returns with a roll of paper towels and blots the red wine out of the carpet and off the nightstand. By the time the cleanup is accomplished Angelica has passed out. He gets her under the covers and straightens up the room. He picks up their clothes which have been scattered all over the room, slips his boxers back on, crawls back into bed and reflects on the day's events. Benjamin is so much in love at this point that he doesn't give Angelica's alcohol consumption much thought. He rationalizes that she is nervous or self-conscious and just got a little carried away. At any rate, it is giving him no cause for concern and he too is soon sleeping.

When Benjamin wakes up in the morning Drake and Izzy are sideways in the bed between Angelica and him. They had crawled into their bed at some point during the night and Izzy has her arms around her mother and her face in her breast. Benjamin smiles, slips quietly out of bed and into the bathroom. Before Angelica and her children wake

162

The Suicide Note

up Benjamin has made a pot of coffee and slipped outside for a cigarette and a cup. He is back and seated on the couch watching the news when Izzy comes out of the bedroom and curls up in his lap.

"Good morning, sweet pea." He gives her a gentle hug.

"Can we watch cartoons?" Izzy asks half asleep.

"Sure!"

Benjamin gets up and moves her from his lap to the couch. He finds a cartoon show on the television, goes into the kitchen area and pours himself another cup of coffee. Shortly Drake comes out and joins Izzy on the couch.

"Well, good morning, Mandrake. Would you two like some cereal?"

"What kind of cereal do you have?" Drake wants to know.

"I want Lucky Charms!" Izzy adds.

"Well, all I have is Trix," Benjamin proclaims.

They both agreed that Trix would be okay and Benjamin prepares them each a bowl.

"Is your mom up yet, Sir Drake?

"Yeah; she's in the bathroom."

"Okay you guys come up here to the counter and eat your cereal."

"Can we eat in here?" Izzy pleads.

"Okay, but don't spill." And Benjamin carries their bowls and spoons and places them in front of them on the coffee table. He pours Angelica a cup of coffee, takes it into the bedroom, places it on the dresser and taps on the bathroom door.

"I put a cup of coffee on the dresser for you," he announces to the closed door.

163

J. McGregor Colt

Just then the bathroom door opens and Angelica emerges with one towel wrapped around her head and another around her body. She has showered and looks fresh and beautiful.

"God, you are gorgeous." Benjamin puts his arms around her and they kiss.

"They're kissing!" Izzy yells out to Drake.

In a moment Drake and Izzy have their arms wrapped around Benjamin's and Angelica's legs.

"Group hug!" Angelica announces with a laugh.

To Benjamin, Angelica doesn't seem the least bit hungover. He knew that if he had had as much red wine as she had the night before he would be quite ill and probably still sitting on the toilet holding his head in his hands begging for God's mercy. In fact, if he had reviewed the prior evening, he would have realized that Angelica drank three glasses of wine at the restaurant to his one and then consumed nearly a bottle and a half by herself when they returned to his room. Her eyes are clear, she is energetic and ready to face the day with enthusiasm.

Benjamin had never been able to handle the next day very well and that was most likely the main reason he had quit drinking. Benjamin is forty-four years old and looks great for his age. The fact that he had quit drinking three years prior accounts for knocking about ten years from his appearance. People are always amazed when they learn his age and compliment him on taking such good care of himself. If they only had known him ten years prior they would realize the ridiculousness of that line of thinking. Benjamin never worked out or really did much exercising of any kind but he does appear fit and his face shows little sign of his age.

164

The Suicide Note

"Tonight I am taking the kids over to my parents' for dinner. Why don't you come along?" Angelica is dressed and is getting the kids ready.

Benjamin reviews, in his head, the scene with Marco the day of his arrival and is a bit hesitant with a direct reply to her offer.

"Well, what are you doing today?" he queries.

"I need to go into work for a few hours." She has the kids ready and appears eager to leave with them.

"What are you going to do with the kids?"

"I need to get them over to Silvia's."

Benjamin thinks about the scene at Silvia's and the Robert factor and does not think that this is an appropriate place for Angelica's kids to be.

"Why don't you let the kids hang out with me while you are at work? They can show me around."

"Yeah!" both kids scream simultaneously and proceed to jump up and down in excitement at such a prospect.

"Well, I don't know." Angelica states but it is obvious that she is not opposed to the idea.

"Look, it's no big deal. We'll have fun. What do you have to do in there?"

"I need to add up all the receipts, make deposits, check the deliveries, all the paperwork stuff. It should only take about three hours. I'll be done around two-thirty or three."

"Okay, so you go to work and the kids and I will go have fun and come by the restaurant at two-thirty."

"Yeah, Mom; pah-leeeze?" Izzy says with her hands folded in prayer.

"Okay; but you guys better not give Benji any trouble... okay Drake?" She looks at him sternly as if there may be some

165

J. McGregor Colt

potential problems with him that she is concerned about and as if her hairy eyeball is really going to do anything to thwart those potential problems.

"Yay!" they both scream and hug Benjamin around his legs.

"Okay, Mom; you better get to work," Benjamin suggests.

"Well, what about tonight? I need to call my Mom and let her know."

"Well, are you sure it's okay? I mean; did they invite me?"

Benjamin is a bit anxious about the whole meet-the-parents deal. Even though he has already met the parents, this is a different situation. He had met the parents on a business and even social level and now he is re-meeting the parents on a potential son-in-law level. It is different, really different, especially after his last conversation with Marco.

"Benji; the cat is out of the bag. My parents and my brothers know about us. Of course you are invited. I'm inviting you. So are you going to come or what?"

"What do you mean the cat is out? Do they know about you moving?"

"Well, no they don't know about that; but, you can tell them tonight."

"*I* can tell them?!" Benjamin says it as both an exclamation and a question.

"*We* can tell them. So? I need to get going." Angelica is being light and friendly but she is eager to get out the door.

"Okay, I guess I'm going to the parents' house for dinner."

The kids are already uninterested in the adult conversation and are back in front of the television as Benjamin and Angelica agree on everything and kiss good-bye at the door. After Angelica leaves Benjamin tells the kids to sit

The Suicide Note

still for a few minutes while he goes in to shower and change his clothes. He promises them that if they are good he will show them a real good time.

Benjamin showers, shaves and dresses as the kids sit quietly watching television. When he is ready he marches them out and gets them secured behind seat belts in the back seat of his rental car. Once seated himself and after the car is running and the air conditioner blasting away he asks them what they want to do.

"Disneyland!" Izzy announces.

"Disneyland!" Drake repeats.

Benjamin knows that Anaheim is fairly close but also knows that Disneyland would have required a much earlier start to make it worthwhile time wise and money wise. It is about a quarter to eleven as they leave the motel parking lot and head up Laguna Canyon Road. If they are going to do something like Disneyland Benjamin figures that maybe Knott's Berry Farm will be more appropriate and less challenging and he knows that Buena Park is fairly close to Anaheim so he offers that alternative as a suggestion.

"Well, it's too late in the day to start a Disneyland day. Why don't we go to Knott's Berry Farm?"

"Disney-land! Disney-land! Disney-land!" Izzy starts out and Drake joins in on the chant.

"Have you ever been to Knott's Berry Farm?" he asks.

"Disney-land! Disney-land! Disney-land!" they repeat.

By the time they reach the I-5 on-ramp to head north toward Anaheim, the chanting subsides and Benjamin has them involved in a game of "I Spy."

"I spy something yellow." Izzy says.

J. McGregor Colt

"No, it's Benjamin's turn." Drake protests.

"It's okay, Drake; let Izzy go."

"No, she's cheating." Drake demands compliance.

"Okay, why don't we just take a little break from I Spy and play something else?"

Benjamin is being very patient with these little ones. He is barely familiar with the care of small children and is handling the whole situation with ease and understanding. A lesser man would have been completely stressed out and ready to drive head-on into the on coming traffic at being suddenly exposed to arguing youngsters in the back seat.

"How about ABCs?" Izzy suggests.

"Slug Bug, yellow." Drake injects as he slugs Izzy on the arm.

Izzy lets out a high-pitched squeal and bawls hysterically until Benjamin can get to the side of the freeway and console her. Drake had turned suddenly brutal in his aggression towards his sister and really has no understanding of the severity of his actions.

"She's faking; I hardly hit her," he protests.

"Drake, maybe you don't understand how strong you are. Izzy is just a little girl. You are much bigger and stronger and maybe you don't think it was very hard but to her it was. Boys are never to hit girls. Okay? Now I am very serious about this, Drake you never are to hit girls. Why don't you tell her you are sorry so we can get back on the road to having fun?" Benjamin is calm but very firm and Drake is humbled and compliant.

"Sorry, Izzy," Drake offers.

Soon Izzy settles down and they are back on the highway. They pass the Disneyland exit at Anaheim and the kids pay

The Suicide Note

no notice. At five and seven neither can read and Benjamin is relieved. Benjamin is following the signs and changes freeways heading east towards Redondo when he spots the Knott's Berry Farm exit just in time to get over and off. The traffic is fast and furious on this warm Southern California Sunday in September. When they get to the gate at Knott's Berry Farm the kids don't even know they are not at Disneyland; all they know is that they are with a whole bunch of other families and there are a whole bunch of other kids their age running around and having fun.

The next two hours are brutal. Benjamin tries to squeeze in as many fun-filled adventures as possible in a short period of time with a thousand other people trying to do the same thing. They make a bee line for Camp Snoopy, ride on several rides and have their picture taken with Snoopy himself. Benjamin wants to visit the only part of Knott's Berry Farm he can remember from his own childhood and in Ghost Town they watch a gunfight, pan for gold and have their pictures placed on a wanted poster. It is a hectic pace that should have been more relaxed but the kids have a great time and become more attached to and comfortable with Benjamin in the process.

It is somewhat of a struggle getting the kids out of there and back into the car but by a quarter past two they are back on the road headed for Laguna Beach loaded down with new toys, candy and pictures memorializing the entire event. The ride back is uneventful as the kids entertain themselves with their new toys and recount in joy what they had witnessed. The traffic is heavy but at just about three o'clock on the nose they pull into the employee parking lot of Centoni's right

169

J. McGregor Colt

beside the Vomit. When they get inside the restaurant they immediately spot Angelica seated at the bar talking to David. The kids run ahead in excitement.

"Mom, we went to Disneyland!" Izzy yells.

"No, stupid; that wasn't Disneyland it was Knott's Dairy Farm." Drake was closer.

Angelica turned and looked to Benjamin and asks in surprise;"You took them to Disneyland?"

"No; I took them to Knott's 'Dairy' Farm," he replies.

"Wow, did you guys have fun with Benji?" she gets off the bar stool and picks up Izzy.

"Yeah, he's fun," Izzy announces.

"They have never been to Knott's or Disneyland before. How did you manage that?" she asks of Benjamin.

"I managed that just fine." Benjamin is almost boastful.

"Hey, Benji; you want something to drink?" David asks

"No thanks, David; I'm cool."

"You comin' over to my folks for dinner?" David continues.

"Yeah, well I guess so. Is it some sort of special occasion or something?" Benjamin is wondering.

"No, not really. We all go over to their house every Sunday for dinner."

"Well, I won't be intruding or anything will I?"

"No, man, it's cool. You are practically family anyway. Jelli told me what you guys are up to. It's cool."

Benjamin is a little uneasy, a little embarrassed and he turns his attention to Angelica and the kids who are showing her some of the toys Benjamin had bought them.

"Well, Benji, you didn't waste too much time spoiling these guys. Knott's Berry Farm, toys, candy." Angelica eyes are

The Suicide Note

a little glassed over and Benjamin notices that she has a large glass with a straw protruding from it in front of the place she had occupied at the bar.

"Yeah, we got pictures too." Benjamin is upbeat and suggests that they go out to the car and check out the pictures and the rest of the stuff the kids picked up.

Angelica says good-bye to her brother and all agree they will see each other later. Benjamin escorts the kids and her back outside to the parking lot. All the stuff the kids had in Benjamin's car is transferred to the Vomit and it is agreed that they will come to Benjamin's motel room between five thirty and six so they can go together up to Newport Beach where the parents live.

Chapter
Thirteen

Angelica's parents live in a development behind a guarded security gate called Newport Shores. As Benjamin pulls up to the gate with Angelica and her kids the security guard stops them and asks Benjamin what business he has there. Angelica leans over and says, "Hi, Walter."

"Oh, hi, Angelica, hey kids. Heading over to your grandma and grandpa for dinner?"

"Yeah, Walter. We went to Disneyland today," Izzy announces.

"Disneyland? Wow that must have been fun." Walter is friendly with the kids and it is apparent that he had known them for a while.

172

The Suicide Note

"It was Knott's Dairy Farm not Disneyland," Drake once again corrects his little sister as Walter pushes a button inside his station and a gate lifts allowing them to pass.

"I think all your brothers except David are up there already, Angelica. Have a good evening, I'll let Jake know you're on your way." Walter waves them through and never really makes eye contact with Benjamin who is very impressed with the entire scenario to this point.

As they weave their way through the palm-lined streets of Newport Shores it is immediately obvious to Benjamin that this is a very affluent neighborhood. The homes are luxurious and the cars in the driveways self-indulgent; Rolls Royces, Ferraris and Mercedes Benz abound. It is apparent that Angelica's parents are not just wealthy...they are filthy rich.

"Pull in here." Angelica indicates a drive to the left with yet another security gate.

Angelica waves to a uniformed guard and the gate is opened.

"Thanks, Jake," she says through Benjamin's open window as they pass through.

Immediately ahead of them is possibly the most opulent home of them all and Benjamin becomes qualmish. The parking lot is packed with about a half a dozen cars of varying degrees of decadence and a six-car garage with all doors open exposing everything from a limousine to a Turbo Porsche. Benjamin timidly parks his economy rental car as they are greeted by a man dressed as a chauffeur.

"Well, hello, kids, and who is your companion today?"

"This is Benjamin Mathews. He is visiting from up in Oregon. Benjamin, this is Ronald." Angelica makes the introductions.

173

J. McGregor Colt

Ronald is a large, well-built, light-skinned black man with graying hair in his mid-sixties. He speaks softly and with a slight hint of a Caribbean accent. He has the demeanor of a well-educated gentleman.

"He has been with our family since before I was born." Angelica has an obvious affection for Ronald and he makes himself easy to like.

"Well, pleased to meet you, young man, and welcome to Southern California." Ronald offers his hand to Benjamin and they shake.

"Everybody is around at the boat, Angelica." Ronald adds, taking Benjamin's car keys.

Angelica leads them around the side of the house through a giant arbor arch to the rear of the house, exposing Newport Bay and a 190-foot Fedship named "Our Angel VI". Benjamin is getting nervous. All Angelica's brothers and several elegant women are congregated around Angelica's parents. Giorgio and Antonio are down from River City, there are other small children playing on the lawn and two uniformed servants are offering things on trays to the guests.

"Who are all these people?" Benjamin whispers in Angelica's ear.

"Just my brothers and their wives and kids...cousins too."

"Oh!" Benjamin is overwhelmed and also under-dressed.

Everyone including Angelica had done themselves up for the occasion. Benjamin is dressed in a pair of cargo shorts, flowered shirt and is wearing flip-flops.

"Jelli!" Giorgio calls out and the entire crowd is drawn in their direction.

174

The Suicide Note

Marco raises one arm in a welcoming gesture and when Benjamin gets closer he offers his hand.

"Welcome to our home, Benjamin. What would you like to drink? How about a very good Scotch? That's what I am having." Marco is friendly and gracious.

"That sounds great. I guess I could use a taste of very good Scotch." Benjamin replies as Marco gestures to someone on the terrace above to bring him another and one for the new arrival.

Angelica's mother is off to the side talking to the wives and a female cousin and Angelica joins that group. Izzy and Drake run off to play with their young cousins and Giorgio joins Marco in a conversation with Benjamin. The rest of the male attendees had boarded the yacht and are messing around with the stereo system. Antonio is with them and has not yet acknowledged Benjamin. When Benjamin's Scotch is delivered, Marco and Giorgio and Benjamin sit down at a wrought iron and glass table which is dockside near the bow and even farther away from the rest of the activity. There are four chairs and the cushions are very comfortable but the whole setting seems out of place and even staged.

"So how are you liking it down here, Benji?" Giorgio inquires.

"Well, this place is pretty hard not to enjoy. I mean; it's beautiful. But I still feel more comfortable in my humble existence up in the Gorge."

"Humble? You are doing pretty well up there. You have a good reputation. People like you. You are a big deal up there." Giorgio is being very flattering.

"Yeah, well, maybe I'm a big fish in a small pond. I guess that's okay with me."

175

J. McGregor Colt

"So, I understand that you want Angelica to move up there with you, Benjamin." Marco cuts to the chase as he leans over the table cupping his Scotch in both hands.

"Yes, Mr. Centoni; that's what we have been talking about."

"Cut the Mr. Centoni shit, Benjamin. You have been calling me Marco for over a year now. Look, Benjamin; I like you. You have been fair and honest in our dealings and I will continue to do business with you based on what I have experienced. What are your intentions with Angelica?"

"I love Angelica very much and I want her around me. I'm not sure what you mean by 'your intentions' but I can assure you that I will never do anything to hurt her or her children."

"Yes, that's very admirable of you but what are your future plans? Do you intend to support her, feed her and her children, marry her? Or, is your intention to simply live in sin and never show her any stability in her fucked-up life?" Marco is blunt.

"Whew!" Benjamin replies and looks into Giorgio's eyes before returning to Marco and adds, "I have thought about marriage to your daughter and admit that I would love to marry her but I have been afraid to bring it up to her in fear that the suddenness of it would scare her off."

Giorgio chuckles and returns a smile from Marco.

"Well, I guess I understand that and I appreciate your honesty as always. Okay, Benji; so here's the deal. Giorgio is needing help at the restaurant in River City. He can't find anybody to do what Ange does for us down here. We are sending her up there with you and she will work in the restaurant four hours a day, five days a week. You keep her straight and make sure she gets to work. You think you can do that?"

176

The Suicide Note

"Have you talked to Angelica about all this?"

"That's what her mother is talking to her about right now"

"Well, Marco, if this is good with Angelica and it is good with you and the rest of your family then I will do what is expected and maybe one day Angelica will agree to marry me and we'll all be one big happy family." Benjamin is animated at this point and perhaps affected a tad bit by the Scotch.

"Okay, Benji!" Giorgio says as he reaches and shakes Benjamin's hand.

"Yeah, okay, Benji." Marco does likewise and adds a pat on the shoulder.

Just then Benjamin looks over across the lawn and notices Angelica looking at him. She winks at him and it lets him know that everything is all right.

"You want another glass, Benji?" Giorgio offers.

"Sure. Thanks."

Giorgio takes Benjamin's glass and walks up to the terrace with it.

"Benjamin, how much do you know about my daughter? Has she told you about her husband, about her kids?"

"Well, not really. But, I haven't asked. Her past is none of my business."

"We learn about one another by their pasts. People are their pasts," Marco proposes in contradiction.

"And, people learn from their past mistakes," Benjamin adds.

Giorgio returns with a glass of Scotch for himself, places another in front of Benjamin and resumes the seat he had been occupying.

177

J. McGregor Colt

"I don't really know anything about Izzy and Drake's father." Benjamin announces after taking a swig from his fresh Scotch.

"Well, that fucking *melanzano* is dead." Marco spits out.

"He means black guy. *Melanzano* is what he calls black guys. It means eggplant in Italian." Giorgio explains with a shrug.

"Black guy? Bullshit, he was a fucking nigger."

"Okay, Pops; he's dead."

"Yeah, big loss to society and now that other one's in jail."
"Other one?" Benjamin asks.

"Jesus, Benji," Giorgio pipes in. "You don't know shit about my sister, do you? Okay, listen! About ten years ago Angelica runs off with this nigger coke dealer boyfriend and they disappear for about three or four months. When she comes back she is married to this dude and strung out on cocaine and whatever else they were into. My dad flipped out and disowned her. Didn't let her in the family for about five years. So, anyway about after two years with this loser husband of hers she starts fucking around with another black guy and gets pregnant. Then Drake was born. She is still married and living with the first guy and still strung out but trying to get straight. She has this thing for black guys. I don't know what that's all about but it broke my parents' hearts. So, anyway the first guy just thinks the kid is his and they keep doin' their thing for a while and then she gets pregnant again. Well, this time her husband figures it out and gets really pissed off and beats the shit out of her and then goes and shoots the fucking boyfriend... Izzy and Drake's biological father. So it's a real mess, right? My dad still isn't having

178

The Suicide Note

anything to do with it. The father is dead, the husband goes to jail for life and me and my brothers get Angelica into a treatment center and her kids to a foster home situation with Beverly, the dead father's sister."

"Yeah; I met her," Benjamin interjects quickly.

"Okay, so Angelica is in a drug treatment center for like six months. She was a real mess. Then she gets out and is looking great and is serious about everything and gets a job doing the books for another restaurant and finally is able to get the court to give her kids back. After about a year she and my dad reconcile. He even accepts the kids now. You gotta know, Benjamin; this has been real tough on all of us but especially my folks. After she and my dad worked things out he put her back in the restaurant. This was a tough decision for him because when she worked there before, she and her nigger husband ripped us off big time before they took off on their little trip. That was eight months ago and she has been doing a great job. She is off the drugs, she shows up for work and there is no missing money. And, now she even has a white guy for a boyfriend...hey, Pops?"

Marco has been sitting in silence as Giorgio is telling all the gory details of his daughter's life.

"Yeah, okay, Benjamin, so now you know. You want a ride to the airport or what?" Marco's eyes are slightly watered.

"No, Marco, you ain't gettin' rid of me that easy. I'm still in."

Just at this moment three loud chimes resound from a bell on board the yacht and Marco stands up.

"Let's eat," he announces.

Everybody starts heading for the gangplank while Giorgio lags behind with Benjamin and lets Marco go ahead.

179

J. McGregor Colt

"There's more to the story, Benji, but I didn't want to say some things in front of Pops."

"Do the kids know all this, Giorgio?"

"All they know is that their father died. They don't know that the father wasn't the husband or that the husband is in jail. So, it's probably a good thing for them to move away from here because someday, when they get older, someone is going to blab."

"Yeah, so we eating on the boat?"

"Yeah, we are eating on the boat. It's our family tradition. Every Sunday the adults in the family share dinner on board Our Angel. The kids eat in the house. When you turn eighteen you get to eat on board. It's a real big deal. Tonight my son will be with us and Antonio's two daughters are here. I don't know where the fuck David is, but it's not cool to miss Sunday dinner unless you're out of town or something. My parents have only missed one of these things in about 40 years since my dad got Our Angel I."

Just at that announcement David comes running around the corner and walks up the plank with them. Benjamin, Giorgio and David are the last ones to enter the massive dining room on board. Benjamin is seated between Angelica and one of Antonio's lovely young daughters. He recognizes almost everyone present from the restaurant opening in River City and he is, once again, overwhelmed with the opulence.

Marco stands, clangs a spoon on an empty wine glass and the room comes to order.

"You all know my friend Benjamin from Oregon. He is welcome with us here by your mother and me to enjoy our family tradition on board Our Angel. I also want you all to

180

The Suicide Note

know that very soon Angelica and her children will be joining Benjamin up in Oregon and that Angelica will be working with Giorgio and Antonio at the River City restaurant. They have your mother's and my blessing and I ask that their success in this new venture be in all of your prayers."

A servant has poured everyone a glass of wine by this time and another is filling bowls with soup from a giant tureen.

"Well, Benjamin," Marco lifts his wine glass to the air. "Here's to you."

"To Benjamin," everyone adds while some add "and to Angelica." They all drink.

After Marco sits down things become a little more relaxed for Benjamin. All eyes and the pressure that came with it are off him as everyone starts talking among themselves about much lighter subjects. Benjamin leans into Angelica and plays a little footsie with her under the table.

"Well, I see they haven't run you off yet," Angelica says quietly to Benjamin.

"Nope... not yet," he jokes back.

Dinner takes a couple of hours, with five courses served in style. Benjamin had never eaten better and is completely bloated as the family starts drifting away from the table to other parts of the massive yacht. Benjamin notices Antonio get up and walk past him and he gets up and follows him out to the aft deck.

"Hey, Antonio, are you okay with all this now?" Benjamin and Antonio had not spoken since the ugly scene in the restaurant in River City.

"Yeah, Benji. I'm sorry about that thing in the restaurant last week. That was uncool. Sorry, okay?" Antonio offers his

J. McGregor Colt

hand and they shake and give a little side-hug. Benjamin takes Antonio as being sincere and everything between them as good.

"Hey, what are you guys talking about out here?" Angelica comes out and puts an arm around Benjamin's waist.

"The weather." Antonio answers as they all relax and enjoy a moment together in the evening air.

"Antonio and his wife have offered to keep Izzy and Drake here with them tonight and tomorrow so you and I can get things together for the big move," Angelica announces.

"That's great. And it's cool with your parents?"

"Yeah, it's cool." Antonio assures him.

After a bit they go back into the dining room and still seated are Angelica's parents and Antonio's two daughters with their mother.

"Benji and I are taking off now, Rebecca; we have a lot to get accomplished." Angelica announces this as a surprise to Benjamin but he plays along.

"Yes, thank you for everything tonight. I don't think I have ever eaten that well in my life," Benjamin addresses the group.

Angelica's mother assures him he is welcome back any time, gratitude is extended to Rebecca for taking the kids and they make their exit. It is all very abrupt.

Once back in Benjamin's motel room there is no further discussion of the move, Angelica's scandalous past or anything else. They get naked, make love for the rest of the night and when Benjamin wakes up briefly at four in the morning, they make love again.

The next day, Monday, starts for them slowly. Benjamin wakes before Angelica, showers and dresses quietly, letting his

182

The Suicide Note

new love sleep. He sneaks out and returns with two double lattes, a couple of croissants and some fruit he had found at a little spot across the street. Angelica is in the shower and when she returns to the bedroom he presents her with a plate he has prepared.

"Oh, this is sweet, Benji. Thank you."

"You only deserve the best, my queen. Hey, I noticed a school bus out there. Isn't Drake supposed to be in school?"

"Well, yes. He is in first grade in Mission Viego. He is going to miss a few days."

"Oh, well I never even thought about that. I guess that's just one more thing to add to my list of things to do in Willow Creek."

"Yeah, when are you going back up there?"

"Well, I guess it should probably be soon. I need to call my secretary and see what's going on at the office. What's the deal with you and the job at the River City restaurant. I mean, when does that start?"

"Giorgio told my dad that he could use me right away and maybe I am going up there with him, like today."

"Today? What about the kids?"

"Suzy was talking about letting them stay with her and then bringing them up with her once we get settled."

"Suzy? Who is Suzy?"

"Giorgio's wife. She still hasn't moved up to River City yet. She has been staying down here because of her job and she works real close to where Drake goes to school."

"Oh, when did all this get figured out?"

"Last night while you were talking to Giorgio and my dad. What did they tell you anyway?"

183

J. McGregor Colt

"They told me pretty much everything. All the things you could have told me... about your first husband, about the kids father, about your treatment, about all of that. I'm still here. I still love you. You can tell me everything, Angelica. I'm on your side. I love you."

"I love you too, Benjamin. I'm sorry. I was just too scared that you would not understand. I guess I was embarrassed. I have had a lot of challenges."

"Challenges?" Yeah, I'll say. That's an interesting way of putting it. Challenges! I like that. You're cool."

Benjamin gives her a big hug, sits down next to the phone and takes the phone book out of a drawer. He figures that he had better get busy back up in Willow Creek and had better figure out how he is getting back up there right now.

"Okay so you are going up with Giorgio when he goes, right?"

"Yeah."

"Well, how do we find out when that is?"

"You could call him."

Angelica takes an address book from her purse and reads off Giorgio's cell number to him as he dials the phone. Giorgio answers on the first ring and he and Benjamin figure that they can all fly up together that evening on a 6:45 flight. With that settled and Giorgio agreeing to take care of the tickets, they hang up.

"Well, I guess we are all leaving today at 6:45. You better go home and pack a bag or two."

"Wait a minute, what about my job here? Who is going to do that today?"

"I know nothing." Benjamin shrugs his shoulders.

184

The Suicide Note

Angelica fishes her cell phone from her purse, calls Giorgio back and they discuss the logistics of it all a little more thoroughly. Apparently someone else is handling the work across the street, Izzy and Drake are being taken care of and she is only coming up for a few days and then returning until she can get moved out of her house and arrange for a permanent move.

Everything is suddenly on a fast track and Benjamin has no time to think about what is happening. He calls up to his office, gets caught up on what was going on and lets his secretary know that he will be in first thing in the morning. He mentions nothing of Angelica or even where he is at the moment. Benjamin is in gear and moving quickly. His next call is to his airlines canceling his return trip with the understanding that he is to be given a credit for a future flight. He then calls the rental car company and lets them know that he will be dropping off the car at about six o'clock that evening at John Wayne. All this time Angelica is in the bathroom with the door open getting ready and listening to his very businesslike handling of everything.

Benjamin displays a certain confidence. He has a commanding air about him when he chooses to. Angelica feels secure with him and even more self-assured being around him. It begins to sink in with her what is happening; she is feeling good about it and even getting excited. They are chatting about the move and the motel phone rings.

Benjamin answered; "Hello, this is Benjamin."

It is Giorgio on the other end confirming that he has tickets waiting for them at the airport. Giorgio suggests that Angelica get home and pack a bag for her trip and some

185

J. McGregor Colt

stuff for the kids. He wants her over at their parent's house by three o'clock so they can take care of some family matters and suggests that Benjamin just meet them at the airport. Benjamin agrees with the plan and hangs up.

"Was that Giorgio?" Angelica asks.

"Yeah." Benjamin tells her the plan.

"Okay, but how did he know where you're staying?" Angelica seems concerned.

"I don't know. Was it a secret?"

"Well, who did you tell you were staying here?"

"I don't know? Maybe Bev, maybe David... the kids knew."

"Oh, yeah maybe it was the kids." She seems a little suspicious of something.

"It sounds like you think something is hinky?"

"Hinky? What a great word." She quickly draws the target off the subject and becomes playful with him.

Benjamin wants to make love to her one more time and after a very short protest from Angelica once again they are in the bed naked, making love. Angelica is very impressed with Benjamin's stamina and is more than the willing partner as she too has a strong sexual appetite. As they are re-dressing Benjamin decides to get something cleared up that he had been curious about. He had grown up around people who had a lot of money but he has never experienced the vulgar amount of money that he has been exposed to over the last twenty-four hours.

"Jelli, there is something that I gotta ask you. I didn't know the restaurant business could make so much money. I mean your parents have a pretty nice house, fancy cars, an enormous yacht. What's the deal?"

186

The Suicide Note

Angelica laughs; "Benji; you don't know?"

"No; I don't. What's the deal? Are you some sort of a Mafia princess or something?"

"Benji; you ever heard of Marco's Pasta Sauce?"

"Jesus, your dad is *that* Marco?"

"Yeah; Marco's Food Products, Incorporated is the largest producer of Italian sauces and pastas in the world. My dad or brothers never told you that?"

"No. I just thought he was some successful restaurant guy from LA. That's all Brad and Jennifer ever told me."

"That's funny. I just figured you knew. Who are Brad and Jennifer anyway?"

"They're my friends in Willow Creek, you know... the pharmacist. They are the ones who introduced me to your dad. They are the one's who own the place I am living in."

"Oh yeah; those are the people I met at the opening. They're kinda weird."

"No, they're not. You just need to get to know them better. They have really been good to me. They've helped me out. I wouldn't even have met you if it hadn't been for Brad introducing me to your dad and telling him that it was all right for him to do business with me."

"Well, how does he know my dad anyway?"

"I don't know."

They are dressed, packed and ready to leave. Angelica takes her car and heads out to do what she needs to do to be at her parents' with Giorgio by three and Benjamin has seven hours to kill before he is to be at the airport to meet them at six.

"Marco's fucking Pasta Sauce... Jesus." He says out loud to himself.

187

J. McGregor Colt

He needs to stay calm but the prospect of marrying into the Marco Pasta Sauce family excites him. All his life he has dreamed of living the life. His friends' parents from high school lived the life. Many of his friends from college are living the life now and Benjamin had always been just on the edge looking in. He had always just been a visitor. He has shared in some perks of the wealthy simply by being their friend but at the end of the day or the end of the vacation Benjamin had always gone home to his own humble reality. Benjamin did okay; he made a couple of hundred thousand dollars a year and that afforded him some luxury, always a new car, trips to Maui. He lived in Switzerland for a couple of years, but this new prospect of great wealth quickly consumed him every bit as much as he had been consumed by Angelica. He has fallen madly in love with an exceptionally beautiful woman and now he learns that she is from an extremely wealthy family. Basically Benjamin, at this exact moment, becomes completely myopic and anything that poses a potential obstacle to his dream is imperceptible and, therefore, not taken into consideration. Angelica becomes even more gorgeous in his mind and her past even further away and more insignificant.

With time to kill Benjamin decides to run into LA. He knew that there was a third Centoni's Italian Cuisine in Beverly Hills and he thinks he will run in and check it out. By about one o'clock he is walking through the doors to the restaurant. This one is by far the nicest and most posh of the three. It is situated on the ground floor of a Sunset Boulevard high-rise on the edge of the Strip just before Sunset turns to a residential neighborhood. He walks straight

The Suicide Note

to the reception podium and is greeted by a friendly, slightly snooty gentleman in his early sixties dressed in an expensive-looking Italian suit.

"Lunch, sir?"

"Yes, please, for one." Benjamin replies as his eyes survey the dining room to observe white tablecloths and gentlemen patrons dressed in suits and women of extraordinary elegance.

"Perhaps you would feel more comfortable dining in the lounge. We have the same menu available in there, sir."

"All right, that sounds fine." Benjamin is agreeable as he did, in fact, feel out of place dressed in blue jeans and an open shirt.

"Yes, just this way, sir." Benjamin is led into the bar. "You may sit where you please."

"Thank you." Benjamin takes a place at the corner of the bar instead of sitting alone at a table.

The bartender is an attractive woman in her mid forties and as she approaches Benjamin she says, "Hey, I know you. You're from up in Oregon. You're my Uncle Marco's friend. I was up there for the opening. So, what are you doing down here?"

"Yeah, I'm Benjamin Mathews," and they shake hands. Benjamin has no recollection of meeting this woman before but he goes along.

"I'm Cynthia. Are you going to have some lunch or you just drinkin'?"

"I'll have some lunch but why don't you bring me a Stoli and soda first."

"You got it, Benjamin." Cynthia walks back down the bar to her pouring station and mixes his drink.

189

J. McGregor Colt

Benjamin starts thinking that Ole Uncle Marco pretty much employed his whole family from brothers and sisters to aunts and uncles and nieces and nephews. He peruses the menu quickly and is ready to order by the time Cynthia returns with his drink.

"There you go, sir."

"Thank you, ma'am," he replies with a nod. "I think I am going to have the linguine with clams."

"Excellent choice. Let me put in your order and I will come back and you can tell me what you are doin' down here."

She is being very friendly and he cannot help but admire the nice way her backside fills the tight black pants she is wearing as she walks away. He acknowledges to himself that the Centoni family produced some very attractive women. The lounge is not very crowded; only two booths have patrons and there is a group of three guys in suits who look like attorneys sitting about midway down the bar eating lunch and talking over something intense. Cynthia comes back through the door to the bar that Benjamin had entered and with her is the host whom he had encountered when he arrived.

"Benjamin, this is my dad, Vincent, Marco's brother."
"Oh!" Benjamin stands and shakes his hand. "Very nice to meet you."

"So, you are my brother's friend from Oregon. It is nice to meet you also. You are in real estate, yes. My wife and I want to move up to Oregon someday. Maybe you can find us a good deal. It's cheap up there, right?"

"Well, it's cheaper than here, but it's getting more expensive everyday."

190

The Suicide Note

"Anyplace is cheaper than here. It was good to meet you. Enjoy your lunch." He is polite but needs to get back to his station and he walks back out the door after waving to the three gentlemen sitting at the bar.

"So, this is a real family operation your uncle has here," Benjamin says to Cynthia.

"Yeah, you could say that. So what brings you to LA?"

"Well, I came down here to see your cousin Angelica."

"Jelli?"

"Yeah."

Cynthia's attitude changes noticeably. It is like she wants to say something but decides that it would be better to not. She makes up an excuse that she has something to do and starts busying herself and tending to the other customers. When his lunch comes she delivers it politely.

"Can I get you anything else?"

"Yeah, I'll have another one of these." He slides his glass towards her on the bar.

He starts eating his lunch and when she returns with his drink she places it in front of him on the bar.

"There you go. So, you all set?"

"Sure," he replies but he truly senses a change in attitude from cousin Cynthia.

He eats the rest of his lunch and finishes his drink without another visit from Cynthia and when it is time to pay he has to walk over to the middle of the bar to where she is talking to the lawyer types so he can pay and get out of there. His warm reception has turned cold upon the mention of Angelica but Benjamin pays no attention to it and leaves.

J. McGregor Colt

It is three thirty by the time Benjamin finds his way onto the San Diego Freeway south bound and all six lanes are a parking lot. He creeps along for over an hour before the traffic starts flowing well past the Harbor Freeway Interchange. By the time he pulls his car into the rental car drop at John Wayne it is quarter to six and he quickly checks in and gets his ticket. He finds a spot to get a cocktail which is within eyesight of the ticket counter so he can see Angelica and Giorgio when they show up and he orders another Stoli and soda.

The flight was for 6:45 and by 6:30 Benjamin has had two Stoli's and there is no sign of Giorgio and Angelica. They announce the last boarding call for his flight and he makes the decision to board. Benjamin doesn't know whether to be mad or worried. He is mad and feels that maybe he has been duped by Angelica or maybe even the entire Centoni family and that getting him out of town is a big plot. Then he thinks that maybe something has happened. Maybe Angelica has been in an accident.

He is tense and considers getting off the plane, but, also; doesn't want to make a scene, doesn't want the drama. Benjamin is one of those guys who would never even consider sending something back to the kitchen. He never wants to rock the boat. He never wants to put anybody out and would become embarrassed if someone with him was rocking the boat or sending something back to the kitchen. He wants to make everybody happy. In a way it is selfish because what he really wants is to have everybody like him. That's what makes Benjamin Mathews happy. The flight takes off and he sits alone next to two empty seats.

192

The Suicide Note

I should have seen from the very beginning that something was wrong with Angelica and her whole fucking family but I was an idiot.

193

Chapter
Fourteen

As soon as his plane lands in Portland and he retrieves his car he dials Angelica's number. It is about 9:30 by then. Benjamin's anger had turned to concern about midway through the flight home and now he just wants to know that she is okay. He has reminded himself that he is deeply in love and that he is going to forgive her no matter what excuse she may have for missing the fight just so long as she is all right. Benjamin is used to roller coaster rides. Angelica answers on the first ring.

"Oh my God, Benji I am sooo sorry," are the first words out of her mouth.

Benjamin is relieved that she is alive and sounds healthy.

"What happened, honey? Is everything all right?"

194

The Suicide Note

"Oh...you know the traffic down here." She is bubbly. "I just didn't give myself enough time and got caught up in a big traffic jam. I'm sooo sorry."

"What about Giorgio?" he quizzes.

"Well, he caught a later flight. He should be in the air now."

"Oh...how come you just didn't come with him?"

"Well I was so mad that I went home. I didn't know that Giorgio changed our tickets until it was too late."

This is another little something that should have raised a giant red flag directly in Benjamin's face. In fact, now, the red flag is starting to show signs of fraying at the edges but he does not notice the flag at all and it is likely the pole on which he is focused. He is more concerned with the illusion of having a family and a trophy wife than with any of the objects being thrown at him to occlude this desire. His love for Angelica that had been festering inside him from the first day they met exploded with excitement when he realized the implications of potentially marrying into the Centoni family.

"Okay but when are you coming up?"

"I don't know. Let me call you in the morning. I'll call the airlines."

Angelica seems anxious. Why hadn't she just joined Giorgio on the later flight? The conversation ends with Angelica promising to book another flight and call him back once she has an arrival time. Benjamin is getting a bit agitated and dials Giorgio. That netted one ring and an offer to leave a message. He tries a couple of more times to reach Giorgio on his forty-five minute drive up the Gorge from the Portland

J. McGregor Colt

airport to no avail. When he gets home he just goes to bed. It is late and he is drained.

When Benjamin had left Seattle three years prior he was soon forgotten by most everyone but Woody Garwood and David Clements. For a while people wondered what had happened to him, where he was but after a bit nobody noticed his absence. Woody and David checked in with him on occasion but knew little about his personal life. The known is that he has pulled himself together and is running a very successful real estate brokerage operation. The unknown is what exactly drew Benjamin to Angelica with such force and vigor. The biggest unknown, however, is why has he blown three years of sobriety without the slightest thought?

In the morning Benjamin reaches Giorgio on the phone. "She's messed up, Benji."

Giorgio's story is that she was not at home when he came over to pick her up. He had hung out for a bit waiting and trying to reach her on the phone but... nothing. On his way to the airport, she called. She was drunk, Giorgio turned around and when he finally found her she was too messed up to travel. Giorgio had to get back to the River City restaurant so he booked a later flight. Angelica had fallen in with old friends that afternoon and one thing had led to another and time had gotten away. That would be the explanation that a reasonable person would go for. Benjamin was a reasonable person and he went for it. By noon of an exhausting morning putting out fires at the office and dealing with Angelica, she is booked on a flight which would be landing in Portland just before 9 p.m.

Benjamin gets busy at his River City office that afternoon and by five o'clock he feels satisfied that he had really

The Suicide Note

accomplished something so he walks across town and drops in to the restaurant. Both Giorgio and Antonio are sitting at the bar and Benjamin grabs the stool next to Antonio. The bar is devoid of customers; it's early and it's a Wednesday.

He gets a friendly "Hey, Benji!" from Giorgio but Antonio is less amiable. Both Giorgio and Antonio know that something needed to happen to intervene with what Benjamin is about to commit to with their sister but it is Antonio who takes it upon himself to try.

"Fuck, Benji... snap out of it. *Goddammo!* I love Jelli very much and only want the best for her but she is fucked up. You need to just run as fast as you can in the other direction. This will never work out."

"Dude." It's all Benjamin could muster.

Both Antonio and Giorgio spend the next several minutes explaining to Benjamin that their sister has a problem with drugs and alcohol and that she can never be faithful to any man. Benjamin objects and protests but at every turn it comes down to, "Jesus Christ, Benji... you have known her for a fucking month and we have known her our entire lives."

The brothers tell Benjamin some more details of Angelica's history. He learns that she had been in treatment more than just the once. He learns that she has had multiple boyfriends and was not faithful to any of them. After a little over an hour and a couple of glasses of wine Benjamin stands, walks out the door, not having been dissuaded, and drives to the airport to pick up his sweetheart. He meets her at the gate. Back in those days one could still do such things, park the car, walk the terminal to the gate and greet the arriving guest or returning loved one... it was a real hassle. Now the

197

J. McGregor Colt

arriving party calls on a cell phone to someone sitting in a car down the road, they pull up to the curb, it's way more sensible, a dramatic embrace and a way-too-passionate-for-the-airport kiss.

Benjamin had decided on the way in that he was not going to mention anything about the conversation he had just had with her brothers nor quiz her on what she had been up to. He is delighted that she is there and all they talk about is the future for the entire ride home and into the bedroom. They sleep well that night and are up early the next morning.

Benjamin lives in an apartment above somebody else's garage. It is a four-car garage, two double garage doors wide and all the spaces in between. It is a pretty large apartment and very nicely appointed but it is, indeed, too small for his newfound family life with kids and everything. Once the loving couple bathes and dresses they head down to the coffee shop for some breakfast and a newspaper. Over coffee they peruse the classifieds for a larger home but nothing sounds interesting so they decide to cross the bridge to River City and see what is there in the way of a rental house. Benjamin has about $100,000 socked away and could use it as a down payment on a pretty nice place. He is making a good living but he has a past and a very poor credit rating. After a couple of days looking at properties in the rental market Benjamin swallows hard and goes to speak to a mortgage broker with whom he had a relationship. Chip Harding looks over his credit situation and tells him that he can probably do something if Benjamin is willing to pay a little higher interest rate and can come up with a 20 percent down payment.

The Suicide Note

Angelica and Benjamin immediately start looking at homes to buy. They scour River City for homes in the $300,000 to $400,000 range and finally determined that they can get twice the house for that price if they stayed on the Washington side of the river. On day five Angelica finds her dream home. This house is perched on the cliff overlooking the Columbia, the Bridge and downtown River City. It is a very large home for the area and it has a swimming pool. Not many homes in Willow Creek have pools. An offer is made and accepted and the loan process is started.

While all this was going on Angelica and Benjamin are hanging out with his landlords, Brad and Jenn Amanson. They socialize in the evenings, go out to dinner or stay in and dine together. There is no drinking involved when socializing with the Amansons. They are very light drinkers, know that Benjamin is a recovering alcoholic and nothing is ever offered. In fact, the Amansons are a very good influence on both Angelica and on Benjamin. During the day the Amansons spend a great deal of time with Angelica, showing her around town and introducing her to their friends. Jenn and Angelica become good friends in only a few days. Jenn is very generous and most accommodating on many levels. When Angelica confides in Jenn about her kids and that she is nervous about how they will be accepted in the new homogeneous, white bread town to which she is moving, Jenn comforts her and promises that there will not be any issues. It is decided that while the home loan is in process Drake and Izzy will live in The Fifth Wheel. The Amansons' camper is parked right beside the garage and is hooked up to water, sewer and electric. The ladies agree that it will be perfect for

199

short term. All is set. In three more days Giorgio's wife will be flying up with Drake and Izzy.

One evening the two couples drive across to River City and dine at Centoni's. They are well received and everyone seems to know Brad and Jenn. The restaurant has survived its first six weeks and the place is packed. Word had gotten out throughout the Gorge that Centoni's serves fabulous Italian food, has a great wine list and makes stiff drinks. Giorgio is tending bar and Antonio is hobnobbing with patrons in the dining room. While waiting for a table Angelica ordered a cocktail. Jenn, Brad and Benjamin stick with club soda. Dinner goes well, Angelica has some wine with her dinner and Antonio joins the table for a bit while dessert is being served.

Everything is all warm and fuzzy until it's time to go. Angelica wants another drink. She has already had a drink in the bar, downed two glasses of wine during dinner and is getting a bit snippy. Now she is insisting on one for the road. Brad needs to open the pharmacy in the morning and convinces the group that it is time to go. Angelica pouts in silence during the ride home. Once she gets up to Benjamin's apartment she opens another bottle of wine, pours a glass and sits down on the couch. As the evening progresses, Angelica's speech becomes slurred and her attitude sours…she is drunk. Angelica is not a happy or fun drunk. She is angry and critical and lashes out at her brothers for not being more friendly at the restaurant. Benjamin thought that they had been very friendly. She criticizes the food. Benjamin thought the food to be exquisite. She proclaims that Brad is a condescending asshole. Her ranting goes on for an hour until she passes out

200

The Suicide Note

on the couch. Benjamin had not seen this side of Angelica. It is like a switch had been flipped in her head and she turned into a completely different person. He is a bit perplexed, covers her in a blanket and goes to bed.

In the morning Angelica is back to her loving, positive-thinking self and the prior evening's events are forgotten and never discussed. In a couple of days the kids will arrive and Angelica has things to prepare. She gets Drake registered in school and helps Jenn clean out the camper and make the beds. The camper has a queen-size bed in the back with a door that closes for privacy and another once a couch is converted.

"The kids are going to love it and maybe there will finally be some stability in their lives," she tells Jenn as she putters around tidying things up for them.

When the kids arrive they are, indeed, thrilled to get to live in a camper. Drake gets the private bedroom and Izzy loves the foldout. A routine starts and soon it is standard procedure for Benjamin to drive Drake to school every morning on his way to work and for Angelica to drop Izzy off at a day care center in River City before reporting in at Centoni's. Within a very short period of time they become a nice normal family doing nice normal family things together. Pretty soon people on both sides of the river get to know them as a family as they are seen at the grocery store together, at school gatherings and eventually at the kids sporting events. Both Drake and Izzy are very athletic and thrive at soccer. Angelica becomes a soccer mom and is quickly accepted by all the other soccer moms who are impressed with her energy and enthusiasm. When it is Angelica's turn to bring treats to

201

J. McGregor Colt

the soccer game, they will not be store-bought treats, donuts or fruit. She will go all out the night before and prepare cookies or muffins or brownies. These will not be just regular cookies or muffins or brownies but rather healthy, gluten-free, organic cookies or muffins or brownies. All the moms are very impressed with her and want to be included in her circle.

There are no more over-drinking incidents and after a couple of months they are moved into their new house. To call Benjamin's new place a house would not be doing it proper justice. It is more of a palatial estate on a three-acre hilltop overlooking the Columbia River. A long serpentine driveway leaves the county road, slithers up the side of a hill and opens up to a large, level paved parking area and a 7,000-square-foot, single-level home. The house was built in the mid-1950s in the shape of an "'L" and inside the "L" is a large swimming pool and paved patio with a built-in bar and barbecue. One end of the "L" is the residential wing and the other is a two bedroom guest quarters with a full kitchen and bath. The middle of the house is consumed by a large formal living room, a 12-place formal dining room and a gourmet kitchen and family room. The house had been built by a doctor so between the guest quarters and the family room is an office with a private entrance. Back in the day the doctor would see patients there. It has its own bathroom and wet bar. To Benjamin, this place is over the top and by no means could he have afforded such a place back in Seattle or even in River City. He only paid $380,000 but it would easily have been $580,000 in River City or $1,000,000 in Seattle. It was a real find and Benjamin feels like he is king of the world.

The Suicide Note

As the months pass Benjamin and Angelica become big entertainers in Willow Creek. Weekends are consumed with dinner parties with their new friends, pool parties for the kids new friends and lots of sleepovers. Parents are always willing to let their kids sleepover at the Mathews. Angelica is as charming as anyone could possibly be. Things are going well for her at the restaurant. Benjamin's real estate business is booming and he soon decides to open up a branch office 20 miles up river in Sunyton, Oregon.

Benjamin had outgrown his first office in Willow Creek after a couple of years and had built a beautiful office immediately at the north entrance to the River City Bridge with a beautiful view of the bridge and the river looking across to River City. Shortly after this office was completed he opened a second office in River City right downtown on Main Street and now he is opening his third in Sunyton. With an economy recovering from an economic downturn due to a closed aluminum plant Sunyton offers a much larger population base. Willow Creek is about 3,000 people, River City is twice that at 6,000 but Sunyton is over 20,000 and has several real estate offices with which to compete. Within six months of meeting Angelica he had bought a house, opened a third office and become a father of two. Soon there is discussion of marriage. Angelica has been on her best behavior and gives no indication that she is anything but a warm loving mother, mate and genuine human being. Benjamin is in love with her and marriage is the next logical step.

It is at a quiet Thanksgiving dinner table at home with only Angelica and the kids that Benjamin makes his proposal. He not only makes the proposal to Angelica but

203

J. McGregor Colt

also to Izzy and to Drake. He explains to them that he is not just marrying their mother but will also be marrying them and wants them to be on board with the whole thing. Izzy and Drake are already calling Benjamin "Dad" and although they are fine with the marriage thing they really don't care one way or another and just want a slice of pumpkin pie. The proposal is accepted and toasted with champagne. The kids are more thrilled by getting to be included in the toast than they are in the subject of the toast.

The Centoni family spends Christmas at the large home in Newport Beach. Benjamin and the kids fly down and secure rooms. Benjamin and Angelica will stay in Angelica's old room and the kids in David's. The home is huge, a three-story Mediterranean-style with seven bedrooms, arched doorways, double curved stairway in a grand foyer and more bathrooms than Benjamin can count. Although there is a library, a den, a sitting room, a movie theater, a poolroom and a full gymnasium in the basement everyone hangs out in the kitchen. The kitchen is what would be expected in a castle. One wall is consumed with refrigeration another with ovens and stoves and a large island in the middle lined with six bar stools. An additional barstool stands at one end with a small television for Marco to sit and watch news, sports and financial reports. Mrs. Centoni always seemed to be cooking things and is therefore always in the kitchen. If Mrs. Centoni is in the kitchen then Marco is in the kitchen and if Marco is in the kitchen then that is the place to be.

Marco has a very interesting story. At the age of 14, in Italy, Mussolini had both his parents executed for treason and was going to come for him and his 16-year-old brother next.

The Suicide Note

They were both able to escape to France and with the help of the French underground, got on a boat to New York along with thousands of other immigrants fleeing the turmoil in Europe... it was 1942. For the next couple of years Marco and his brother, Vincent, lived in the street and survived by doing odd jobs for several of the restaurants in Little Italy. Elena Maria Regio's father owned one such restaurant.

Elena, at the age of 14, was preparing food in the kitchen of her father's restaurant when Marco, by then 16, was delivering fish. He fell in love with her at first sight but she rejected his advances. She told him that he smelled like fish and that he would never amount to anything. Marco would not be deterred. He had been in the country two years already and his English was getting pretty good. One day he told her that someday he would be a very important businessman with lots of money and that she had better latch on to him now before someone else does.

"I will be a very big man and you should grab me while you have that chance."

She would laugh and the game would go on for another year. Marco would hit on her and she would push him away.

One day, on a fish delivery, he witnessed two men threatening Elena's father. After some inquiries he learned that these men worked for The Don, the neighborhood mob boss, and were extorting money from her father. Marco went to The Don and tried to make a deal with him. He would work for The Don for free collecting money but The Don had to let Elena's father and his restaurant alone. The two guys that had been arguing with the father challenged Marco on his proposal, arguing that there was no way that he could alone collect from all the people from whom they were extorting. Marco then challenged the one who appeared to be the tougher of the two to a fight and if he lost he would drop the matter but if he won then he would choose which of the two would partner with him in the collections.

The Don approved of this challenge and then witnessed Marco beat the crap out of his best man. For the next year The Don left Elena's father alone. Eventually the neighborhood heard the story and eventually it trickled down to Elena. She was still not buying in to Marco's advances but she was warming up a bit because he was charming and very good-looking. But; now he was working for the mob and she was apprehensive. A little over a year passed and Elena's father died suddenly of a massive heart attack. This unexpected disaster left her helpless. She was an only child. Her mother had died giving birth to her and her father had never remarried. He had raised her alone with the help from an aunt when she was younger.

For a week the restaurant was closed and the father was buried. It was Marco who stepped in and helped her re-open. She had already been doing most of the cooking and Marco became a most gracious host for the front of the house. He quit his job with The Don and eventually the two thugs reappeared asking for a percentage of the restaurant's income for "protection."

At first Marco just paid them but after a couple of months, after he had achieved getting the restaurant doing better business than it had ever done, he stopped. Two more times the thugs came by for their percentage and two more times they left empty handed. The third time The

The Suicide Note

Don came with them. The Don liked Marco. He had been a good loyal worker for him but he was not going to make any exceptions. He told Marco that if the money were not paid by the next day that he had better start to worry about potential disastrous repercussions that could befall him, his loved ones or perhaps the restaurant itself.

The next day came, there was no payment and early the next morning the restaurant burned to the ground. Elena was devastated. She had nothing. Her living quarters were on the second floor above the restaurant and although she was able to escape the fire, she was not able to get any of her personal belongings. She had nothing. When Marco showed up for work that morning Elena was sitting on the curb in front of the smoldering remains. She was not crying, she was just sitting there in a stupor in a nightgown and a robe. Several of the neighborhood women were trying to talk her into coming with them so they could get her cleaned up and dressed but she just sat there. It wasn't until Marco showed up that she broke down.

"You did this," she screamed at him. "Why didn't you just pay them? Now I have nothing. What am I supposed to do now, Marco?"

She was hysterical. This went on for several minutes but eventually one of the women calmed her down, took her home and got her cleaned up and dressed. Marco knew exactly what he needed to do but first he needed to get Elena to agree. They had gotten to the point where Elena no longer found Marco repulsive and had, in fact been flirting with him, offering him encouragement. Marco had been socking away money. He had been living very meagerly, not spending on things that were

J. McGregor Colt

not absolutely necessary and had also been stealing from The Don. He knew where The Don kept his money. The following day Marco sat down with Elena and told her that he had enough money to rebuild a restaurant but it would have to be in California.

"California? Are you crazy? I can't go to California."

At that point Marco quickly pulled her in to him and they kissed. This was the very first time that they had kissed. At first she was stunned but within seconds was a willing participant and they kissed again, longer and harder.

"Okay, so when do we leave for California?" she asked.

"Tonight, pack your things. Oh, that's right, you don't have any things. Here, take this."

He surreptitiously handed her a roll of bills. When she pushed it back and tried to say something he insisted.

"Buy some clothes, whatever else you need, and a suitcase. I will meet you at 9:30 tonight at the train station."

Once Elena realized that she had nothing in New York, no family, no real friends and that Marco was really her only option, she caved. That night they boarded a train for Los Angeles. The next morning The Don was found dead in his office, with his throat slit, in front of an open and empty safe. Nobody ever found out who did it and eventually nobody even wondered what had happened to Marco and Elena.

As promised, Marco found a failed restaurant in Newport Beach with a For Rent sign in the window. Elena and he worked very hard for weeks cleaning it up and converting it with a Tuscan flair. Elena insisted that they name it "Centoni's Italian Cuisine." Although Marco could barely even boil water, Elena was an exceptional chef and made all her own

208

The Suicide Note

sauces from scratch and her own pastas. She was amazing in the kitchen and loved being there. With Elena in the kitchen and Marco greeting the guests the restaurant was an immediate success and was being frequented by celebrities, movie stars and producers. Centoni's Italian Cuisine was the place to see and be seen. Pretty soon pictures of Marco and various celebrities were displayed on the walls throughout the restaurant. They were making a good living, got married and started having babies.

It was not the Newport Beach restaurant, nor the second Los Angeles restaurant that brought them the incredible wealth but rather Elena's sauces and pastas. After the second baby, Giorgio, Marco did not want his wife slaving away in a restaurant kitchen. He wanted her to tend to the children so they hired and trained chefs to make the dishes exactly how Mrs. Centoni directed them.

The Centonis were living well in a more affordable Long Beach neighborhood but when Elena became pregnant for the fourth time they bought a new, bigger home in a gated community closer to their restaurant. The new home was not anywhere as large as the home they currently occupy but large enough to house four children and a massive kitchen. While pregnant with Angelica Mrs. Centoni worked in her new kitchen perfecting her sauces. One evening, a dinner guest in their home, suggested that she package and sell her sauces. Bingo! That's what made them filthy rich. Marco locked on to that idea, created a company called "Marco's Sauces" and eventually "Marco's Pastas" and within in a couple of years they were on the shelves of every major grocery store in America.

J. McGregor Colt

Angelica's fifteenth birthday was celebrated in the new kitchen of the new house in which Benjamin was sitting at that very moment waiting for the rest of the family to show up so he and Angelica could announce their intention to marry.

Christmas at the Centoni house is nothing like Benjamin had ever experienced. There is a large twelve-foot tree that must have been professionally decorated in a corner of the massive living room. Presents are stacked high under the tree hiding the bottom third. The smaller children could not reach the gifts on the top. Thirty-five stockings hang on the mantel and adjacent walls, each with an embroidered name. There are sixteen kids running around hyped up on sugar, Marco and Elena's four children and their spouses/mates, Marco's older brother Vincent and his wife, Marge, and their three children with spouses and children. Cynthia, whom he had met at the LA restaurant, was single and did not come with a boyfriend. It's a circus.

Upon the arrival of each family the stack of gifts under the tree got higher and everyone went around and put things in the various stockings. Benjamin has a stocking; Elena has made one for him. She has figured out that he was part of the family now. About half the adults are seated in the living room keeping an eye on the tree and the younger kids, a few were in the poolroom playing games and all the rest are in the kitchen where Elena is holding court. It is not until this day that Benjamin realizes who wears the pants in the Centoni family. Although Marco had been the only one with whom Benjamin had conducted any business and although Marco ran the family business, it is most definitely Elena Centoni who runs the family.

The Suicide Note

Everyone defers to her, including Marco's older brother and his wife. Vincent and Marge had come out west several years behind Marco and Elena to run the second restaurant. Marco would not have opened the Los Angeles restaurant if he could not find someone that he trusted absolutely and the only person who could meet that expectation would be a family member. Vincent had been struggling in New York. Marge was a seamstress and he ran a restaurant for somebody else. They had four teenage children all of whom were getting into trouble with law enforcement. It was petty trouble until Vincent's oldest child Vincent, Jr., or Vinny as he was known, was under suspicion of rape by the New York City Police Department. Vincent knew that if he did not remove the rest of his children from their current environment that things would get even worse. They moved to California and are now part of the Centoni family businesses. Three of Vincent's children work for the family; a son is in the pasta plant, an older daughter in the corporate office and Cynthia in the restaurant. Vinny is a different story.

Benjamin notices right away that none of the cousins are all that friendly with Angelica... especially Cynthia. Whenever Angelica would enter a room that Cynthia was in Cynthia would get up and leave the room. He never sees them exchange any cordiality and the same goes for the spouses of the other two cousins. There is something strange about the whole thing. The cousins are not very friendly towards Benjamin either. He thinks that maybe they feel threatened by him so he just stays away from them.

By late morning everyone has arrived and it is Elena who decides when it is time to start passing around and opening

211

J. McGregor Colt

the presents. First she assigns two of her grandkids to pass out the presents. This is a great honor to be bestowed. Every year the grandkids would lobby for this honor. This year it will be Drake and Maria. Maria is one of Antonio's daughters, is a couple of years older than Drake and is very bright. The two of them make a good team. Maria keeps Drake in line and all goes well as presents are ripped open, hugs exchanged, gratitude displayed and mayhem. The process takes a couple of hours and at the end there are still a few gifts under the tree and a very large fire in the fireplace burning all the wrapping paper and boxes.

The kids are all playing with their gifts, the ladies are showing each other theirs and the guys make their way to the kitchen for beers. Breads and cheeses and charcuterie had been laid out in the kitchen for those who wanted to snack and after about an hour Elena gives permission to pass out the stockings. It is tradition in the Centoni family that everyone drop a little something in everyone else's stocking. Some are overstuffed and others are not. Benjamin only has four or five little trinkets in his but he is new and not known by the entire family. Giorgio's wife, Suzy has the most overstuffed stocking. All the kids love Suzy. She is the go-to person for babysitting and they all love hanging out with Zia Suzy.

Once the stocking transfer has taken place in the living room everyone disperses into smaller groups. Most of the kids remain in the living room playing on the floor, Suzi and a couple of the other ladies stay with them. A group goes to the poolroom, a group down to the boat and a group to the kitchen to help Elena prepare dinner. There is no shortage of servants around the house but Elena insisted on overseeing the preparation of all food served in her home.

The Suicide Note

Benjamin feels a bit awkward. He tries hanging with the guys in the poolroom and then on the boat but it is clear that he is an outsider and not privy to any of the conversations and kidding that is going on. All these guys have history together and Benjamin is not getting the "inside jokes." He finally settles on a bar stool in the kitchen with Angelica and Marco and a small group of females: Antonio's wife, David's girlfriend and Vincent's oldest daughter Valerie.

The conversation is lighthearted, a little politics, a little sports but mostly about how things are going on up in River City. People pop in and out for some food and comment. Benjamin feels comfortable there and Marco pours him a glass of Scotch.

At one point Angelica gets up to go to the bathroom and once she clears earshot Valerie asks, "How's she doing anyway?"

Antonio's wife furrows her brow at Valerie and cocks her head quickly toward Benjamin as if to say, "Don't ask that question in front of him."

Elena pipes up and says, "She's doing great, just great now that she has found Benjamin here," and she gives him a big hug from behind.

It's awkward, Benjamin blushes and everyone laughs. It is apparent that there are some family secrets. When Angelica returns there is an awkward moment of silence but that passes quickly.

Valerie breaks the silence. "I really appreciate the financial reports that you are sending down from Oregon, Jelli. They are very thorough and well done. Much better than what Antonio was sending me."

J. McGregor Colt

Valerie is the comptroller for the family operations, the restaurants and food processing plants. She holds a masters degree in economics from UCLA and is very well respected by all. It is Valerie who discovered that Angelica and her first husband had been embezzling from the Newport Beach restaurant several years ago and it is also Valerie who persuaded the family to keep law enforcement out of it and get her into treatment. Benjamin is not aware of this detail but Angelica is and thanks her sincerely for her statement. Everyone in the room, with the exception of Benjamin, knows what the acknowledgment means to both women.

Christmas dinner is enormous. There are twenty-five adults and older children seated around the long dining room table and the ten younger children are seated around a large round table in a smaller dining area off the formal dining room; all are being served by staff. Marco is carving a turkey on one end while Antonio slices a large baron of beef on the other. Plates are being passed around and getting mixed up, kids are spilling things and crying, it's mayhem. Benjamin loves every bit of it. He is elated and overjoyed to be included in such a family experience, one like he has never had before but towards which he has always strived.

At the end of the meal Marco clangs a spoon on a wine glass, stands up and gets everyone's attention.

"Benjamin and Angelica? Do you have something that you would like to share with the family?"

Benjamin turns red. This catches him by surprise but he stands and pulls Angelica up with him.

214

The Suicide Note

"Yes. First of all I would like to thank everyone, even you guys over there in the side room, for including me in your Christmas. I have never experienced anything like this before."

There is laughter and acknowledgment all around.

"And, I would like there to be many more Christmases in my life just like this one. Angelica has agreed to be my wife."

There is cheering and excitement and the kids join in and run around but there is also some eye rolling and even some glaring from Cynthia. Benjamin notices this and adds it to the long list of mental notes he has been tabulating. Elena insists that the wedding take place in the house and Marco is in full agreement with her insistence. Marco is prepared to make a big deal out of it. This is his only daughter and he was not able to give her away the first time she got married because she had just run off and done it with some guy of whom he did not approve. Marco had convinced himself that his daughter had snapped out of whatever she had gotten herself into and is finally on the right track.

The date is set for the first Saturday in April. In 1993 that was April third. There are a lot of preparations to be made.

Chapter
Fifteen

After an exhausting family Christmas in sunny Southern California Benjamin and his cell of the family arrive back to the Gorge in a snowstorm. Having never seen snow before the kids are both very excited and although Benjamin just thinks it to be a big hassle, he takes delight in playing with them, making snow angels and snow men and such things. He really is a great father to these kids and they had taken to calling him Dad fairly quickly in the relationship. Angelica, on the other hand, stays inside during most of the snow events and doesn't really participate in any of the kid-oriented activities.

All I really ever was to her was a day-care provider for her kid.

Once everything returns to normalcy, Benjamin back to work, Angelica back to work, Drake in school and Izzy in

The Suicide Note

preschool, Benjamin feels a sense of warmth, he is comfortable and happy. He is now living the life that he feels he was always meant to live. He starts getting very involved in school activities, after-school sports and gets the whole family skiing. Mt. Hood Ridges Ski Area is less than an hour drive from the house.

One Friday in mid-January he comes home from work and says, "Let's go skiing tomorrow." The kids screech with joy.

"Wait... none of us know how to ski." Angelica protests.

"Come on, Mom... please."

"Please, Mom."

"I can get you all lessons," is Benjamin's answer.

"But the kids have nothing to wear, no skis, we can't just go skiing." Angelica is quick to point out.

So the next day Benjamin takes everyone to a ski shop in River City and rigs them all out with everything except boots, skis and poles. He buys everyone helmets, gloves, goggles, pants, jackets and long underwear, figuring that they will rent the rest up at the mountain. They are all very excited with all their new gear, including Angelica, and the next day they get up early and drive up to the mountain.

Drake and Izzy are enrolled in a kids camp program and Angelica is signed up for a morning private lesson. Benjamin goes skiing and meets up with Angelica at noon in the lodge as planned. When he catches up to her he finds her being very flirtatious with her all-too-receptive ski instructor. She acts as if she doesn't even know Benjamin when he approaches. It is very awkward and Benjamin finally, after too long a period of time, leans in to the conversation and says, "Hey, come on, Ange, let's go get some lunch."

217

J. McGregor Colt

"Oh, Justin and I already ordered," she replies glibly.

Benjamin is a bit astonished that Angelica had not waited for him and now he seems to be the third wheel in a conversation between his fiancé and some ski instructor dude. He sits quietly through lunch and after Justin finally leaves the table he tells Angelica that he thinks that she had been very rude to him. He tries to explain how he feels but she just blows him off and accuses him of being jealous. He holds back his temper.

"Okay, let's go skiing. Let's see what you learned this morning."

Angelica is very athletic and Benjamin is surprised at how well she is doing after just one three-hour lesson. They ski the easy green runs all afternoon, pick up the kids and return home with the idea that they are going to come back the following weekend. They ski almost every weekend that winter and Angelica starts referring to them as the "Skiing Mathews Family."

The incident with the ski instructor was not an isolated one. Angelica is a flirt. She loves the attention paid to her by men and returns their attention whether Benjamin is around or not. Whenever they would go out in the evening there will always be a group of single guys flirting with her, asking her to dance and she will never discourage it. Benjamin will protest and she will always say; "Don't worry, Benji... you're the one I'm going home with." After a time he just learns to accept this and is happy that she does, indeed, go home with him at the end of the evening.

Angelica soon gets a reputation for being a "party girl" and once she starts making friends there are nights when she

218

The Suicide Note

will go out with the girls. After a few of these "girls night out" ordeals Benjamin puts his foot down and explains to her that she needs to make a decision.

"Do you want to be single or do you want to be married? This is getting ridiculous. In three weeks we're supposed to be getting married and you're out gallivanting around town like a crazy person." Benjamin is concerned.

Angelica takes him seriously and admits that he is right. She agrees to stop all the socializing and for the next three weeks she stays home and then they are off for a wedding and a honeymoon.

The wedding is an extravaganza. The ceremony and the reception are held at the Centoni home in Newport Beach. To the Centonis it's a small family wedding but to Benjamin it is over the top. The small family wedding consists of about 300 family members and close friends. The reception is catered by a very high-end Beverly Hills company and among the guests are a few movie stars and movie business moguls. Benjamin had never seen anything like it. He is now part of the rich and famous, he is shell-shocked.

After leaving Drake and Izzy with Giorgio and Suzy the newlyweds are off on a flight to Cancun for two weeks in the sand and the sun. Benjamin had purchased two regular airline tickets but when they get to the gate they find that Marco had upgraded them to first class. Benjamin had reserved a regular "Junior Suite" at the JW Marriott but when they arrive they discover that Marco had upgraded them to the "Presidential Suite." They spend two weeks living luxuriously and have a wonderful time. There are no flirtations from Angelica with other men and the couple

219

J. McGregor Colt

seem very much in love to the rest of the guests and staff at the resort.

They return back to Willow Creek as husband and wife. Within days of being back Angelica pushes Benjamin to start the adoption process for Izzy and Drake. Benjamin agrees that would be the logical next step and never considers any downside to the proposition. A lawyer is hired, papers signed and filed, it is all very official and very proper. Bada bing, bada boom, Benjamin now has a wife and kids and is very content.

Time passes quickly, without incident and soon it's summer. The kids are out of school and the days are filled with lots of activities. Angelica enrolls them in the local swim team, signs Izzy up for dance classes and Drake for Little League. They are the picture of the All American Family. Through the kids they meet other parents and extend their social circle quite a bit. At first it was just family, an occasional friend of Benjamin's and always Brad and Jennifer Amanson but now they have grown their social circle significantly and are always attending or hosting barbecue parties with some new friend or another.

Three years go by quickly. Benjamin's business is still thriving, he is doing very well financially, has gotten involved in the Chamber of Commerce and is a very highly regarded business mogul on both sides for the river. Angelica and Benjamin are great entertainers, involved heavily in the community and always on the A-list for social events. Every summer their house is a hub of activity with friends and their children enjoying the pool. On Sundays their small core group of three other couples get in the habit of throwing a

220

The Suicide Note

rotating barbecue party. Once a month or so it will be at the Amansons' place.

At one of these Sunday afternoon barbecue parties, late in the summer, Benjamin is presented with a potential problem, an issue with Angelica. The usual four couples and their kids had been at the Amansons' since early afternoon. There is drinking and eating and everyone is having a great time in the late summer sun. At dusk it is time to go home. The kids have school the next day and the parents have work. Everyone packs up and heads out except the Mathews. Brad and Jennifer encourage them to stick around a little longer. More drinks are served and after about an hour Benjamin notices the kids getting tired and he also notices that Angelica is drunk, slurring her words, speaking loudly and has become confrontational. All agree that it is time for her to get in the car except her. It is Jennifer who finally convinces her that they all have to work in the morning and that the party is over.

The ride home is unpleasant and once they arrive things escalate. Angelica gets abusive with Benjamin and with the kids. Whatever Benjamin tries to do to calm her down only make matters worse. The kids are crying and begging her to stop. She perceives their pleas for peace as them siding with Benjamin and that makes her even more livid. Angelica demands complete and unequivocal loyalty from her children. She screams at them to go to their rooms and pack a bag because she is taking them away and when they did not comply she starts chasing them around the living room. They become very frightened by her, run into the kitchen and huddled under the kitchen table trembling in fear.

221

J. McGregor Colt

At one point in all the commotion Drake cries out, "Why does it always have to be like this?"

Eventually Angelica tires and passes out on the couch in the family room. Benjamin quietly gets the trembling children in their beds and stays with them until they fall asleep. He leaves Angelica to sleep it off on the couch and goes to bed. The next morning everyone acts like nothing is wrong and after the kids are delivered to school Benjamin comes back to the house and confronts Angelica with the events of the night before. She is quick to pass it off like it is no big deal but agrees to stop drinking. She must have had a very bad hangover so it would have been very easy for her to agree that she should probably stop drinking. Benjamin is concerned but the incident is forgotten. Angelica does stop drinking, the family life returns to normal and the incident is not mentioned again.

When Angelica and Benjamin first started dating there was alcohol consumption. It was as if it was part of the whole dating ritual. Benjamin had been completely clean and sober for a few years prior, had kicked the cocaine habit and decided that he was okay with becoming a social drinker. He justified it by telling himself that the alcohol had not really been problem, that it was the cocaine. Whenever they would go out there would be drinking. Benjamin never drank enough to get drunk, Angelica would get flirtatious and amorous and sometimes a little over the top but Benjamin, at first, just thought it was cute. And; at first, they never had any alcohol in the house unless they were having people over. Eventually, as they made more and more friends and started having people over more and more Benjamin started to maintain a full liquor cabinet.

222

The Suicide Note

Angelica's vow to stop drinking only lasted a couple of weeks. On the weekends when they did not go out or have people over the alcohol consumption actually got worse. It would start with a martini or two after work on Friday and then a bottle or two of wine with dinner. Usually they would just go back to the bedroom and have wild drunk sex but sometimes Angelica wanted to fight. At first it was more sex and less fighting but after a couple of years it became less sex and more fighting and then one night Benjamin had had enough. There had been several occasions when Benjamin got home from work that it was obvious to him that Angelica had already been drinking. There was no glass, no physical evidence but her eyes would be glazed over and she did not want any direct eye contact. Whenever he called her out on it she would deny it. If he pressed the issue she would get angry and defensive. As the kids grew older they caught on to this routine.

On one evening after work Izzy meets Benjamin outside as he pulls up the driveway. She begs him not to say anything when he goes inside. She does not want to endure another night of screaming and yelling. When he gets inside and sees the shape Angelica is in he loses it. She is completely shit-faced and it isn't even six o'clock yet. He walks back to the bedroom, packs a suitcase, storms out the door, drives into Portland and gets a hotel room where he stays until Monday morning when he drives back and goes directly to the office. At about noon he receives a phone call from Angelica, who is accusing him of having an affair.

"No... I just cannot stand to be around you when you have been drinking. It's like a switch goes off in your head at some

223

J. McGregor Colt

point and you become this completely different person... a very ugly person."

"So now I'm ugly and you don't want to be around me."

"That's not what I said. I said that I don't want to be around you when you have been drinking."

This goes back and forth for a while. Angelica has a knack for turning the finger back on the pointer. Whenever she is challenged she will get very defensive and then quickly change to the offense.

"You've been drinking."

"No, you've been drinking."

Nothing is resolved with the exception that Benjamin makes her understand that he is not coming home until she gets help for her drinking. He is gone, staying at friends, for the whole work-week and on that following Saturday she calls and says that she will agree to counseling if he will come home. Benjamin goes home and they talk about Angelica's drinking very little that weekend other than the promise made to call Dr. Paul Ravens first thing Monday morning for an appointment. Dr. Ravens is a licensed psychiatrist who specializes in issues with alcohol and had come recommended by a recovering alcoholic who works in Benjamin's office.

On Monday morning Angelica is up before anyone, makes breakfast, packs lunches for the kids and kisses Benjamin goodbye as he heads out the door. Life is good, Benjamin is happy to be home and encouraged by Angelica's attitude. When he returns from work that evening Angelica is in the kitchen making dinner and Drake and Izzy are sitting at the kitchen table doing homework. Life is good. After dinner,

224

The Suicide Note

after the kids are put to bed, Benjamin asks if she had called Dr. Ravens and her reply is that he is booked out two weeks but she has set an appointment and the subject is dropped. The next two weeks are great. It is, once again, the perfect little family. Benjamin too does not drink in support of Angelica's effort. There is no mention of Dr. Ravens and after two weeks Benjamin asks Angelica when her appointment is.

"Oh, we don't need to waste any money on that guy. I quit drinking. I canceled the appointment."

"Look Ange, Dr. Ravens has been very successful helping other people deal with this stuff and you should really just go in and talk to him."

"How do you know about this guy, anyway?"

"Suzanne Britt in the office. He helped her."

Angelica becomes spontaneously unglued at this point.

"You've been talking to people in your office about me?" she screams.

She is furious and runs down the hall to the bedroom. Benjamin goes down and tries to console her. He explains that Suzanne is a recovering alcoholic and that he confides in only her and that she would keep it confidential.

"It's called Alcoholics Anonymous because everything is anonymous. She's not going to be blabbing everything around town."

"Oh, bullshit. Now everyone is talking about me behind my back. I hope you are really enjoying yourselves."

There is nothing that Benjamin can say or do to calm her down. He sleeps on the couch that night and in the morning there are no words spoken between the two of them and it is very cold around the house for several more days.

225

J. McGregor Colt

By the weekend things warm up, life goes back to a strained level of normalcy, the couple continue a sober life with the kids to school, dance classes, weekend trips to the coast, a couple of trips down to L.A. to visit Nonna and Nonno and eventually it's Thanksgiving. At this point they had been married for six years and had almost always spent Thanksgiving with Antonio and Giorgio and their families at one house or another but this year Angelica just wants to have a quiet family dinner at home with Benjamin and the kids.

Angelica studies recipes, makes a list of ingredients and goes shopping. She is very enthusiastic about preparing a Thanksgiving feast all by herself. She employs Izzy, now eleven years old, to help in the kitchen and when Benjamin gets home on Wednesday evening the kitchen is abuzz with pie making. Even Drake is helping out. By then the thirteen-year-old Drake is not involved in much to do with family life as he has grown, in his own mind, above all that. Benjamin notices three bottles of red wine sitting on the floor of the pantry when he went in search of something to snack on. He doesn't say anything. At this point neither of them has had a drop of alcohol in nearly three months. After a small dinner and after the kids wander off to their respective room Angelica suggests that they have a glass of wine.

"Ange; we don't drink... remember?"

"Well, this is a special occasion. I didn't say I wasn't going to drink on special occasions." She is being very convincing and very flirtatious and, not wanting to rock the proverbial boat, Benjamin caves.

Angelica brings out two glasses and one of the bottles and Benjamin opens it. They cozy up on the couch together, watch

226

The Suicide Note

television and over the next hour consume the bottle of wine. Benjamin is apprehensive that "the switch" will go off but it doesn't. They enjoy a romantic evening together, go back to the bedroom and make passionate love under cover of Van Morrison music. It is one of the best love-making sessions they have had in a number of years and Benjamin wakes up the next morning with a big smile on his face.

Thanksgiving Day is spent around the house with the aroma of a baking turkey and the sounds of the Macy's Parade emanating from the television. As dinnertime approaches Benjamin notices another bottle of wine on the table along with four wine glasses. When dinner comes Benjamin slices the turkey and Angelica pours everyone a glass of wine. The kid's glasses are diluted with water but they are thrilled to have been included. The meal is fabulous. Angelica truly has a knack for following directions from a cookbook. By the end of the meal the bottle of wine had been consumed and while the table is being cleared Benjamin notices Angelica chugging the wine that Izzy had not touched after the first sip and a "Yuk."

When the wonderful family event is over, the kitchen is cleaned up and the trash taken out everyone retires to different corners of the house. Benjamin is lying on the couch in the family room watching the evening news and Angelica appears with two glasses and the third bottle of wine. Now Benjamin is getting annoyed but he holds back. Angelica has already opened the bottle and pours them both a glass. He judges by the level of wine still in the bottle that Angelica has already had a glass. Now she is showing open signs of intoxication and when Benjamin expresses concern she explodes in rage.

227

J. McGregor Colt

"You are always criticizing me. I just made you a fantastic dinner and you don't even appreciate it. Fucking asshole!"

This outburst of overreaction catches the attention of the kids and they hide in their rooms with the doors closed. The fight escalates into physical violence when Angelica digs her nails into Benjamin's side, breaking the skin. All he can do is remove himself from the scene. He grabs a coat, runs out of the house and hides in a dark section of the yard on a bench. From there he can see Angelica inside the illuminated house pacing back and forth in the kitchen yelling at the kids. He wants to go back inside and rescue the kids but figures that it will only make matters worse so he sits tight outside in the dark. After about twenty minutes or so of ranting and raving things die down inside the house and everyone goes to bed. He sneaks back in and, once again, sleeps on a couch. As he lies there trying to fall asleep he recognizes that nearly every special event had been ruined by Angelica's alcoholic rages. This needs to stop.

The next morning Angelica, once again, acts as if nothing had happened the night before and the rest of the long weekend is consumed with normal family-type fun activities. This is the life to which Benjamin had acclimated himself. Angelica's drinking bouts, periods of sobriety, violent outburst and times of simple domestic normalcy all blended together. In the evenings as Benjamin would drive home from work he wondered which Angelica would meet him at the door but he is determined to keep the marriage together. He wants to be centered, he wants a family, he wants to be normal and he loves Izzy and Drake very much.

228

The Suicide Note

After a while into their seventh year of marriage Benjamin begins to notice that Angelica is not always home when he gets there. The kids will always say that she has gone to the store and are vague about how long she has been gone. When she returns she does not always have groceries in her hand or any evidence of having been to any sort of a store. Of course Benjamin is suspicious that she is up to something but, again, he doesn't want to rock the boat. The ice is getting pretty thin around the Mathews house so he just puts it out of his head and makes do.

Angelica is often tardy or even absent altogether for Izzy and Drake's sporting events and dance recitals. She always seems to have one excuse or another mostly centered on work. She is still working at the restaurant so Benjamin buys off on it for the most part but he is still a bit suspicious. Angelica is very secretive about her whereabouts but life goes on and to an outside observer life with Benjamin Mathews is good.

Chapter
Sixteen

B ack a few years, after he had built a successful business, had the fabulous house but before the troubles started with his gorgeous wife, Benjamin reached out to old friends in Seattle. Benjamin and Angelica would run up to Seattle a couple of times a year without the kids and visit with his old friends. Benjamin was proud to show off Angelica and share stories of his business successes. On one of these trips he reconnected with Woody Garwood and Woody's second wife Marsha. Marsha is younger, about the same age as Angelica and the two hit it off immediately. Benjamin feels very good about reconnecting with his old friend.

A few years after the break-up of Mathews, Garwood & Clements, Inc. Woody divorced his first wife and became

The Suicide Note

a homebuilder. Woody's business thrived throughout the 1990s and he is doing very well financially. By now he is quite possibly the largest spec home builder in the ever expanding suburban areas surrounding Tacoma and lives in a very nice home on the shore of Ponder Lake. David Clements had gone to work for his family's timber company. He started out working under an older cousin in the real estate division and by the mid 1990s is running that division. David too was doing very well financially. Woody had not spoken to David for years and when Benjamin tries to reach out to him he is treated to a cold shoulder.

David is not interested in rekindling a friendship with Benjamin but Woody and Marsha are. Very soon the two couples start doing things together with their kids. Woody and Marsha have a son just one year older than Drake so it makes it easy for them to take trips together to Palm Springs, Sun Valley and to each other's homes. Woody and Marsha come down to Willow Creek on numerous occasions and stay in the guest house. The two couples lounge around the pool and drink and laugh and when the Garwoods are around Angelica is always on her best behavior. She is fun and witty and very charming. Benjamin always likes doing things with the Woody and Marsha because there are never any angry outbursts from Angelica and she always seems to keep a handle on her alcohol consumption.

The spring following the disastrous Thanksgiving the two couples, without the kids, go to Italy together. Benjamin had purchased a week at a villa in Tuscany from some benefit auction in River City supporting some organization that purports to do good for some needy group and pay the salary

J. McGregor Colt

of some overpaid executive director. He knew it was a rip-off but it's an opportunity to get dressed up in fancy clothes, hobnob with other eminent citizenry, and show off how much money he could afford to throw away.

Angelica and Benjamin planned to spend one week at the villa and another week traveling around other parts of Italy. It is Angelica's idea to invite the Garwoods along. Benjamin agrees that it would probably be a lot more fun with another couple so they start planning. Angelica and Marsha both go overboard, new luggage, a new wardrobe, they spend weekends together shopping. Benjamin doesn't care about the money Angelica is spending so long as she is staying somewhat sober and not screaming at him or at the kids. She is always in a good mood when she is buying things for herself. When it comes to birthdays and Christmas she is always cheaping out on the gifts for others but when it comes to buying things for herself there are no limits to her extravagance.

Italy is a disaster. The villa in Tuscany is fabulous, a three-bedroom estate of brick and stucco with a large shaded outdoor dining and entertaining area and a pool surrounded by a four-foot wall in the middle of a large vineyard. Nothing could have been lovelier; it is straight out of a romance novel. The two couples spend days venturing out in their rented BMW and evenings back at the villa making dinner and drinking the local wines. Each day after they leave to venture around the countryside, a little Italian woman comes in, makes the beds and leaves clean towels. It is perfect and they see a great deal of Tuscany on their daily adventures out. They take in Cortona, Montepulciano, Siena and all

232

The Suicide Note

the Renaissance art and Gothic cathedrals these ancient villages have to offer. Their days are fulfilled careening over winding roads through rolling hills of vineyards. The weather cooperates and they all enjoy each other's company, indulging themselves in the local wines and epicurean delights.

The disaster starts during week two. After they leave the villa they drive down to Rome and that's where the trouble begins. Benjamin had been to Rome before. He and Carly had spent time there some 15 years prior so he knows a bit about the place. Things start getting testy between the two couples after the long drive to Rome and that first night they just decide to dine separately. The next day the two couples walk around Rome together, looking at the sites, the Colosseum, the Pantheon, the Spanish Steps. Benjamin takes it upon himself to be the tour guide. All day he guides the group to this or to that and by the end of the day Angelica has had enough. Around the corner from the Spanish Steps is an America Express office and Benjamin insisted on sharing a story about how he and Carly, out of cash, had sat in front of that office for five hours waiting for a wire of funds from home so they could continue their travels.

"Would you just shut the fuck up about you and Carly. I am sick of this shit. It's all you've talked about all day." Angelica's voice is loud and attracts attention from nearby tourists.

Woody and Marsha are caught off guard and embarrassed by the audience they have attracted. Benjamin is dumbfounded and apologizes quietly to Angelica. He tries to calm her down but the switch had been flipped. Angelica storms off in what she thinks is the direction of the hotel. When Benjamin tries to direct her she screams.

233

J. McGregor Colt

"Fuck off... leave me alone." She has derailed.

Benjamin gives up and watches Marsha take off after her. At this point Benjamin too has become upset and it is Woody's duty to console him. The trip is breaking down. The two couples are tiring of one another and Angelica and Benjamin aren't even speaking. On day ten of a fourteen-day trip everyone is ready to go home. Woody and Benjamin make it back to the hotel first and go to the lobby bar for a drink. After about twenty minutes or so they see Angelica and Marsha come through the front door. Angelica goes straight for the elevator and Marsha comes into the bar and orders a glass of wine.

"She's really pissed. I think she's going home," Marsha informs them.

"She's not going home. She does this," Benjamin announces, seemingly unconcerned.

"You should go up and talk to her," Woody suggests.

"Bullshit, I'm not going anywhere near her when she gets like this."

There are a few moments of silence while each one of the three analyze their personal version of the situation and what ramifications it has. It is Marsha who breaks the silence.

"Okay, fuck it then, I'm just going to sit here and drink wine."

The mood relaxes and the conversation turns the subject of where they should all have dinner. After a decision is made regarding dinner and after Marsha's second glass of wine the Garwoods return to their room to freshen up a bit and agree to meet back down in the lobby in twenty minutes. Benjamin does not want to confront Angelica so

234

The Suicide Note

he stays in the bar instead of freshening up and has another drink. He is drinking Scotch and by the time Woody and Marsha meet him back in the lobby he has polished off three and is feeling quite chipper. All acknowledge that none of them has seen Angelica so they leave the hotel and head down the sidewalk to a restaurant the bartender had recommended. When they sit down at their table Benjamin orders another Scotch, and Woody and Marsha order a bottle of wine.

La Cucina Rosso is a small family-owned restaurant and when they arrive they are greeted by the owners, who speak no English, and a daughter who speaks a little. They are very welcoming. There are plenty of vacant tables but it fills up quickly and becomes quite loud with all the conversations going on around them in an assortment of languages. The mother is in the kitchen cooking things up while the father and daughter wait diligently on a packed house. It is a wonderful experience and the food is fabulous. During the meal Benjamin opens up to Woody and Marsha about the state of his marriage. The four Scotches help with the free movement of thought spewing from his lips. He tells them that after about six months into his marriage he had become concerned that there was something wrong with his wife. He relays the stories of her drinking and her violent behavior and tells them that it is, at times, unbearable to the point that he will have to leave the house. He tells them that she is abusive to the kids and to him.

"Well, I can't believe that," Woody interjects.

"She seems like such a warm and caring mother," Marsha adds.

J. McGregor Colt

"She can be but then again... there is like this switch that goes off in her head and she just becomes this raving maniac. It's incredible. It's not the person I fell in love with."

"How often does it happen?" Marsha asks.

"How long does it go on for?" Woody adds.

"I don't know. It's usually when she drinks. I'm telling you... there's this switch. I can be sitting there having a good time and 'click' a monster appears. It's unbearable and the shit she will say... right in front of the kids... the foulest language."

"Have you been to a psychiatrist or something?" Woody wants to know.

"She won't go. She can go for periods of time with nothing, no alcohol and no outbursts and then she just thinks that everything is all right and she, she thinks she doesn't need any counseling. Stupid!"

"How much of the time is she like this?" Woody asks. "What percentage of the time are you miserable versus happy together? I mean, shit, no marriage is one hundred present peaches and cream... believe me."

Marsha pokes Woody in the ribs.

"Watch it, Robert, or you'll be sucking on peach pits and sour cream tonight." They laugh and take another sip of their wine.

By now Benjamin has switched to wine and they have ordered a second bottle.

"No, seriously, Benjamin, how often does she get bad? Is it twenty percent of the time, fifty percent, eighty? What percent?"

236

The Suicide Note

Benjamin sits a moment and contemplates the question.

"You can live with twenty percent but probably not eighty. What is the threshold? When do you throw in the towel?" Woody prods.

"I'm not going to throw in any fucking towels. I love her deeply. I want to be married. I like having kids and shit and going to soccer games and going to fucking PTA meetings. I love my life most of the time."

"Okay...what percent of the time do you love it?"

"I don't know... maybe seventy-five percent."

"Seventy-five percent? Well, shit, you're doin' great. You can endure twenty-five percent of the time in hell. Think about it. How many people are happy and blissful seventy-five percent of the time? Shit, even heroin addicts are only high fifty percent of the time. The other fifty they are miserable, looking for more shit or scrounging for money to get more shit. You are high in your marriage and enjoying family life seventy-five percent of the time? You are very fortunate... as am I," as he winks at Marsha. "You can handle that."

Woody has made a good point; they pay the bill, hug the owners, stumble out the door and get back up the sidewalk to their hotel. When Benjamin gets back to his room he is drunk and Angelica is not in the room. He lies down on the bed and moments later passes out. The next morning he is completely hung over and sick to his stomach. He downs five ibuprofens with a large glass of water. As his head starts to clear he realizes that not only is Angelica missing but so is all her stuff and her passport. He showers, shaves, gets dressed and walks down to the lobby. As he approaches the front desk he stops short and thinks, "What the fuck am I going to say to this

J. McGregor Colt

guy?" but at that moment notices Woody and Marsha having breakfast in the lobby bar and walks over and joins them.

"She's fucking gone. That cunt, excuse my language, Marsh, took her passport and all her shit and she's gone."

"If she took her passport and left then she is a cunt." Marsha shoots back.

"You know, Benjamin, every woman you have ever brought to Europe has flown home alone. Perhaps you need to rethink this whole bringing women to Europe thing." Woody tries to lighten the air and they all chuckle.

They still have two more days in Italy before their scheduled flight home. This is still a couple of years before cell phone communication was easy between Europe and The States so Benjamin doesn't even bother trying to call home and he doesn't want to call and alarm anybody so the three of them just continue on without Angelica. It's awkward for Benjamin but by this time he has become accustomed to awkwardness in the aftermath of an Angelica meltdown.

When Benjamin finally gets home it is late in the evening on a weekday. The kids are watching television in the house alone and do not know where their mother is. They tell him that she had gone to the store but it has been a couple of hours. Benjamin tries calling her cell phone but gets no response in six attempts. After a while he tells the kids to go to bed and he does the same.

In the morning he finds Angelica in the kitchen feeding the kids breakfast and making lunches; she doesn't acknowledge his presence when he enters the room, it's tense. Benjamin needs to get to the office but he also needs

238

The Suicide Note

to figure out what is going on with his wife; she is avoiding him and what had started out as a little misunderstanding in Rome has escalated into a major battle. In fact, at this point, Benjamin can't even remember what it was in Rome that had gotten them to this point. Angelica loads the kids in the car and drives them off to school, Benjamin stays home waiting for her to return so they can sort things out. Benjamin isn't as mad as he is concerned, maybe even scared. He loves Angelica very much, despite her shortcomings, and doesn't want anything to break them apart. When Angelica returns to the house he confronts her.

"Are you going to talk to me?" he asks timidly.

"What do you want to talk about?"

"Come on Ange, really? You left me in Rome. What was that all about?"

"Really? Well, I just figured you and your friends would rather have been with Carly. Why don't you just call Carly? Maybe she can make you happy."

"Ange! What are you talking about? You are the only person who can make me happy. What's all this crap about Carly? I haven't even laid eyes on that woman in twenty years."

"Well, she's all you and your friends could talk about in Europe. Carly and me did this, Carly and me went to this place."

"Wait... my friends? First of all I thought Woody and Marsha are *our* friends and secondly I don't recall talking about her at all. I just related a story about waiting for money at an American Express office."

This conversation goes back and forth for a while and nothing gets resolved. When Benjamin tries to hug her

J. McGregor Colt

and tell her he loves her she pushes him away and screams for him to not touch her. Benjamin leaves and goes to the office.

After a couple of hours of getting caught up and returning phone calls Benjamin receives a call from Antonio who wants to meet him for lunch. Antonio had never invited Benjamin to lunch before and he sounds pretty serious. Antonio doesn't want to meet at Centoni's so they choose a little diner out by the Interstate where none of the locals would go unless they wanted to get away from the other locals.

When Benjamin arrives Antonio is already seated in a booth with his father. Antonio and Marco are seated together on one side of the booth and indicate for Benjamin to sit across from them. Neither one of them look happy and neither one extended their hand in greeting.

"Hey Marco, I didn't know that you were in town. What's this all about?"

The son and father look at one another and there is an awkward silence before they both look back at Benjamin.

"Look Benjamin, my father and I know that Angelica can be difficult." Antonio starts to get angry and his father places his hand on his forearm to calm him.

"There is absolutely no excuse for hitting a woman. This is my sister for Christ sakes. I will fucking kill you if you ever lay a hand on her again." Antonio is furious.

"What? I have never laid a hand on Angelica. I have never laid a hand on any woman. What the fuck are you talking about?"

"Ange told us that you hit her. She told us that you got drunk and beat her up in Italy. She told us that she was so

240

The Suicide Note

scared that she snuck out after you fell asleep and flew home." Marco spoke softly but sternly.

"This is not something that will be tolerated in my family. We do not deal with these things lightly. We deal with them very seriously with very serious resolution inside the family... no authorities. You understand what I am saying?"

"Marco! Antonio! I have never hit Angelica. Never! I don't know where this is coming from. Angelica flipped out in Rome because she thought I was talking about an ex-girlfriend too much. She just flipped out and left. I never touched her. We really never even got into a fight. This is ridiculous. I swear."

"Well, she seems very upset." Marco answers. "We think it would be a good idea for you to move out of the house for a while."

"But Marco, where am I supposed to go? This is crazy. I never touched her."

Marco slams his palm on the table, attracting attention from nearby patrons, and tells him, with a clenched jaw, that he does not care where he goes but to stay away from Angelica and he slides out of the booth and exits the restaurant.

"Benjamin. I hope you understand that we are serious. Come with me. I have something for you." Antonio had calmed down but he is all business.

When they get out to the parking lot Marco is just driving off. Antonio opens a back door to his car, reaches in and pulls out a suitcase, Benjamin's suitcase.

"Go find a place to hang until we can get this all sorted out."

That is the end of the conversation. Antonio gets in his car and drives off. Benjamin stands there for a moment,

J. McGregor Colt

dumbfounded, holding his suitcase. When he gets to his car he opens up the bag and does a quick inventory. Someone had packed everything he needs; clean clothes and toiletries, the essentials for about a week. Essentially, Benjamin has been booted out of his house, excommunicated from his family with the shirt on his back and a toothbrush.

I should have known from the very beginning that something was wrong with Angelica and her entire fucking family.

By the time he gets back to his office he is furious. He immediately calls an old attorney friend of his in Seattle and after some catching up and reliving old times he settles down enough to explain to Ross Goodman the events of the past couple of weeks and his now homeless situation. Ross advises him to find a local lawyer and get a restraining order as soon as possible so Angelica cannot remove any of the personal property from the house or incur any debt against the community of their marriage. He further advises him to file a legal separation document while this all plays out. When Benjamin hangs up he is less mad but more worried.

Benjamin does not want a divorce or a legal separation or anything of that nature; he wants to be home with a loving wife and dote on their children together. He had come to love his domestic life and was living in a bubble of unrealistic fantasies. Considering the wild and crazy days of his youth and the extravagant lifestyle he had been living prior to meeting Angelica it was somewhat amazing the person whom Benjamin had become but he was very content with it. Now, Benjamin is scared. He makes some more phone calls: Angelica, who did not pick up; a local lawyer, who is out but will call him back; and Woody. Woody puts him on

242

The Suicide Note

speaker so Marsha can hear the story. They are both shocked and surprised that Angelica could do what, apparently, she had done and further urge him to do what Ross Goodman had suggested.

At about 6 p.m. he locks up the office and finds a motel out by the interstate where his car won't be conspicuous. He never speaks to the local attorney with whom he had left a message and just figures that he will deal with it in the morning. That evening he gets a bite to eat at a fast food joint and watches television in his room with a bottle of Scotch. He tries Angelica on the phone a couple more times but nothing. He calls the house and nothing. After a couple of tumblers of Scotch he even thinks about driving up to the house but catches himself after reflecting upon the lunch meeting with Marco.

Eventually he falls asleep and at 5:30 in the morning there is a pounding on the door to his motel room. Groggy and disoriented he opens the door dressed only in underpants. A River City police officer asks if he is Benjamin B. Mathews and when he acknowledges that he is, the officer hands him an envelope. Benjamin has been served with a restraining order. It takes several minutes for it to kick in but a judge has issued a temporary order restraining Benjamin from going within five hundred feet of his own house and fifty feet from his wife and children. The order claims that he is a threat to their wellbeing and that he has ten days to show cause why it should not be a permanent restraining order.

"What the fuck!" he says out loud.

It is still dark, he has been blindsided and he isn't sure why. He makes coffee, showers and gets dressed but there is nothing he can do as it is still only 6:15 and the local

J. McGregor Colt

attorney he had called the day before would not be in his office yet. Benjamin paces back and forth in his room, tries to concentrate on the morning television news and at 6:45 a.m., after checking his watch every three minutes or so, he gets in his car and drives to a restaurant for breakfast.

There are three or four restaurant options in River City for breakfast, Benjamin chooses Denny's because he figures he won't know anyone there and therefore not have to explain why he isn't home with his family at that time of day for breakfast. Before his breakfast order is served a group of people he knows comes in and sits at the booth directly across from him. It is Mike Bonds and the crew from Bonds Home Builders. He knew Mike through business and has sold one of the members of his crew a piece of land.

"Benjamin Mathews? What are you doing here so early in the morning? Old lady kick you out of the house?" Laughter all around.

As Benjamin's breakfast is being served he completely over-informs.

"Well, yeah, she did."

Benjamin didn't know Mike Bonds well, they had not been to one another's homes for dinner or anything but he knew him well enough, they liked each other, and he completely spills the beans. He tells Mike and his crew the entire story from Rome to home. It is way more information than they wanted to listen to but they sat politely, listened and once in a while one of them would say; "That sucks."

Benjamin had always worn his heart on his sleeve; now he is distraught, blabbing about it, and getting some superficial support from people he barely knew seemed to help. It doesn't

244

The Suicide Note

help his audience much but that had not occurred to him. After breakfast it is still too early for the attorney's office to be open but he drives over the bridge to Willow Creek and sits in his car in the parking lot. At about five minutes before 9 a.m. Bill Summerset and his wife pull into the lot in their big white Cadillac. Bill is a white-haired old country lawyer. He is a large man in his seventies and well dressed in a suit and tie. His wife accompanies him because she is his receptionist. They both smoke and are smoking when they get out of their car. Benjamin knew them, he had used Bill for some minor real estate things in the past, easements and fulfillment deeds, nothing complicated. Bill handled the adoption papers for Isabella and Mandrake.

"Good morning, folks." Benjamin approaches them in the parking lot.

"Oh, good morning, Mr. Mathews." Mrs. Summerset answers.

Benjamin could not remember her first name and she could not remember his, but Bill replies.

"What's up, Benjamin?"

Benjamin apologizes for accosting them in the parking lot and by the time they have unlocked the door and turned on all the lights he has told them the entire story.

"What can I do about this restraining order?" He hands Bill the document.

"Marilyn?"

"Yes, Bill."

"Can you come in here a moment please?"

The law office of William T. Summerset consists of a small reception area with four old chairs and a coffee table

245

J. McGregor Colt

loaded with old magazines. Behind a glass screen with a sliding window sits Marilyn Summerset and beside her is a door that leads down a narrow hall past a copy machine room with a bunch of supplies and file cabinets to William T. Summerset's private office. His office is strewn with files of unfinished business, the walls are decorated with pictures of race horses he has sponsored over the years, and it doubles as his law library. It is a large room, holding a conference table with half a dozen chairs around it and a large mahogany desk with two beautiful red leather chairs to accommodate clients. Lining two walls are bookshelves loaded up with law books. Bill sits behind the desk in an impressive executive chair with a burning cigarette hanging out of his mouth. The conference table is stacked with files and law books, a couple of which are actually open.

"Bill, isn't it against the law to smoke in a public building in the State of Washington?" Benjamin says jokingly.

"So sue me. You'll need a lawyer for that."

He hands his wife the restraining order and asks that she make a copy of it and set up a file. He explains to Benjamin that he has a busy day but will be over at the courthouse in an hour and will find out what is going on. Bill assures Benjamin that he will have information for him before the end of the day. Benjamin leaves feeling somewhat relieved that his case is in good hands. Bill Summerset is very well respected in town, had served as a district court judge for several years and knows all the prosecuting attorneys well.

By the end of the day Benjamin has blabbed his predicament to anyone within earshot. Nobody is really all that interested but Benjamin doesn't care. He is overly excited with

The Suicide Note

stress and telling everyone he encounters about his situation lets some of the pressure building up inside of him get out. One day he had been sitting on top of the world, a king in his castle with a beautiful wife and loving children and the next day he is living in a motel room down by the interstate out of a suitcase under questionable circumstances... it could be stressful.

At about ten to five Benjamin has not yet heard from Bill Summerset so he gets in his car and drives back over to his office. When he gets there Marilyn is just putting her coat on and getting ready to leave.

"He's back there. Just go on back but don't take too long. We need to get home. My son and his wife are bringing our grandkids over for dinner."

She locks the front door, takes her coat back off, sits down and lights a cigarette.

"Mr. Mathews is coming back there." She still can't remember his first name.

"Okay, Benjamin, sit down." Bill is just stubbing out a cigarette in the large overflowing ashtray on his desk.

"Benjamin, you have a problem. Your wife claims that you beat her and she has what the judge deems to be a believable witness. You will not be getting back into your house anytime soon."

Benjamin blows up.

"That is total bullshit. I have never laid a hand on her in my life. I have never laid a hand on any woman... ever."

"I know, I know. Calm down, it gets worse. She is also filing for divorce. You will probably be getting served those papers this evening or tomorrow morning."

247

J. McGregor Colt

"What the fuck?"

"Watch your language, young man." Marilyn yells out from the front.

"This is crazy, Bill. We just spent two weeks in Italy together. I just got back two days ago. What is going on?" Benjamin stands and starts pacing around the office nervously.

"She is claiming that you and another couple wanted to have group sex and when she refused, you slapped her and bloodied her nose. She claims that she had to sneak out in the middle of the night and catch a flight home."

"That is the most preposterous story that I have ever heard. The couple we were traveling with I have known since junior high school. The husband is my former business partner. She's talking about Woody Garwood and his wife. You know Woody. That is preposterous."

"Okay, Benjamin, look, there is nothing I can do about this right now. I suggest that you get an affidavit from these friends of yours explaining their version of what took place in Italy."

"Nothing took place. There is nothing to explain."

"Okay; have them explain that in writing and at the end it will need to say 'I swear the above statement is true to the best of my knowledge under penalty of perjury in the State of Washington.' Now, I need to get out of here or Marilyn is going to kill me." He stands, puts his coat on and escorts Benjamin out to the front.

Benjamin is upset, embarrassed and very confused when he calls Woody to explain what he has been going through the past several days. Marsha is on speaker phone and they suggest that he come up to their place for the weekend and

248

The Suicide Note

sort things out. Benjamin can't keep paying for motel rooms so he decides a trip up to Ponder Point is a good idea.

Before he leaves he rings up Brad and Jennifer with the idea of getting his old apartment back for a while. Jennifer answers the phone and tells him that she and Brad have split up and that she has no idea where he is. This is a bit perplexing to him but he knows that Brad has been struggling financially. The Amanson Pharmacy on both sides of the river had closed. A Walmart had been built over in River City and many of the small locally owned retail businesses that are not related to the windsurfing industry are suffering as a result. Amanson's could not survive and it put a severe burden on Brad and Jennifer's relationship. They had split up, Jenn did not know where Brad was living and she does not think it will be a good idea to rent out the apartment as she is not certain what her immediate future beholds. Benjamin heads north with this new information, not knowing where he will live when he gets back.

Chapter
Seventeen

The weekend up north with Woody and Marsha is like a scene from *The Lost Weekend* starring Ray Milland, complete with all the desperate humiliations. After a brief discussion about how horrible Angelica is the three immediately start drinking heavily and eventually order up some cocaine from a friend of theirs. Benjamin had not even seen cocaine for about ten years but apparently Woody and Marsha have not totally given it up on that career-destroying nose caviar and Benjamin jumps on board at the first suggestion. By late evening the Garwoods' house is filled with six or seven revelers, most of whom Benjamin does not know, and a party rambles on all night, fueled by alcohol and ignited with cocaine.

The Suicide Note

There is one particular female friend of Marsha's who takes a liking to Benjamin. Cindy Skyler worked with Marsha at a law office in Tacoma before Woody and Marsha started dating. They had all been friends for about ten years and had all never grown out of the cocaine thing. Benjamin has just the right mixture of heartache, fear and alcohol to take a big snort every time it is offered. His years of sobriety and his even more years of abstinence from cocaine have been completely forgotten in a flash. The party continues into the early hours of the next morning. Had it not been for all the alcohol Benjamin had consumed and all the cocaine he had inhaled he probably would have gotten Cindy into bed with him but at about 3 a.m. everybody goes home and Benjamin crashes hard in the Garwoods' spare bedroom.

The next morning, late morning, around 11 a.m. the three arise and assemble in the kitchen for Bloody Marys. Woody and Marsha have a teenage son who is away at a friend's all weekend so Saturday is spent nursing a hangover in front of the television set watching movies on Pay-Per-View. It is a completely wasted day except that Benjamin is able to persuade them to write a letter to the court explaining what really happened in Italy. Benjamin reflects on how his life has suddenly taken a nose-dive and as he drinks more he gets more gloomy, more silent.

Woody and Marsha share a story about Angelica that they had been reluctant to tell him before. On one of the visits he had made with Angelica up to the Garwood house Angelica had come on to Woody. After Benjamin and Marsha had gone to bed and left Woody and Angelica in the kitchen together she unbuttoned her blouse, exposed her breast and

251

J. McGregor Colt

rubbed them, seductively, in Woody's face. She begged him to make love to her in a sloppy drunken seduction attempt but the awkwardness was interrupted when Marsha returned to the kitchen for a glass of water. Upon hearing the story Benjamin is flabbergasted.

"Why didn't you tell me this before?" he asks.

"We just figured that she had had too much to drink and didn't know what she was doing." Marsha quickly interjects.

"We got her down to your bedroom and she fell in bed with you. We just figured that you took care of her. She was very horny," Woody says coyly.

Marsha is supportive of Woody. They both apologize for not saying anything about it sooner but conclude that since Angelica didn't say anything about it the next morning she had probably no recollection of the incident and that it was a one-off sort of a thing.

Saturday night consists of more heavy drinking but without the cocaine. They all agree that the night before had been a mistake and resolved not to repeat it. In the morning, hung over again, Benjamin gets in his car and heads back to the Gorge. River City is about a three-hour drive and it gives him plenty of time to reflect and figure out what he is going to do. That night he takes a room at the same motel, resolves to figure everything out in the morning and gets a good night's sleep.

On Monday he is anxious. He hasn't figured out anything and doesn't really know where to start. His wife had thrown him out, her family had threatened him, his own family is a distant bridge he had burned years prior, and all Woody Garwood knew what to do was to pour him a drink. He still has his office and on the way there he swings into Walmart

252

The Suicide Note

to get some aspirin as his head still hurts from the weekend. While perusing the shelves he glances up to the pharmacist window and there is Brad Amanson behind the counter, dressed in a white, heavily starched jacket.

"Brad? What are you doing back there?"

Brad looks up briefly and walking away says, very coldly, "I can't talk now, I'm working."

Benjamin stands there for a moment in disbelief that he has been treated by Brad in such an abrupt manner. He understands that if Brad is working as the pharmacist at Walmart and that if his wife didn't know where he was that things couldn't be all that good for him either but they are friends. Benjamin figures that friends don't treat one another the way that Brad is treating him and he is perplexed. What is up with Brad, he wonders as he pays for the aspirin and continues on to his office.

When Benjamin gets to the office it seems like a normal, business as usual, day around a real estate office. Nobody seems to know about what he has been going through. Everyone at The Mathews Group has a great deal of respect and admiration for Benjamin but no one really has any time to show it... they are busy. The real estate market is hot, had been for a couple of years, and Benjamin has the hottest agents in the Gorge with three offices, all out-producing their competitors with very little guidance from their leader.

The Mathews Group is on auto pilot, as it had been for the past couple of years. Benjamin rarely even shows up to the sales meetings anymore so when they see him in the office it is a pleasure but they really don't need his input on anything. He has become more of a figurehead, representing the company's

253

J. McGregor Colt

interests with the Chamber, Rotary and City/County governmental issues. After picking up his messages from the receptionist he goes back to his office and closes the door.

He slumps down in his chair behind his desk and stares at a blank computer screen for a good fifteen minutes before he snaps out of it and starts clicking on the keyboard. He figures that he should probably just get to work and opens up the company Transactions in Progress page to get a quick view of what is in the pipeline. He goes to the accounting page to see what is in the bank account. He peruses the Multiple Listing site to get himself up to speed on what is on the market and what is not and before he knows it...it's time for lunch.

When he opens his door and comes out into the reception area a couple of his agents are talking about what to get for lunch. Benjamin suggests a deli up the street and offers to buy them both lunch. They are enthusiastic and eager to hear all about his trip to Tuscany. He covers all the good things about Tuscany on the walk up the street, leaving out the dramatic ending, and by the time they sit at a table in the deli with their sandwiches, the subject changes to business. Benjamin is engaging but his head is clearly elsewhere.

After lunch he pays a visit to his Willow Creek office and from there he calls Jennifer Amanson. She is not warm and friendly with him. She knows that Brad is working at Walmart, makes it clear that she really doesn't want to talk to him, nor to Benjamin, and she hangs up abruptly.

"What the fuck is going on with everybody?" he asks aloud to himself.

Once he makes the rounds at that office and chats a bit with the agents that are there he gets in his car and drives up

The Suicide Note

river to Sunyton. He isn't really all that comfortable in the Sunyton office. It had been a Century 21 office and when the owner died one of the agents in that office talked Benjamin into taking it over. Century 21 has a completely different game plan and philosophy than does The Mathews Group but once he was able to get rid of the baby-shit yellow jackets they all wear and acclimated them to his philosophy, things began to run smoothly. A couple of agents quit but for the most part everyone stuck around and is happy. He kept everyone's favorite agent, Joyce Remy, and made her the branch manager. Joyce is from one of the large cherry orchard families and is very well respected in town. She was never a top producer but knew the law better than any of the others, is honest and always has a positive mental outlook. She is jolly and she is loved but the Sunyton is not producing as well as the other two offices and before he leaves he promises Joyce that he will start coming to their sales meetings and help her with getting the production up. Benjamin's mind is still elsewhere but it is not obvious to Joyce.

Benjamin needs to find a temporary place to live and on his way back down the freeway to River City he remembers that a builder friend of his has a furnished apartment on the lower level of his place in Willow Creek. After a quick call he learns that it has just become available so he arranges to take the place after the carpets dry. They had just been cleaned and need another day to dry before the furniture can be put back in place. It was good timing.

Back at his motel room Benjamin flops down on the bed and stares up at the ceiling. What has become of his life? Just when he thinks things can't get any worse his cell phone rings.

255

J. McGregor Colt

It's Bill Summerset and he informs Benjamin that Angelica has filed for a permanent restraining order and temporary maintenance in the amount of $5,000 per month while everything is being settled in the divorce. He further explains to him that she has filed signed affidavits from witnesses claiming that he has been physically and mentally abusing her and her children for years.

"Are you fucking crazy? Are you out of your goddamn mind?" Benjamin is screaming into the phone.

"Hey; settle down. Don't yell at me, goddamn it. I'm only telling you what I got today. Don't shoot the messenger. I'm on your side here." Bill is exasperated.

He knew Benjamin pretty well and finds it difficult to believe what is being said about him in the affidavits.

"Who is this Bradley B. Amanson? Isn't he that pharmacist in Willow Creek?" Bill asks.

"Yeah, why?"

"Well, he's one of the people in the affidavit claiming that you beat your wife."

"What?"

"Yeah, it's pretty damaging stuff."

Benjamin is numb.

"How the fuck... what the fuck... We were friends. His wife and him were friends of ours. I rented an apartment from him when I first moved down here. We were very close. I don't get it."

Bill reads one of the more scathing accusations from Brad's affidavit and Benjamin seethes with anger. He cannot understand why Brad would say such things. What is his motivation for making up stories about him?

256

The Suicide Note

There are two more affidavits; one from Mandrake Mathews and another from Isabella Mathews. At this point Benjamin and Angelica have been married for seven years; Drake is 15, Izzy is 13. Drake's affidavit validates and confirms that Benjamin has been mistreating his mother and also refers to a specific incident in which Drake himself had been physically abused. Everything Drake claims in regard to his mother is a complete fabrication but the incident regarding himself does have a shadow of truth to it. Benjamin recalls the incident a couple of years prior to all this, back when they were one big happy family, back when everything was rainbows and butterflies, Benjamin came home from work and discovered that some of his tools were laying in the driveway. He picked up a wrench and a couple of screw drivers and went in the house. Angelica and Izzy were in the kitchen making dinner and Drake was spread out on the couch watching television.

"Drake! Were you messing around with my tools?"

"No." An emphatic denial.

"Well, I found these in the driveway just now." Benjamin holds up the wrench and the two screw drivers and waves them in front of Drake's eyes.

"I didn't put 'em there," Drake insists. "Maybe you left 'em there."

This conversation went back and forth a couple of minutes before Angelica broke it up and told Benjamin that she had not seen Drake playing with any tools. Benjamin then asked Izzy if she knew anything about how the tools mysteriously got left in the driveway. Nobody knew anything and in frustration Benjamin dropped the subject but not before a short proclamation.

257

J. McGregor Colt

"Okay but just understand that I am not mad about someone using my tools or about someone using my tools and not putting them away but if I find out later that someone is lying I am going to be furious and somebody will be punished. There is nothing worse than a liar."

"Okay... dinner's almost ready. Everyone get washed up." Angelica broke the tension.

"You got one last chance to tell the truth." Benjamin yelled at the kids as they walked down the hall to a bathroom.

"Good grief...just drop it, Benji."

"I know damn well Drake is lying." Benjamin insisted but he did drop it, they ate dinner and there was no further mention of the tools or the lying.

After dinner Drake went outside, Izzy went to her room to do homework and Benjamin helped Angelica clean the kitchen and do the dishes. There was no more talk of the tools and the man and wife were pleasant in the sharing of domestic after-dinner chores. When the kitchen was clean Benjamin went out to the garage to put the tools away and found Drake skateboarding around their large paved parking area with one of the neighbor kids.

"Hey, Neal. Were you and Drake using these tools today?"

"Yes, Mr. Mathews. Sorry we didn't put them back." Drake had been ratted out.

Drake had been busted and he knew he had been busted. Mr. Mathews sent Neal home and Drake in the house and returned the tools to their proper place in the garage. When he got back in the house Drake had already found the shelter of his bedroom hoping that being banished to his room would be his punishment. Room isolation had always been the method of

258

The Suicide Note

punishment for misbehaved actions in the past. He found out very quickly that this time was going to be different. Benjamin was furious when he entered Drake's room. He had never given anyone a spanking before but he knew how it was done, having been the recipient of one on several occasions himself in his youth. The Sarge was a prolific spanker. Benjamin, in a fury, reiterated to Drake as he attempted to take him over his knee that he was not being punished for using the tools, or for not putting the tools away, but for lying about the tools. Taking Drake over his knee turned out to be not such an easy task. Drake, at 12, was strong and he was squirmy. Benjamin could not hold him down and in frustration wound up slapping Drake on the back of his upper leg a couple three or four times. It was an ugly scene and wore Benjamin out. Drake's screaming drew Angelica and Izzy's attention and Benjamin angrily brushed passed them in the hall outside the bedroom door as he huffed his way back down to the kitchen.

When Angelica came back down to the kitchen to join him she smiled and said, "Well, that went well," sarcastically.

"Yeah," Benjamin retorted. "That little fucker is strong."

"And, probably too big to spank. I don't know what you were thinking."

"I am just trying to teach him the importance of not lying," Benjamin announced in exasperation.

The version of this incident in Mandrake's affidavit is far more violent and exaggerated than was the reality and makes Benjamin out to be a tyrant who thrives on making everyone's life at home miserable. It is a very bad man Drake describes but not as bad as the man Isabella describes in her affidavit. Izzy claims that Benjamin was sexually molesting her.

259

J. McGregor Colt

When Bill reads him some of the claims in Isabella's statement Benjamin just goes silent. He is drained of all emotion and cannot utter a word. Inside of him a psychological balloon keeps getting larger and larger, inflated by his belief that he is being wronged. He could burst at any moment.

"Benjamin? You still there?" Bill asks through the phone.

"Yeah, Bill, I'm still here. I just can't hear any more of this. Every single thing those kids are saying is complete and total bullshit. I have no idea how they could possibly say those things. I was a good father to them. They were living in a trailer park when I took them in. I showed them a good life. Sorry, I gotta go now. Let's pick this up again tomorrow."

"I'm in court all day tomorrow and the next day. I can see you on Friday. Can you make it in at two o'clock?"

"Yeah, okay, see you then."

Benjamin puts down his cell phone, buries his head in his hands, and cries, uncontrollably, for several minutes.

260

Chapter
Eighteen

enjamin spends the rest of the week sobering up. He talks with Suzanne Britt in his office about concerns he had been revisiting about his own alcoholism and she takes him to an Alcoholics Anonymous meeting. He is very familiar with the protocol and procedure at such meetings, having been to several in the Seattle area years earlier, and does not feel uncomfortable. He is a little surprised to see a few familiar faces around the room but feels no apprehension. The meeting takes place at 6:30 in the morning in the basement of the Episcopal church. The group is situated in chairs formed in a circle in the center of the room. There are coffee and donuts on the counter against the back wall. Benjamin pours himself a coffee and sits down in one of the vacant chairs. The pastor of

J. McGregor Colt

the church, a recovering alcoholic himself, is sitting in the chair on his left and Suzanne sits to his right. Benjamin chuckles to himself about the pastor but quickly reminds himself that alcoholism invades all walks of life. After reciting the Serenity Prayer and listening to a few others speak Benjamin feels comfortable telling his story.

"Hi, my name's Benjamin and I'm an alcoholic."

He speaks for a good ten minutes and explains how he had been a wild and crazy guy in Seattle a decade ago. He admits to heavy cocaine use and destructive behavior and relates his prior experience through treatment. He admits that he had been clean for three years when he first moved to the Gorge, only started drinking again when he met his wife and explains that it had started out as a social thing but has now morphed into a reckless thing. He gives the group a short version of the circumstances of the divorce filing, includes that he has just returned from a binge-drinking weekend with friends in Seattle but leaves out the part about the cocaine. He doesn't think Suzanne is ready for that bit of information and he is, after all, her boss. A few in the circle give him some encouraging words, congratulate him for showing up and say they hope to see him back.

The pastor pats him on the knee and says: "One day at a time."

Benjamin leaves feeling pretty good about the whole thing until thoughts of Angelica start drifting back into his head.

The next morning is Friday and Benjamin goes again to the AA meeting. This time he just sits and listens. The pastor, Father Ed Stead, speaks and Benjamin is very moved by his words. Father Ed has a good sense of humor and barely

The Suicide Note

plays the God card at all. Alcoholics Anonymous dwells really heavily on a higher power to help guide one through a life of sobriety but Father Ed explains that it doesn't need to necessarily be the God in the Bible. He explains that a higher power can be anything you want it to be so long as it isn't yourself. Being an atheist, Benjamin really likes the way Father Ed explains it and leaves that morning with that thought in his head.

That afternoon Benjamin meets with Bill Summerset.

"Look, Benjamin, I'm just going to be blunt... you're screwed. She has employed a very high-powered divorce lawyer from Southern California. I'm not going to do you justice. I'm just a small-town guy who helps old ladies with their wills and gets people off D.U.I charges. You need a specialist, my friend."

"Jesus H. Christ," Benjamin replies. "What's that gonna cost me?"

"I don't know. Call this guy." Bill reaches across his desk, flicks an ash off the end of his cigarette and hands Benjamin a business card. It is for a lawyer at a law firm in Vancouver, Washington. Benjamin studies the card a moment and just shakes his head.

"What the fuck?" He stands up and walks out. There is little else he can say or do.

Roger P. Parsons, Esq., a partner at Parsons, Stebbins, Flatbern & Cole P.S. After a little research Benjamin learns that Parsons is the highest-rated family law practice in the State of Washington and that Parsons himself specializes in representing the husband in divorce cases. He has a very good track record for not letting the husband get the shaft in

263

J. McGregor Colt

a divorce. This comforts Benjamin a bit but he's still worried about what all this is going to cost and he is very disturbed by what his old friend Brad and his own stepchildren are saying about him.

A phone call to Parsons's office nets him a time to have a telephone conversation with Roger Parsons at some point in the future. Bill Summerset has already called and greased the skids for him getting in, as Parsons doesn't take just anyone; he is too busy and is able to cherry-pick who he represents. A legal assistant gets Benjamin's case number and asks Benjamin to fax over everything he has received so far. She agrees to call him back for an appointment once Roger is able to review the file. Benjamin faxes the restraining order, the divorce papers and the three witness affidavits he has received. Then he waits, he goes back to work and tries to keep his mind clear from everything by getting involved with matters around the office. He even attends a sales meeting in Sunyton as he had promised. He also continues to go to AA meetings.

A week goes by and finally Roger Parsons's office calls. The legal assistant tells Benjamin that Roger has read his file and can meet with him a week from Tuesday at 8 a.m. She also tells him to find as many people as possible to write affidavits that will discredit the ones that have been written about him and tells him to bring those with him. An affidavit defending himself and answering all the accusations against him will also be helpful so Roger can start building a case.

For the rest of the week Benjamin calls everyone he can think of that knows him, that knows what a great father he had been to Angelica's kids. Most have not even heard that he is getting a divorce but word starts getting out and

264

The Suicide Note

spreading through the small community. Several people say they don't want to get involved but a few agree to write something. He calls Marsha Garwood and she agrees to write something up and send it down. He gets a couple of his agents to write something and a neighbor at the Willow Creek house who had spent a great deal of time with him and the kids. He is not able to connect with Jennifer Amanson until Saturday morning, when he finds her in the grocery store parking lot. She tries to slip away from him but he confronts her.

"Jenn, what's going on? Why are you dodging me? What's up with Brad? What's up with Brad saying all that bullshit about me to the court?"

"You really don't know? You have no idea what is going on, do you?" Jennifer starts to tear up.

"What are you talking about?"

"Your wife has been sleeping with my husband for months. He is living at your house now. We are getting a divorce."

Benjamin is frozen; his body is frozen, his mind is frozen. He stands in silence for a moment before he can speak.

"What?"

"I can't believe that you are oblivious to this, Benjamin." She is emphatic.

"They have been sneaking around behind your back for at least six months. I found out just before you guys went on your Italy trip. The idiot left his email open and I found the disgusting love letters they were exchanging with each other. I kicked that son-of-a-bitch out that day. I was actually surprised that you took that hussy to Italy."

"I didn't know. I had no clue. Why didn't you say something to me then?"

265

J. McGregor Colt

"I was grossed out and wanted nothing to do with any of you."

"Well, shit, Jenn, I had nothing to do with it. Did you think I encouraged them to have an affair?"

"I don't know what I thought but Brad and I are divorcing and I am moving back to Portland. Good luck." She gets in her car and drives off.

This new development is absolutely shocking to Benjamin. He is completely blind-sided by this latest revelation, and the thought of a drink is very attractive... he resists. Instead he drives to Centoni's Italian Cuisine. It is just about the time that the staff will be showing up for lunch. He walks through the doors and his eyes immediately find Giorgio.

"Look, Benji, you better get the fuck out of here before Antonio sees you."

"Hey, come on, Giorgio. I have never touched your sister or her kids. This is all a bunch of bullshit. She has been having an affair with Brad Amanson for months. This is just a big ploy to make me look bad."

"Benjamin, look, Brad is a family friend and has just been consoling her through this very difficult time. You need to get out of here. You are only going to make things worse for yourself."

Just then Antonio walks through the front door.

"What the fuck is he doing in here?" he asks Giorgio, then turns to Benjamin and puts his fist in front of his face.

"Get your sorry fucking ass out of my restaurant."

Antonio escorts Benjamin briskly out to the curb and tells him that if he ever comes anywhere near the restaurant or Angelica again that he will "fuck you up really bad."

The Suicide Note

Benjamin leaves, shaking his head in disbelief, and Antonio goes back inside. When he gets there Giorgio is waiting to talk with him.

"Antonio, what are we going to do about this?"

"What are we going to do about what? That son-of-a-bitch needs to stay out of here."

Antonio is angry and starts folding napkins aggressively while they continued talking in whispered voices.

"Can you blame him? Angelica is at it again. Benji is getting fucked over completely."

"Look Giorgio, Jelli is family. Regardless of how fucked she is or how much she is fucking somebody else over... again, she is family. Benji is not family. You need to respect the family. Papa told us what we needed to do."

"Yeah, but really, Benji is a good guy. I feel like we owe him something."

"Shut the fuck up about that. We owe him nothing. I warned that dumb shit what he was getting himself into but he wouldn't listen. He was letting his dick do the thinking. Just drop it. We gotta get open for lunch."

Giorgio is torn. He really likes Benjamin and knows that his sister has some pretty serious issues. Angelica's problems are not just drug- and alcohol-based but the drugs and alcohol certainly contribute. Angelica is a sociopath. She lacks any sense of ethics regarding others. Her lack of conscience allows her to manipulate others without any sense of wrongdoing. Benjamin had become a victim of her manipulation many years ago and all this is soon to become evident to him.

Benjamin tries to concentrate on work but when he gets back to his office all he can do is sit and stare at his computer

267

J. McGregor Colt

screen. After an hour or so Suzanne Britt notices him sitting there and comes in and asks if he is all right.

"Well, no, not exactly. I just found out that Angelica has been cheating on me. So, no, I'm not all right."

"Do you feel like drinking?"

"No."

"Would you like to go get a cup of coffee somewhere and talk about it?"

"No, thanks, Suzanne. I appreciate it but I think that I just need to go home and sort things out."

"Don't isolate, Benjamin. That could prove to be disastrous to your sobriety."

"No, I'm fine." He stands up and starts loading things into a briefcase; a laptop and some papers.

"Okay, but promise that you will call me if you get overwhelmed. We could hit a meeting or something. I know there's one in the back room of the Elks this evening."

"I promise to call if I need a meeting. Right now I just need to go home and sort things out in my own mind. Thanks a bunch, Suzanne. I really appreciate you." At that Benjamin leaves the office and Suzanne returns to her desk.

When Benjamin gets home he is overwrought with visions of Angelica making love to another man. He slumps over in a big chair, puts his face in the palms of his hands and begins to cry uncontrollably. He just breaks down and can't shake the vision of Angelica and Brad together in bed. Shortly his emotions turn to anger. He gets angry about Brad, whom he had considered to be one of his best friends, sleeping with his wife. He gets angry wondering for how long the affair has been going on. He gets angry wondering if there have been others.

268

The Suicide Note

Then, he diverts his anger to the Centoni family. He reflects on how poorly he has been treated by Marco and by Antonio since this all came to light. He does have a twinge of understanding, however. If they believe the accusations Angelica is making then he understands why they would be upset with him, but he has a hard time believing that they really believe these preposterous scenarios. He starts reflecting on the conversation Marco had with him years ago. He reminds himself that Marco had told him that Angelica was bad news. Had he really been that big of a sap? He fantasizes about waiting in the Walmart parking lot for Brad to get off work, bludgeoning him to death with a baseball bat, blood spurting everywhere, Brad begging for mercy and Angelica sitting in her car witnessing the whole thing in fear that she would be next. It gave him some satisfaction but, in reality, he knows he isn't capable of such a thing. Benjamin is, basically, a jellyfish; he knows he is lacking any substantial vertebrae, and this angers him even more.

The evening before his appointment with Roger Parsons, Benjamin drives into Vancouver to locate the law offices and get a motel room close by so he won't be late for his early morning time allotment. That accomplished, he gets a room at the Comfort Inn, not walking distance, but close to Parsons's office. His room has a kitchenette but there is a restaurant and bar right next door so he walks over and gets a table in the bar. Monday Night Football is displayed on half a dozen television monitors throughout the bar; a waitress comes over and asks him what he wants to drink and if he is going to order some food.

"Yes, I'm hungry. Leave the menu and I'll think about that drink. Thank you."

269

J. McGregor Colt

At this point Benjamin struggles. Does he want to break his sobriety? Does he want to get drunk and be hung over for his appointment in the morning? It's a real dilemma for him. He really does want a drink and he figures that he could have just one or maybe even two and be fine. Then he ponders what he would have. A beer? A glass of wine? A Scotch? Scotch is what he enjoys most... a good 12-year-old single-malt Scotch.

The waitress returns as he is mulling it all over.

"Have you decided on what you are going to have?"

"Yeah, I'll try the clams and linguine and maybe a little side salad."

"Excellent choice. How about something to drink?"

"I'm fine with just water. Thanks." He studies her ass as she walks back to the bar and then diverts his attention to the football game.

The Denver Broncos are playing the New York Giants in the first regular season game played at Invesco Field at Mile High in Denver. The announcers are making a big deal about it but all Benjamin can think is how disgusting it is that corporate interests are renaming all the iconic stadiums. He vows to continue calling it simply Mile High Stadium. He doesn't care for the Broncos because of past rivalries with the Seahawks so he cheers for the Giants.

After his meal he returns to his room, crawls into bed and turns the game on there. He turns the volume down so he can't hear the commentators jabbering and falls asleep with the television on about halfway through the fourth quarter. The Broncos were ahead and it didn't look like the Giants had much of a chance of a miraculous comeback.

The Suicide Note

In the morning the television is still on and it looks like the morning news is airing a premier of some disaster movie. He watches a plane fly into a tall building and goes back to the bathroom and gets in the shower. While he is brushing his teeth he comes out and turns up the volume on the set so he can listen to the news while he gets ready. It is while he is shaving that he begins to realize that the scene that he had seen earlier might not have been a disaster movie after all.

He comes out of the bathroom, sit on the edge of the bed, watches a second plane, on live television, fly right into the side of the second tower of The World Trade Center in New York City and explode into flames. This is no disaster movie, this is a real live disaster playing out on live television right in front of his eyes. He sits, frozen, watching people jump out of windows from fifty or so stories up to their deaths. The personal pain and agony he had been suffering suddenly pales in comparison. He continues watching in disbelief while he gets dressed and packs his overnight bag.

When he gets down to the lobby to check out and grab a quick motel-lobby-breakfast and some motel-lobby-coffee there is a small crowd that had formed a semi-circle around the television hanging from the ceiling in the corner. Nobody is speaking, several women have tears in their eyes, and it is a very somber scene. He wonders if Roger Parsons will be canceling his appointment.

As he is pulling into the parking lot for Parsons, Stebbins, Flatbern & Cole and being directed by the signage to the client parking area a flashy silver 308 GTS Ferrari zips past him and disappears to the parking lot behind the building. Behind the building is reserved for the employees and the

271

J. McGregor Colt

partners. Whether the Ferrari belonged to an employee or to a partner Benjamin knows that this is going to be a very expensive experience. Inside the lobby of the law firm a very smartly appointed man in his mid-forties is standing, brief case in hand, talking to the very attractive young red-headed receptionist who is handing him a stack of pink "While U Were Out" notes. The redhead smiles at Benjamin.

"Yes, sir, may I help you?"

"I'm Benjamin Mathews and have an appointment with Roger Parsons at 8 a.m."

"Oh, good morning, Mr. Mathews. I'm Roger Parsons."

The well-appointed man reaches out his hand and they shake.

"Please take a seat over there and let me go back and get situated. I just got in. Sheila will get you some coffee if you like."

Roger turns and exits the lobby. He is brief, businesslike, and makes no indication that he is even aware of what had taken place in New York City just moments ago.

After asking Benjamin if he wants coffee and how he preferred it, the redhead disappears for a couple of minutes and returns with a small tray holding a carafe of coffee, an empty cup with saucer, a serviette and a small spoon. She places the tray on the side table beside where he is seated.

"Did you see what happened in New York this morning?" Benjamin asks.

"Oh yes, it's all over the news. Isn't it horrifying? I thought that maybe the partners would be canceling the appointments today but it's business as usual around here," she says with a slight hint of disgust.

272

The Suicide Note

"Yeah, I assumed that may be the case. I mean I thought that maybe they would be canceling my appointment. I live up in Willow Creek and came in last night and got a motel room so I wouldn't have to get up so early. It was a real shocker to wake up to... that's for sure."

Just when he is about to turn on some Mathews charm with the young and attractive receptionist her buzzer rings and she tells him that he can go back now. She stands up and escorts him down a long hall and around one corner to the open door of Roger Parsons' office. For the entire journey down the hall Benjamin can't take his eyes off Sheila's behind. It is a very fine behind, accentuated nicely by the tight knee-length straight skirt she is wearing. It occurs to Benjamin that he is very horny and that even the events he had witnessed on television earlier, nor the fact that he is about to meet with a very expensive attorney to discuss what part of his net worth he could potentially keep, does not distract him from his wanton lust for the receptionist.

Parsons' office is lavishly furnished and looks out to the Columbia River waterfront over the Amtrak station and the southwest side of downtown Vancouver. Benjamin remembers taking trips up to Seattle on the train with Angelica and the kids. He remembers a huge argument in the parking lot to the Amtrak station just before they were to leave on one such trip. He remembers all sorts of huge arguments with Angelica just before they were about to do a lot of things and then he remembers why he is standing in front of a divorce lawyer on the morning of what will be one of the most iconic days in American history.

"Well, I wasn't sure we would be meeting after what happened this morning." Benjamin says nervously.

273

J. McGregor Colt

"I can't just close down. The courts aren't closing down so I guess we can't take any breaks." Parsons is dry and direct.

"Yeah, I guess not. So where do we start?" Benjamin sits in a comfortable chair across a very large mahogany executive desk facing his lawyer.

"Let's start with these accusations your wife and kids are making. They say that you aren't a very nice guy. You beat your wife and molest your kids."

"Hold on a sec. Those are complete fabrications. I never laid a hand on her or any woman for that matter. I have got to believe the children have been coerced, in some way, to say those things. I was a very good father to those kids. This whole thing completely blindsided me and now I learn that she has been having an affair with one of our friends. I'm getting screwed." Benjamin is getting agitated.

"Okay, first of all, this is a 'no-fault' divorce state so the fact that she was cheating on you is irrelevant to the case."

"Well, look, I am out on the street with only an overnight bag and three changes of underwear. I had to go to Walmart and buy sheets and towels and underwear and such. I have nothing. My wife cheated on me and I am the one out on the street with a restraining order and these outlandish allegations against me. I just don't think it's fair."

"Very little in life is fair, Mr. Mathews."

"Well, this is ridiculous."

"Okay, let's see what we can do about it. She says that you have been mentally and physically abusing her and she has this Bradley Amanson person backing up her story in his affidavit. So tell me who he is."

The Suicide Note

"He's the guy she's been sleeping with. Brad and his wife were good friends of ours. I rented an apartment above their garage when I first moved to Willow Creek. He owned the local pharmacy until Walmart put him out of business recently. We were good friends... so I thought."

"Okay; what proof do you have that they are having an affair?"

"His wife told me."

"Does she have evidence? Did she catch them in the act? Can you get her to testify under oath to this?"

"I thought you said it was a 'no-fault' deal."

"Yes, but if we can show that there is some motivation for them to make you out to be that bad guy then we may get some sympathy from the court."

"Okay, look; the only bad guy here is Angelica. I have been suffering her alcohol and drug abuse for years. She gets very violent and is both physically and mentally abusive to both me and her kids. What she is saying in this affidavit is what is true of her... not of me. She is projecting. I never did any of these things but she certainly has."

"Bill Summerset sent over half a dozen or so statements from people testifying to your upstanding nature. A couple of them state how good you were with the kids. None of them say anything about your wife's alcohol or drug abuse or anything about her violence. If there is any hope of refuting her statements we will need evidence to the contrary. Can you get anyone who will back you up on your claims?"

"She is very cagey. She was all smiles and bubbles in public and around friends. The monster side of her only came out when we were alone or at home. She was very calculating. She

275

J. McGregor Colt

could be yelling and screaming and carrying on and when the phone would ring she could instantly flip a switch and become a completely different person... all loving and bubbly with the person on the other end of the phone like nothing was wrong. It was uncanny how she could just do that."

"Okay but we have to prove it. Right now it's just your word against hers and the judge tends to take the woman's side in these situations especially when there are school-age children involved. We have a show-cause hearing in two weeks. It would be nice to have some statements discrediting her accusations and I'll see if I can get you your clothes and maybe some other personal belongings. You'll need to make a list."

"I'm getting screwed."

"Probably, but we're gonna try our best to make it less painful than it can be."

Before Benjamin leaves the office he signs some papers acknowledging that Parsons, Stebbins, Flatbern & Cole P.S. is the attorney of record in the matter and he is given a checklist of things he is to supply as quickly as possible in preparation of the show-cause hearing in two weeks. On his way out to his car the red-headed Sheila stops him and makes sure that she has his billing address. He could swear that she winked at him but knows really that it was just a fantasy.

When he gets back up the Gorge he swings into his River City office and finds that nobody is there except the receptionist. She has a small portable television on her desk and has been watching the non-stop coverage from New York. It is obvious that she had been crying.

The Suicide Note

"What is wrong with this world?" She breaks down.

"Okay; let's just close everything up. You go home. Take some time off. I'll let you know if there is anything important that I need you for."

They close up the office and walk out together. It is an eerie feeling on the sidewalk. Nobody is around, most of the shops are displaying "Closed" signs and when he drives down Main Street it looks like a ghost town. He crosses over into Washington, stops in the Willow Creek office, and finds several people there. They too had been watching things and are all huddled around a small portable television set. By then the news of a plane going into the Pentagon and another crashing in a field in Pennsylvania is dominating the story. All flights are canceled coming in or going out of the United States and the military is on super high alert. After about an hour huddled around the television with five or six of his agents he puts a stop to it and sends everybody home.

"Look, you guys, you all need to go home and be with your families. Give your kids a big hug."

Benjamin closes down the office and goes home himself. It's about three in the afternoon; nobody is out and about, the streets are empty. He flips on the television and discovers that all the network stations are dedicating full coverage to the attack. By now a radical Muslim terrorist group has taken claim for the incident, the attackers are being identified and reports are coming in about how they pulled it off. While Benjamin is processing all of this horror he keeps coming back to his own personal horror and is reviewing, in his head, what had transpired at the lawyers office earlier that day.

277

J. McGregor Colt

All of a sudden it dawns on him that Angelica has a very troubled past, a husband in jail for murdering the person with whom she had been having an affair, and past drug addictions. Surely there would be some record of all this in the courts of Southern California. He immediately digs out his laptop and sends Roger Parsons an email explaining everything he knew about his wife's past. He suggests that there will be court documents regarding her first husband and that there will probably be something discrediting about Angelica herself. He gives the attorney the husband's name of Tyrone Biggs and suggested that his wife could have been an Angelica Biggs or an Angelica Centoni. Benjamin is very enthusiastic about this new revelation and truly thinks that he is on to something. He is hopeful, almost cheerful.

Once he sends off the email he returns to watching the news coverage. It is depressing but it takes his mind away from other depressing thoughts. He makes something for dinner and eats it in front of the television. A little after six o'clock his laptop makes a little ringy-dingy sound indicating that he has a new email. He slides the laptop across the couch and reads the reply from his lawyer. The lawyer is interested in investigating more but needs the county in California where all the shenanigans took place. And he needs Angelica's date of birth. Benjamin gives the date of birth and guesses that it was Orange County.

He goes to bed that night feeling hopeful; still depressed, but hopeful.

Chapter
Nineteen

For the next couple of weeks the entire nation is consumed with the events of 9/11, except Benjamin... he is consumed with other things. His wife, he is learning, had been sleeping around with men other than just Brad. Apparently it is common knowledge that Angelica is a raving sex addict and had seduced the pool man, the chimney cleaner, as well as encouraged a great number of men who had come to the house while Benjamin was at work, and now, one of them is occupying his beautiful home and sleeping in his bed. Benjamin is consumed with other thoughts and has no room to burden his mind with the events of 9/11.

His first court appearance is in the County West District courtroom in Willow Creek. The purpose of this first

279

J. McGregor Colt

appearance is to answer to the abuse allegations and explain why the restraining order should be lifted. His attorney also wants the venue moved to Vancouver so it will be close to his office. He tells Benjamin that this will save him travel expenses and also give him the home court advantage.

Benjamin meets Roger in the hallway prior to entering the courtroom for a quick rundown of what is going to happen. While they are talking Angelica, Antonio, Brad Amanson and two guys in very expensive suits walk by them and into the courtroom. Nobody acknowledges Benjamin. Angelica is dressed like a librarian. She has on a white blouse buttoned up to the neck under a blue suit, her hair is pulled back in a bun and she is wearing very little make-up. She is putting on quite the show and her entourage is pretty intimidating as well.

They give the entourage a few moments to get seated inside the courtroom and then follow, seating themselves at the opposite end so as not to be too close. The court cases that precede the Mathews matter include a teenager fighting a speeding ticket, a domestic violence issue and a DUI. The seats in the courtroom are about half full; it is busy, with attorneys walking around and whispering to one another. When the judge calls Mathews vs. Mathews the two men in expensive suits escort Angelica to a table in front of the bench and Roger and Benjamin move up to a table beside them. The judge then reads the restraining order, describing, in detail, the disgusting allegations so the entire courtroom can hear all the ugly acts of which Benjamin is being accused. He is completely embarrassed, not realizing that the proceedings are going to be public. Benjamin does not realize a lot of things in his pitiful innocence but all that is about to change as abruptly as a match thrown on a gasoline-soaked log.

The Suicide Note

Roger Parsons stands and speaks, denying everything and presents the affidavits from three of Benjamin's witnesses countering the allegations just read. Then one of the suited men at Angelica's table paints a much more sinister picture and explains that his client and her children have been living in constant fear. At this point Angelica begins to cry. It is all very dramatic. She could have won an Academy Award for her performance. Benjamin just sits and shakes his head in disbelief.

"We would like to see the restraining order renewed for another six months and further ask that the court order the respondent to pay a temporary separate maintenance of $3,600 per month and temporary child support in the amount of $700 per child for two children. We further ask that the court order Mr. Mathews to keep the mortgage payments current and also the payments on the 1999 Cadillac Escalade currently in Mrs. Mathews' possession."

The very well spoken man then turns to his sidekick and is handed some papers which he in turn hands to the court clerk.

"If it please the court we have submitted herewith an itemized list of Mrs. Mathews' monthly expenses which will clearly justify the separate maintenance amount."

He then turns and sits back down in his chair behind the table next to a tearful Angelica.

"Excuse me, your honor, but we have not had the advantage of seeing this list and would ask for some time to review. Further we would like to point out that the children are not the children of Mr. Mathews but rather children Mrs. Mathews had prior to this marriage."

281

J. McGregor Colt

"Hold on a moment, counselor," the judge says sternly to Roger.

"Mr. Greenly," now directing himself to the other table. "please provide a copy of this to the Respondent." The judge then asks, "Is it true that the children are not Mr. Mathews' children?"

"Mr. Mathews has adopted these children. I offer these adoption papers as proof of this." Mr. Greenly passes forward the adoption papers Benjamin had signed several years prior.

"And has thereby taken upon full responsibility for their well being."

"That's enough, thank you. I am prepared to rule on what has been proposed today without further comment. I will extend the restraining order but will add that it is a mutual restraining order meaning that neither party will come within 50 feet of the other. I will grant the $3,600 per month in separate maintenance and will further stipulate that the Respondent maintain the mortgage and the car payments. I am also going to rule in favor of the child support amount and will suggest that Mr. Mathews take a full accounting of the promise he made to these children on the day he agreed to adopt them. The law does not give me leeway to waive child support responsibility for the children in this matter. Is there anything else?"

Roger stands up.

"Yes, your honor. I have a petition for a change of venue for the divorce proceedings. My client is well known in this community and much of this is going to get ugly, it seems. My office is in Vancouver and the Petitioners attorney are in the Los Angeles area so Clark County would be much more

282

The Suicide Note

convenient to the Portland airport for them. I think it would be more beneficial to both parties to have this moved out of the county where they both reside."

"Are you on board with this, Mr. Greenly?" the judge asks.

"Yes, your honor. That sounds reasonable."

"Okay, I'll tell you what I'm willing to do. I'll compromise and meet you half way. I will move the proceedings to Skamania County. Stevenson is a lot closer to Vancouver and the Portland airport and I am the district court judge for that county as well so we will all see more of each other very soon. Clerk, submit the paperwork and I will sign it."

The gavel comes down and the whole thing is over and done in about 15 minutes. Benjamin is to pay his manipulative, conniving, unfaithful wife $5,000 per month and continue making the payments on the house she is living in with his old best friend Brad. He is more astonished than he is furious.

Brad and Antonio bustle Angelica through the courtroom, down the hall and out of sight very quickly. The LA attorneys hang out in the hallway with Roger for a while and shoot the shit as if they were old college buddies or something, only adding more fury to Benjamin's astonishment as he hangs out down the hall waiting patiently to talk to Roger.

"What was that all about? Did you actually know those guys? You sure seemed pretty buddy-buddy." Benjamin asks when Roger approaches.

"No. What good does it do us to piss those guys off at this point? Eventually we're gonna want something from them. Relax."

They talk while walking down the hall and out to the parking lot. As they stand in the parking lot continuing their

283

J. McGregor Colt

talk Benjamin notices his silver Escalade pull out with Brad behind the wheel and Angelica in the passenger seat. He just shakes his head in disgust. He is getting completely screwed over, he figures, and he hadn't even really seen it coming. After Roger gets in his fancy Ferrari and drives off, Benjamin heads across the lot to his own car when a black sedan pulls up next to him. Antonio is in the passenger seat with the window down.

"Okay; motherfucker, you only get one warning. I don't give a rat's ass what that fucking judge says. You pay $5,000 per month to Angelica or you are going to regret it very badly. You understand?"

Antonio is sounding like a mobster at this point and when Benjamin looks at the driver and another scary looking dude in the back seat he realizes that there is a strong possibility he is dealing with dangerous people.

"Jesus, Antonio! Give me a break."

"You ain't gettin' any fuckin' breaks. Don't test me. If I hear you aren't payin' you're gonna regret it. Don't fuck up," he says as he gestures for the driver to go.

As the car pulls away Benjamin notices that it has Nevada license plates. He isn't sure what that means but it certainly arouses his curiosity. He imagines real mobsters. He is shaking a bit by the time he gets in his car, drives straight to his basement apartment and locks the door behind him. After he is home for a few minutes mulling everything over he hears footsteps upstairs and knows that his landlord is home. There is an interior stairway that provides access to the upstairs kitchen. Benjamin climbs the stairs and knocks. He just needs somebody to talk to and he knows the landlord is neutral

284

The Suicide Note

and has a good take on things. Randall opens the door and welcomes him in.

"Hey, Benjamin, I was just gonna have a beer. You want one?"

"No, thanks."

Randall Spears is a local home builder and accomplished windsurfer. He and Benjamin had spent a lot of time together windsurfing and chasing women back when Benjamin had first moved to the Gorge, back before Benjamin had fallen hook, line and sinker for Angelica. Randall had not seen much of Benjamin for the past five years mainly because Benjamin had quit windsurfing and had sequestered himself with his new family.

"How is everything going with you, Benjamin? I imagine it's been rough." Randall asks with sincerity.

Benjamin sits down at the kitchen counter and tells Randall everything that has been going on. He tells him about Angelica cheating on him with Brad. He tells him all about being banned from his own home, the allegations the kids are making and the subsequent restraining order. He tells him what the judge has just ruled. And he tells him about the threats the Centoni family is making, the car with Nevada plates, and all.

"Holy shit, Benjamin, do you own a gun?"

Benjamin chuckles at his question.

"No, seriously man, you need to pack a gun. These guys aren't messing around."

At first Benjamin scoffs at this line of thinking. Benjamin has never owned a gun and has never had any desire to do so. The entire idea is alien to him but Randall insists that he gets a gun right away.

J. McGregor Colt

"You need a nice little 38 Special like this one."

Randall slides open a drawer he is sitting in front of and shows Benjamin a .38 caliber Smith & Wesson handgun he keeps handy in a drawer in the kitchen.

"Good grief! What do you have that for?"

"Protection, my friend... protection. Follow me."

Randall puts the gun back in its place in the drawer, leads him out to the living room, and opens a large stand-up gun safe. The opened door displays a wide assortment of rifles, handguns and an antique shotgun.

"Are you expecting an invasion or something?" Benjamin asks sincerely.

"Ya never know. These are strenuous times. We need to get you a gun. What are you doing in the morning?" Randall is being very serious and quite insistent.

Benjamin has no idea what he would be doing in the morning but agrees to go with Randall to Jack's Guns & Ammo. The two have dinner together, talk over some good times they had shared together and part ways at about ten o'clock.

With all that is weighing on his mind Benjamin does not sleep well that night. He keeps visualizing his wife having sex with Brad. He gets more and more angry thinking about the judge ordering him to pay what he thinks to be an outrageous sum of money to his lying and cheating wife and it prevents him from sleeping. He just can't understand how anyone can do to another human being what Angelica is doing to him. Benjamin struggles all night thinking about Angelica's complete lack of guilt, her lack of empathy. He can't understand how she could convince others, so convincingly,

The Suicide Note

that someone else is the bad guy. It's like she has a split personality or something he figures.

Angelica is a sociopath and Benjamin is only beginning to realize it. She actually gets enjoyment from making others feel guilty. She only values herself, believes that she is better than everyone else but, above all, Angelica is a liar. She lies about everything: big things, small things, inconsequential things. She lacks accountability for her actions. But, like most sociopaths, she is well-liked. She comes off as being very friendly and approachable. This is how Angelica will gain a person's trust and get them to open up their vulnerabilities. Angelica was on stage that first time she met Benjamin. She lured him into her web. Benjamin cannot sleep.

In the morning Randall comes around and pounds on Benjamin's front door. The home they live in is a daylight basement arrangement. Randall occupies the upper levels and Benjamin lives in the apartment below. Benjamin is still in bed and asks Randall to give him a few minutes to get dressed. After a bit, they leave in Randall's big pick-up truck, drive into downtown Willow Creek and park in front of a coffee shop. The gun shop isn't going to be open for another twenty minutes so they go in the coffee shop and get bagels and coffee.

"Crap, I didn't really sleep much last night," Benjamin offers.

"Yeah, I don't guess I would either with all the shit you got going on."

One of Benjamin's agents comes by the table where he is sitting and discusses a little business with him. A few other people wave over at him. To everyone in town it is just

287

J. McGregor Colt

another day. To Benjamin it is far from normal, he is torn up emotionally but makes no indication of such.

When Jack's Guns & Ammo opens Benjamin and Randall are the first ones through the door. Jack is a hard-nosed red neck sort of a fellow. There are American flags, Confederate flags and bumper stickers that say things like "America, Love it or Leave it" and "Don't Tread on Me" displayed all over the walls... and, of course, there are guns and probably ammo.

"What can I do for you boys? Oh, hey there, Randall?" Jack asks.

Benjamin figures that Randall is probably one of Jack's better customers.

"Benjamin here needs a firearm. I'm thinking a .38."

"Automatic or revolver?" Jack queries.

"I don't know. Show him both. I prefer a revolver but let's let him make the choice." Randall is doing the talking.

Jack looks at Benjamin and asks if he currently owns a gun and Benjamin acknowledges that he does not.

"Okay; give me a minute." Jack disappears into a back room.

Benjamin and Randall browse around the shop. Benjamin finds some more interesting bumper stickers: "I Was Raised RIGHT," and "Just Another REPUBLICAN. Working Hard So You Don't Have To." Randall thumbs through a gun catalogue. Benjamin feels really out of place in Jack's but doesn't let on.

"Okay, boys, here's what I got." Jack says as he re-enters the room and places three handguns, in their boxes, on the counter.

288

The Suicide Note

"This first one is a very fine Smith & Wesson .38 caliber revolver with a two inch barrel. Randall; I believe you have the same piece."

"Yep, that's the one I showed you last night, Benjamin."

"This one here is the Automatic Colt, General Officer. It's a bit more compact and is also a very fine weapon. The last one is another revolver made by Taurus. It's less money but not as good a handgun as these first two."

Benjamin picks up the Colt.

"I like this one."

"Okay, this comes with a clip that holds seven cartridges. Are you gonna need ammo?"

Jack is a bit gruff and to the point as he slaps a box of cartridges on the counter next to the pistol Benjamin has chosen.

"Yeah, okay sure. What's all this gonna cost?" Benjamin asks.

"You're gonna need a holster." Randall chimes in. "Jack, you got a holster you can show him?"

"Yeah, I was gonna throw in this little belt clip-on job. You probably don't need anything fancier than this."

Benjamin indicates that he is good with everything and is ready to pay and get the hell out of there but Jack informs him that there is paperwork to fill out, a background check and a waiting period.

"They don't let me just let you walk out of here with a firearm any more... the bastards. I'll call you once everything has cleared and you can come back and pay me then. Here, fill this out too. You're probably going to want a concealed weapons permit. No sense owning a gun if you can't carry it around with you."

J. McGregor Colt

Benjamin completes the paperwork and they leave. Three days later he returns, pays for the gun, holster and ammo and walks out of the store with it all in a bag. The concealed weapons permit was to be mailed from the sheriff's office and that will take a couple of weeks, Jack explains, so technically he isn't allowed to carry the weapon on his person yet. When he gets home that night Benjamin grabs Randall and they drive out to a remote area for a little target practice. Benjamin feels good with the weapon in his hand and he is empowered when he fires it. Randall gives him a few pointers and after about thirty minutes he has become a pretty good shot. He likes the way the gun feels in his hand. When he gets home he doesn't put it away right off but plays with it for a bit, pointing it at various things around the apartment. Benjamin is now a macho-man gun owner.

Chapter
Twenty

A couple of days later Jennifer Amanson calls his cell. Benjamin is sitting in his car when the call comes in, about to get out and walk into his Sunyton office meeting. It's about twenty minutes before the meeting is to start so he sits there and speaks with her. She is distraught.

"Benjamin, I know that you're an innocent victim in all this. I know that the accusations being made about you are complete bullshit."

"Thanks, Jenn."

"Let me talk. I don't have but a few minutes. You have got to be very careful. The family you have married into is very dangerous. Don't mess with them. They will hurt you, believe me." Her voice is getting shaky as she speaks.

J. McGregor Colt

"What do you mean? I haven't done anything. It's your husband who..."

"Fuck Brad. He has always been very secretive in his dealings with the Centonis. I'm not sure what is going on there but their relationship dates back before Brad and I met. I can tell you this; Brad is not only sleeping with your wife, he is also supplying her with drugs."

"What!?" Benjamin asks emphatically.

"Cocaine and Adderall. Pharmaceutical cocaine. It started out with the Adderall. She got a prescription for Drake and she took it herself. When that ran out Brad would just supply her with it... he owned the pharmacy. It was very easy to cover up. It's been going on for a couple of years and so has the sneaking around behind our backs."

"Good grief! Cocaine?"

"Yeah. Brad and I used to do cocaine together years ago but we stopped. At least I thought we had stopped. Apparently Brad didn't. I uncovered all this when I was closing out our books when we finally had to close the shop down."

"Fuck. What a mess. Will you testify in my behalf? She is trying to take me for everything I have."

"No, absolutely not. That's why I'm calling. You have got to leave me out of this. I'm moving away. They are dangerous people, Benjamin. You have got to be very careful. They do not play by the rules."

"But I just can't let them take away everything I have."

"Benjamin! I can't say any more. Be careful. I've gotta go." She hangs up.

Benjamin sits in shock for a couple of minutes before he goes inside and attends the sales meeting. He isn't focused at

The Suicide Note

all on the issues being discussed at the meeting. The agents and staff know something is wrong but nobody inquires. None of them really know him all that well and they have no idea about any of his latest personal life challenges. Sunyton is only twenty miles away physically but a thousand miles away on a socioeconomic scale and the citizenry does not mix much with those in River City or in Willow Creek.

Every day there is new information coming in about Angelica and her family. Benjamin has learned more about Angelica in the past couple of weeks than he did the entire eight years of their relationship. Why had he not seen these things before? Is he too naive, too trusting in his fellow man? Yes, to both. Benjamin is a sap, for sure, but Angelica is a truly evil person. To what limits can this person go and what is her motivation? The questions consume Benjamin's thoughts.

Angelica Elena Centoni was born on February 2, 1960, the third child of Marco and Elena Centoni in Newport Beach, California. When she was about fifteen years old her family moved from a modest home in Long Beach to the opulent estate in Newport Beach. Her parents had made a very good living, very quickly. Angelica grew up with privilege, but she had secrets that haunted her for her entire adult life.

When she was thirteen she was sexually molested by an older cousin and this was, most likely, the pivotal point in her life. Vinny, as he was called, was the oldest of Marco's brother Vincent. Vinny was a rough kid. He had always gotten into fights and was in trouble with the law more than Marco wanted. Marco did not want any attention brought to his family. If there was a dispute in the neighborhood he just wanted to take care of the matter himself. He felt no need to get the authorities involved. Vinny was constantly drawing attention to the family and, although Marco didn't like it, his young thirteen-year-old daughter did. Angelica was very impressed and enamored with Vinny, who was six years her senior. She looked up to him and idolized everything he did.

One afternoon Vinny came over to the house in Long Beach for a visit with his cousins to find that the only one home was Angelica. It was a hot summer day and Angelica had been sun bathing in the back yard in a skimpy bikini. She was only thirteen but physically she was a fully developed young woman. She had high firm breasts, a shapely midsection and a nice round bottom. When Vinny arrived Angelica began to flirt with him. This did not go unnoticed and Vinny became aroused. He made an advance and gave her a kiss. The kiss was returned and Vinny got aggressive with her. When he tried to lay her down on the couch and remove her bikini bottom Angelica resisted. By this point there was no turning around for Vinny. He raped her. He was void of any thought of guilt, remorse or repercussion. He took the virginity of a thirteen year-old child in a violent and aggressive act of power. He was sexually satisfied quickly and Angelica was devastated and in pain.

When the ugly matter had come to a conclusion Vinny helped Angelica back to her bedroom and told her that she had better not tell anybody about what had happened. He promised her that he too would keep it a secret, convinced her that it was she who was to blame, that it was she who should feel guilty.

Over the next several months Vinny and Angelica would meet secretly and have sex. Vinny at one point started

The Suicide Note

supplying her with cocaine and alcohol and they continued to have a secret sexual relationship for the better part of Angelica's eighth grade year in school. Vinny would supply Angelica and her friends with booze and drugs and Angelica would supply Vinny with sex.

It was all very reprehensible and then they got caught. It was Vinny's younger sister Cynthia who caught them. First she discovered Vinny giving Angelica and a couple of her girlfriends some beer. She got mad at her big brother and threatened to tell their parents if he didn't stop. Then she found evidence that he was also giving them drugs. At that point Cynthia was furious and barged into Angelica's bedroom to confront her but found instead something far more alarming: her brother in bed, naked with Angelica. She ran fast out of the house and right into Antonio who was just getting home. It was obvious that Cynthia was upset about something. Just when Antonio tried to find out what was wrong with her Vinny came around the corner still putting on his clothes. It didn't take Antonio long to put two and two together especially after seeing his little sister in the final stages of straightening herself up.

At that point all hell broke loose. Vinny and Cynthia slipped out while Antonio was reprimanding his little sister. He knew that Angelica was probably no little angel but had only now just realized how un-angel like she truly was. Antonio could not contain his rage and slapped Angelica square across the face when she told him to mind his own business. The slap brought a momentary conclusion to the argument, Angelica retreated back into her bedroom, and locked the door behind her.

295

J. McGregor Colt

In time the rest of the family came home and concluded that something had transpired. Antonio took his father aside out of earshot of his mother and brothers and told him what had happened. Marco was furious but calm. That night at the dinner table there was no discussion of the matter. Everyone sensed something was wrong but no one but Marco, Antonio and Angelica knew what it was. The rest knew better than to pry.

Things moved quickly after that. Marco had Angelica enrolled in a private girls boarding school in San Diego County and she was shipped off in two days. She went quietly. Vinny also left. It is uncertain whether or not he went quietly. Vinny just disappeared and nobody knew, including Antonio, if he had run away never to be seen again or if he had been disposed of by Marco. The subject of Vinny never came up in conversation. Cynthia told her father, Vincent, what she had stumbled upon as soon as she got home that day. Vincent, who had given up hope that his son would ever amount to anything good or meaningful much earlier, just shook his head and kept his thoughts to himself. After Vinny disappeared, Cynthia, not really knowing for sure what had happened to him, never stopped blaming Angelica. She never forgave Angelica for her part but the matter was never discussed. Cynthia just stayed away from Angelica from that point on.

After Angelica had been shipped off to boarding school Vincent went to Marco to offer support, maybe even some sort of an apology for his derelict son's actions. Marco was not sympathetic. This had not been the first time that Vinny had caused the family embarrassment or humiliation. Vinny's bad behavior in New York was the main

The Suicide Note

reason Vincent had brought his family out to California and Marco had warned him at the time that he needed to keep Vinny under control. Marco reminded his brother of this and Vincent agreed to what had to happen next.

That next day Vincent convinced his son to go for a ride with him out into the desert with the story that they were going to look at a real estate opportunity. On Highway 91 somewhere between Corona and Riverside Vincent turned down a side road and then again down a dirt road. About a mile down the dirt road they came upon Marco standing next to a sedan, with Nevada plates, talking to two other men. Vincent and Vinny pulled up and both got out of the car. At this point Vinny just figured that this was the real estate they were looking at and that the two men had something to do with that. There were no cordialities. Marco looked at Vinny and said, "You're going with these guys." He then took his brother by the elbow and they got in Vincent's car and drove off. As they departed Vincent looked in the review mirror and saw his only son being forced in the back seat of the sedan with Nevada plates. This was the last time he would see his son and the last time Vinny's name would be spoken in the Centoni family.

Angelica stayed away in boarding school for the next four years. The school in San Diego was not the only school, however. She got kicked out of that one after the first year. There would be two more schools for her before she finally completed her high school education and returned to the family home in Newport Beach. By that time the Centoni Italian Cuisine restaurants had been in operation for several years and were thriving. Marco decided to give his

297

J. McGregor Colt

daughter a chance and set her up with a job in the restaurant bussing tables.

For a while Angelica behaved herself and was eventually moved up to waiting tables. In the evenings she took some bookkeeping and accounting courses at Coastline Community College and started helping out a bit in the office. The bookkeeper for the restaurant liked Angelica and took her under her wing. She showed Angelica how to tally the daily receipts and prepare the deposit slips. This arrangement continued for several months. Marco noticed the change in his daughter and began trusting her, giving her more and more responsibilities around the restaurant.

After about a year and a half Angelica had become a trusted employee and in good standing with the family. She had completed bookkeeping courses at the community college, wasn't doing drugs and didn't seem to have any issues with alcohol. On her twenty-first birthday Marco announced that Alice, the restaurant bookkeeper, was retiring and that Angelica would be taking over that position in the Newport Beach location. Everyone in the family was surprised at this announcement but wished Angelica well and congratulations abounded.

Perhaps Angelica had finally grown up and was going to be a responsible member of the family. She quit waiting tables and now spent her days in the office upstairs doing the books, ordering the alcohol, the produce, the meats and such. She also inventoried everything. She knew how many plates, knives and spoon were supposed to be in the building and knew when it was time to order more. She had become very diligent.

298

The Suicide Note

Another year went by before she felt comfortable hanging out in the bar after her work was done. It was on her little brother David's twenty-first birthday that she joined a crowd in the bar to celebrate. David was promoted to daytime bartender that day and after that it became a habit of hers to hang out in the bar when she got done and wait for David's shift to end at 5 p.m. On an occasion or two she may have had a drink or two too many but it wasn't often and she didn't cause any damage or make any scenes.

On one such day that she may have had one too many, an old friend of hers from middle school came in with her boyfriend and another guy. Beverly Washington introduced Angelica to the other guy, Tyrone Biggs, and the two connected right off the bat. The fact that Tyrone was a black man was no deterrent to Angelica; she had never had a boyfriend and a relationship with Tyrone was launched immediately. They left the bar together that evening and went over to Tyrone's place and had wild passionate sex. For several weeks Angelica made up for the sex she had not been having since she had been staying away from booze and behaving herself. Tyrone was the lucky beneficiary of her passion. They hung out for the next year as boyfriend and girlfriend and then snuck off and got married. When he learned of this Marco was furious, he did not like or trust Tyrone, and especially did not like that his daughter had married a black man.

Angelica and Tyrone got a place together and lived as husband and wife faithfully for at least six, maybe seven months until Angelica started to get the itch. Her sexual passion had been re-released, the feeding trough filled; she

299

J. McGregor Colt

couldn't get enough and started fooling around with other men behind Tyrone's back. Tyrone was an abusive husband and she confided this to Beverly, who had become her closest confidant and friend. Beverly and Angelica would get together and console one another on the trials and tribulations of their lives and soon Beverly's older brother, James, started hanging out with the two ladies as well. James was a tall, good-looking man a year or two older than Angelica, and she was very attracted to him. Eventually, as is Angelica's modus operandi, the two became secret lovers. They would sneak away behind Beverly and Tyrone's back and have sex whenever the opportunity arose.

Angelica also started drinking more and getting into cocaine. The cocaine was something that Tyrone had introduced into the equation. He was a small-time dealer. The nighttime bar scene in Newport Beach and the surrounding area was swimming in cocaine users and Tyrone was a willing supplier. He also dealt out of the bar at Centonís. Angelica was very good at keeping her brothers and father in the dark about all this. She was always on her best behavior around them and when she became pregnant with Mandrake she got completely sober. For her entire pregnancy she was clean as a whistle and once Drake was born she made a valiant attempt to be a nurturing and caring mother. As far as everyone could see she was doing the right thing. There were, however, her uncontrollable sexual desires and within a year she was pregnant again.

This second pregnancy aroused Tyrone's suspicion. He thought that he had been careful to wear a condom whenever he and Angelica had sex. Angelica became furious

The Suicide Note

when he dared to question the second pregnancy. She threw a fit, accusing him of not loving her, of looking for an excuse to abandon his family. Tyrone was immediately put on the defense and never brought the subject up again. After Isabella was born Angelica and Tyrone got heavily into drugs and alcohol, and their lives, everything Angelica had mended with her family, just fell completely apart. It was not too long after the birth of Isabella that Tyrone figured out that Angelica had been sleeping with Beverly's brother. Tyrone himself was not the picture of virtue, having enjoyed his own unfaithful encounters but he cracked, went berserk and shot and killed James in a fit of rage. During his murder trial it was discovered that both of Angelica's children were fathered by James.

Beverly was emotionally devastated by the death of her brother but did not blame Angelica. She understood that Tyrone was abusive, she understood, through previous conversations with Angelica, that she had been looking for a way out of the marriage, and she accepted, now, that she was the aunt to two young children. Beverly took the responsibility willingly, protected Drake and Izzy from the ugliness of their lives when she could and tried to help Angelica deal with her demons. Beverly was a good friend and wore the mantle of Aunt well.

301

Chapter
Twenty One

Benjamin continues the struggle of dealing with the new reality that has caught him completely unaware and slammed him in the face, full force, like a blast from a fire hose. He has lost his house and family and is living in the furnished basement apartment of someone else's house. At night he lies in bed and fumes at the thought of some other guy enjoying the luxury that he struggled hard to build for himself over the years. He torments himself with visions of his Angelica making love with another man.

The torment only gets worse as his divorce case progresses. Things are dragging on for way too long as far as Benjamin is concerned. There are delays and continuances and every time there is a court hearing Benjamin is not allowed

302

The Suicide Note

to say a word in his own defense; the entire system is flawed as far as he is concerned. The only ones who are allowed to speak are the attorneys and nothing is going his way. Angelica wants everything. The longer she is able to string out the proceedings the longer he is required to continue to pay her expenses and, on top of it all, as if there is one more thing that he could possibly endure, he is ordered to pay her attorney fees. A stab in the eye would have been less painful.

Now it has been over a year since this matter had begun, a year since he learned his wife had been cheating on him, a year since the events of 9/11, and, by now, he has been accused of being an unfaithful husband, a wife beater, a child molester, a drug addict and the judge seems to be buying off on the whole thing. Angelica has also accused the Garwoods of being drug dealers. This accusation came after the Garwoods had submitted an affidavit vouching for Benjamin's character and validating his ability to be a loving and doting father to his stepchildren. Basically, Angelica is accusing Benjamin and anyone else who will speak up in his defense, of being the kind of person that she actually is herself. She is truly the master of projection.

All Benjamin can do is work. He knows how to work. He does not know how to deal with his emotions and the divorce proceedings are draining him. Matters only get worse for him when the news of what is happening in the Stevenson courtroom makes its way up the river to the communities of Willow Creek and River City. People are starting to talk about it, long-time clients are turning away, a couple of his agents quit with the thought that they cannot work for a man who beats his wife or molests children. Most understand that

303

J. McGregor Colt

Benjamin is being used but some side with Angelica and keep their distance. The he-said, she-said mentality seeps out of the courtroom environment and into the community. Benjamin just wants the entire thing to come to a conclusion but at the same time he is not willing to give up everything he has to a conniving, lying, unfaithful sociopath.

In an attempt to prove his innocence of the accusations Angelica has been making in court, Benjamin submits to a lie detector test. The administrator of the test tries to conclude whether or not Benjamin has molested his young stepdaughter. Benjamin has absolutely not done anything that could possibly be construed as molestation but the lie detector test is inconclusive. This is devastating to Benjamin and magnifies further doubt of his innocence.

His attorney is able to get a court-ordered psychiatric evaluation of the children. Angelica takes both children for three sessions each to a local child psychiatrist for a full evaluation of their mental health, to try to determine the validity of Angelica's claims, and, again, the evaluation proves inconclusive. Angelica has brainwashed and threatened the children so much that they are either afraid to tell the truth or sincerely believe that Benjamin is a bad man. The psychiatrist claims in his report that it could be possible that the children are lying but he cannot be positive and, in all likelihood, they are probably telling the truth.

At this point all Benjamin is trying to do is protect at least fifty percent of his net worth. Angelica is going for much more than that. She is suing for the emotional distress she had been made to suffer and the lifetime damage that Benjamin had done to her children. She plays the judge like a virtuoso plays

304

The Suicide Note

a violin. At every courtroom session she gives the appearance of a simple, modest housewife and is able to muster tears at each appropriate moment. Benjamin, on the other hand, plays himself and guffaws at her performance, incredulous that anyone could possibly believe her. It does not go well for him. He gets outplayed at every turn.

The property settlement is what is at stake, what will determine the material things in his life he is going to be left with. Benjamin knows that he isn't his car or his house. He knows that he isn't his business, or his children, or his wife. He isn't sure who he is but he knows that he isn't any of those things. Benjamin has given up on the judge believing that he is the good guy and that she is the bad guy. He knows that at this point none of that matters. All he wants to do is to retain a fair settlement of the property.

The Willow Creek Bluff home has increased in value significantly and is now worth about $1.5 million with only about $190,000 left owing on the mortgage. He owns the Willow Creek office building which is worth about $800,000 but has a mortgage of about $650,000. He is only a tenant in his River City office and his Sunyton office so there is nothing of value to consider there. There are some partnerships he is involved in that own as much as 3,000 acres of rural land for future development purposes, but his equity in this land is minimal and can be viewed as more of a liability than an asset in that he has monthly payment obligations in order to keep it. Basically, his entire net worth was in the Willow Creek residence. He does own a real estate brokerage company.

Benjamin propose that the house be sold and the equity split on a fifty-fifty basis. He suggests that Angelica's share of

305

J. McGregor Colt

the equity in the other real estate holdings be subtracted from his side and they just go on their merry, separate, way. This is not good enough for Angelica. She wants much more than half and hires a business appraiser out of Seattle to come up with a value for The Mathews Group. The appraiser, whose integrity should have been scrutinized, claims that Benjamin's business is worth $1.2 million. This, of course, is completely preposterous as far as Benjamin is concerned. To him, a real estate brokerage business isn't worth much of anything other than the fair market value of its used furniture and computers. Agents have no obligation to stay and the real estate market fluctuates so drastically that there is really nothing to appraise. Benjamin feels he would be lucky to get $30,000 as a business opportunity for all three offices combined. But, again, the judge does not see it this way.

In the end, after eighteen months of traveling back and forth to Stevenson for court every four or five weeks, the judge is ready to rule on the property disbursement and final divorce decree. Angelica will get the residence and has 90 days to refinance the $190,000 to get Benjamin's name off the mortgage. Angelica will get the Escalade she is driving and Benjamin will get the pickup truck his company is leasing. Benjamin is to pay off the Escalade and he is given 90 days to do so. Benjamin is awarded full ownership of The Mathews Group and any real estate that is included with that. In Benjamin's way of thinking, he gets completely screwed out of $1 million in equity in the house and is, in turn, awarded a job for life.

Benjamin had made every attempt to be a good husband, a loving father and an upstanding citizen in his community

306

The Suicide Note

and had gotten completely blindsided by a psychotic sociopath and her entire family. For the next couple of weeks after the divorce is finalized Benjamin is very difficult to be around. A few more of his agents quit and go to work for his competitors. His Willow Creek office falls from a high of ten agents down to three. He loses half of his River City agents and now only has eight. The Sunyton office only had five agents to begin with and they all remain as they really have no idea what is going on in the first place. Things are not going well for Benjamin financially but he doesn't seem to care. The only thing that survives through it all is his sobriety. He continues going to AA meetings and gets to be pretty close with Father Ed Stead and also with Suzanne Britt and her husband; they have all stood by him throughout all the ugliness. They know him to be a good person, they are among the few who believe that he is not a wife beater or a child molester.

Benjamin's real estate business is suffering and he is not spending any time trying to change that. He is too busy feeling sorry for himself. He is spending most of his time in his River City office just staring at a computer screen. He enjoys the company of his agents in that office and he gets his best moral support from Suzanne. Oftentimes Ed Stead will come down and the three of them will go out to lunch together. Their favorite place to go is the dining room at the River City Hotel. The owner there is friendly and often sits and talks with them over lunch. Occasionally they will cross paths with one of the Centonis but eyes are averted and no words are spoken.

The city parking lot where Benjamin parks his car every morning is right across the street from the entrance

J. McGregor Colt

to Centoni's Italian Cuisine so it is inevitable that their paths cross eventually. One evening as Benjamin is getting into his car to drive home he notices his Escalade pull into the lot. Brad is driving, Angelica is seated in the passenger seat and in the back are Izzy and Drake. They park, get out and walk happily right past him sitting in his car and into the restaurant. Izzy makes brief eye contact with him and he can almost make out a smile of sympathy on her face but they keep walking. Nobody says anything. Benjamin is heartbroken.

Benjamin had never stopped being heartbroken. From the River City waterfront he can look across the river and easily make out his old house on the Willow Creek Bluff. Benjamin will often drive down there and just sit in his car looking at his old house, remembering what joy he used to have there. He remembers the day they all moved in and the delight he had in realizing that he had finally made it. He reminisces about all the parties they hosted in the house and the visitors they would have stay with them but it is all lost now, he has lost everything. When he speaks about his troubles at the AA meetings he is attending Suzanne and Ed Stead become more and more concerned about his mental health and encourage him to go see a professional... he refuses.

One morning he pulls into his space in the city parking lot and when he gets out of his car Antonio and Giorgio are both standing in the lot between where he parked and the route he needs to walk to his office.

"Hey, here comes the loser." Giorgio proclaims.

"Look at the pitiful cocksucker." Antonio chimes in

"Are you having fun at your little cry-baby AA meetings bad-mouthing our family?"

308

The Suicide Note

They have both gotten right up in Benjamin's face now and continue to be very intimidating.

"We warned you already a couple of times, douchebag. You keep your fucking mouth shut about Angelica."

Just as Antonio utters those words and is about to punch Benjamin in the stomach the meter maid comes around the corner to check the lot. Antonio backs up and lets Benjamin continue on his path without further word. Benjamin knows he has dodged a bullet and also knows that the matter is not concluded. After that Benjamin will carry the new revolver whenever he leaves the house. He also starts parking his car in a different city lot. The new lot is further away but does not require him to go near the restaurant.

In the next few weeks things start getting really tough financially for Benjamin. His two main offices are not producing enough business to pay the overhead and the Sunyton office is only producing enough to sustain itself. This, coupled with the fear he has of running into the Centoni boys, causes him to close the River City office and move those agents over to Willow Creek. Now he has little reason to go into downtown River City unless he is going to an AA meeting. He loses another two agents over this move but Suzanne sticks with him as do five others. After everyone gets adjusted to the new arrangement things seem to settle down in Benjamin's life. He now only has two offices to manage and is able to spend more quality time in both. He also spends a lot less time in River City. His agents have business over there and he has an occasion to go to the title company over there but his visits are stealth and brief. Every time he crossed the bridge he feels uneasy and is always looking over his shoulder.

309

J. McGregor Colt

With the exception of Suzanne and Ed Stead and maybe Randall, his upstairs landlord, Benjamin does no socializing. He will go to work and then go home. Occasionally he will go to an AA meeting and occasionally he will go to the grocery store but that's about it. Eventually he even stops going to AA meetings. Benjamin isolates. After having built a successful business and being the life of the party socially he now finds himself with a failing business and no social life whatsoever. His old friends have all abandoned him and his new friends are people he meets in AA.

He is home alone feeling miserable and his phone rings. The caller ID identifies the number as his old house phone. It's Izzy.

"Dad, you gotta come home and get me. Mom is drunk and trying to hit me with a hammer." Izzy is screaming and very upset.

"I can't, honey. You gotta call 911."

"Nooo. I can't. You gotta come get me. Please, she's..." The phone goes dead.

Benjamin's heart is racing. He isn't sure what to do at this point. There's a restraining order, there's the Centoni brothers and there's just no way he is going to chance anything. He calls 911 and tells the dispatcher what Izzy had said. When he hung up he is very nervous and paces around his apartment for several hours before finally lying down and getting some sleep.

In the morning he calls the Willow Creek Police to find out what had happened. They are very vague. They tell him that when they got up to the house, the only one home was the teenage daughter. The mother was not on the premises and the daughter said that everything was fine. Benjamin

310

The Suicide Note

is very confused. It isn't for a couple of days that the story becomes clear. Izzy calls him again from a friend's phone and tells him the horrible things that are happening at the house. She paints a very disturbing picture. Apparently, Brad has moved out, Angelica is drinking heavily and is into some sort of drugs. She is throwing wild parties with Drake and all his friends and buying them booze. She is also having sex with one of Drake's friends. Drake and his friends are seniors in high school now and Angelica is having sex with one of them.

"Can't I just come live with you, Daddy?" Izzy begs.

"Wow, Izzy. I don't know what I can do about that. You told the court that I molested you."

"I know, I know. Mom and Brad made me write those things. They told me what to write. I was afraid. I'm sorry, Dad. I will tell them the truth now."

"Izzy, I will look into seeing what I can do. But I think that there isn't going to be a whole lot. Where are you now? Are you safe?"

"I'm just over at a friend's house but I've gotta be home for dinner."

"Okay. Let me make a couple of phone calls tomorrow. I can't call you so you're gonna have to call me but don't do it again from the house phone."

"Okay, try really hard, Daddy, I'm really scared. It's really bad at home."

So now Brad is out of the picture and Angelica is up to her old tricks again with the sex, drugs and rock and roll. But, what is Benjamin going to do about it? The first thing he does is call his divorce attorney. Roger Parsons tells him to stay out of it. He warns Benjamin that it could very well be a set-up.

311

J. McGregor Colt

He tells Benjamin that there is nothing that he can do about it and adds that if Benjamin pursues it with the police it could backfire on him big-time.

Benjamin then calls his local attorney hoping for a better answer. Old Bill Summerset is of no more help than was Parsons. He too warns Benjamin off.

"Benjamin, stay out of it. It's over. Move on with your life."

Suzanne and Ed Stead say pretty much the same thing. But Benjamin won't listen. He, instead takes his gun, gets in his car and drives over to his old house. He just sits in the dark at the end of the driveway and has only been there for about 15 minutes when a patrol car pulls up behind him and turns on the blue lights. Benjamin quickly hides the pistol under the front seat before the officer tap on the window.

"Benjamin Mathews? Please step out of the car." One officer says very sternly as another officer flashes a light into the car from the passenger side.

Benjamin gets out and is immediately turned around and placed in handcuffs from behind.

"You are under arrest for violation of a restraining order."

Benjamin is hauled up to Goldendale some 30 miles away and spends the night in the Klickitat County Jail, BOOM, just like that. He is able to make one phone call. He calls Ed Stead. Father Stead bails him out the next morning and drives him to the impound yard to retrieve his car. After thanking Ed and saying goodbye Benjamin checks under the driver's seat and finds that his gun is still there. The cops obviously had not searched the car. This is a big relief as Benjamin knew that had they found the gun he would really be in deep trouble.

312

The Suicide Note

Benjamin is now wrought up in anger, imagining all sorts of scenarios. Was it a set-up? Was Izzy complicit in getting him arrested? Was she making up the sex story? Was it all a big hoax? But what would her motivation be? Now, after a big, long, drawn-out divorce in which he lost everything, he is arrested, thrown in jail and will have to defend himself, once again, in a court of law. He is guilty of breaking the restraining order. He figures that he had a good reason to do so but how is he going to prove it? What Benjamin does not know is that his pick-up had been spotted by Drake who had been hanging out at a friend's house across the street. Drake called his mother at home and his mother called the cops. She could have called Antonio so, basically, Benjamin dodged that bullet. But the next day Angelica does call Antonio.

That night Benjamin is upstairs visiting with Randall when they hear something downstairs in Benjamin's apartment. Someone had broken in and is making enough noise to be heard upstairs. Randall signals Benjamin to be quiet as he goes to his gun safe, grabs a rifle and quietly sneaks around the outside of the house. He catches two guys quietly sitting in Benjamin's apartment waiting for him. He surprises them before they are able to do anything in their own defense and runs them off at gunpoint. They move quickly into a dark sedan with Nevada plates and disappear before Randall can catch the license plate numbers.

"I'm calling the cops," Randall proclaims when he gets back upstairs.

"Wait. Why? What was it?"

"There were two thug-looking characters waiting for you in your apartment. I ran them off with this little baby." Randall raises his rifle proudly.

313

J. McGregor Colt

"What?"

"Yeah. You know anybody from Nevada who might want to hurt you?"

"Nevada?"

"Yeah, They drove off in a car from Nevada. I couldn't read the numbers."

"Fuck! Don't call the cops. Those are bad guys. They work for the Centonis. Calling the cops will only make it worse."

"The Centonis? You mean the restaurant guy? What do you mean, are they gangsters or something?" Randall is confused.

"Or something," is Benjamin's only response and he goes back downstairs.

When he gets down there he makes sure the doors are bolted, checks all the windows and pulls the shades. He sits at a small dining table with a lamp turned on and starts writing something on a yellow pad of lined paper. Benjamin is shaking; his hands tremble as he fills an entire page with his thoughts.

I still love Angelica and the kids very, very much and would forgive her and take her back if I could only have my life back. Sorry to whoever I have hurt.

When he's done he stands up, leaving the yellow pad on the table, puts on a jacket, grabs his gun and walks out the door to his pickup. He crosses the bridge and drives around River City for a while. He cruises by his old office and remembers what good times he has had with his agents building that business. He drives by some of the buildings he has sold over the years and reminds himself of all the fine people he had met and the large commission dollars he had

314

The Suicide Note

made doing so. He is in a nostalgic yet melancholy mood when he finally drives down to the waterfront and parks.

He sits in his car at the waterfront and stares up across at the Willow Creek Bluff to his old house. After about an hour, with tears flowing from his eyes and drenching his face, with his sweaty palm, hands shaking and entire body trembling, he slowly raises the gun to his head and pulls the trigger.

Chapter
Twenty Two

Thirteen days later Benjamin wakes up in an ICU room hospital bed in Portland, Oregon with a splitting headache. Fortunately, or unfortunately, depending on which side of the headache you are sitting, a doctor and his wife had been walking their dog along the waterfront when they heard a gunshot and saw a flash coming from inside a parked pickup truck. They immediately called 911 and stanched the blood flowing from Benjamin's head until paramedics were able to stabilize and transport the patient via helicopter to the roof of Oregon Health Science University in Portland.

Benjamin remains in a drug-induced coma long enough for brain specialists to reduce the swelling in his brain and, with some sort of metal plate, replace the portion of

The Suicide Note

Benjamin's skull which had been blown off. It is all very scientific, elaborate, complicated and Benjamin is still alive but the extent of his brain damage is yet to be determined.

Rumors start circulating around the Gorge. Within days most people know that Benjamin was shot in the head down on the River City waterfront. Some speculate that it was a suicide attempt but most believe that he has been the victim of an attack. The staff and agents in his office are most concerned and Suzanne Britt takes on the role of liaison between the office and the hospital. She reports on Benjamin's condition and assures everyone that he is going to make it. Although she knows that it was indeed a suicide attempt, she keeps that knowledge to herself only discussing the matter, in private, with her husband, with Ed Stead and eventually, with Randall.

Randall becomes instantly involved in the whole ugly mess when a police investigator and a social worker knock on his door three days after the incident and ask to search Benjamin's apartment. Randall escorts the two downstairs and watches as they politely, yet diligently, search through Benjamin's belongings. It is Randall who first notices the yellow pad of paper with Benjamin's writing lying face-up on the table. He reads what Benjamin had written before he brings the note to the attention of the others. When the investigators leave they take a few of Benjamin's personal items and the yellow pad with them. Later that same day Ed Stead stops by to talk with Randall and to find out what, if anything, he knows about Benjamin's mental state.

"He was upset about everything that had been going on in his life. He told me that he was afraid of his in-laws. There

317

were some guys snooping around here a couple of days ago." Randall let Ed know what had been going on. "You don't suppose that the Centonis had anything to do with this do you?" Ed seems very concerned with that possibility.

"Well, it's possible I guess but probably not. Benjamin left a note. The cops took it." Randall's words fall on Ed like a boulder.

"Oh, no. This is not good."

The two speak for another hour, reflecting on what a great guy Benjamin is and agree that he didn't deserve any of what he had been going through. They sympathize with his suffering. At this point Benjamin is still in a coma in the ICU. Before they depart they agree to keep the knowledge of the note to themselves out of respect for Benjamin and his family.

The next day Benjamin's sister, Deloris, comes down from Ponder Point and stays in Benjamin's apartment for a couple of days. Benjamin's only other family member, his brother Joe, Jr., or JJ, as he was commonly called, had followed in his father's footsteps and is serving in the Air Force stationed in Hawaii. Benjamin and Deloris were not close but are certainly closer than are Benjamin and JJ. After Benjamin had gone away to college he hardly ever returned to the family home and paid very little attention to JJ whenever he did. The two barely even knew one another but Deloris had made a genuine effort to stay in touch over the years, sharing Christmas cards, birthday greetings and the occasional phone call.

She was vaguely aware of what Benjamin had been suffering the past year and a half and is concerned. She gets to know Randall and listens intently to stories about her brother. Although neither of Benjamin's siblings stayed in close contact

The Suicide Note

with him they knew he had become pretty successful, had his own business and a nice home. They had met his stepchildren and Angelica only once, when Benjamin brought them to his mother's funeral.

Randall does not mention a note in his conversations with Deloris but at one point she asks if he had heard that it was a suicide attempt.

"Yeah, I know that's what some people are saying. I don't know." Randall is vague and evasive and the subject is dropped from her line of questioning.

After Deloris returns to Ponder Point, Randall, Suzanne and Father Ed spend a great deal of time together. They make a couple of car trips to see Benjamin in the hospital but all they can do is stare at him through a glass partition and watch him sleep. The doctors are very good at keeping them apprised as to his condition. Deloris had put them on a list that allowed the doctors to share this information before she went home. When it becomes apparent that Benjamin is going to survive the bullet wound, the prevalent issue becomes the state of his mental health. For the first several weeks of his regained consciousness the hospital staff concentrate on getting him to walk and talk again. His left side has suffered major paralysis and his speech is severely hampered.

He is moved into a rehab wing of the hospital after two month of therapy. Eventually he is able to walk with a crutch but cannot hold a glass of water steady with just one hand. His speech is labored, he remembers little for longer than a few moments and is usually disoriented. His head is filled with a variety of imagined sounds. He hears birds chirping; sometimes he hears a train rumbling towards him or a pack

319

J. McGregor Colt

of bloodhounds barking and howling and getting closer. Psychiatrists will come into his room and talk with him for an hour each day but they find him to be delirious and quasi-incoherent at best. At a time of lapsing clarity, Benjamin does not know how he had been shot, he tells one psychiatrist. He really has no memory of it whatsoever. In fact, he had little memory of anything regarding his most recent life.

As the months pass, still in the mental rehabilitation ward of the hospital, he starts to remember that he is in the real estate business and he thinks that he may be married with children. It's the visits with Father Ed and Suzanne and Randall that finally bring his memory around to realizing that he is no longer married, but that memory will fade in and out and occasionally he will need to be reminded. On the occasions that he is reminded, he just shrugs it off like it was no big deal. His rehab lasts for over eight months before he is released from the hospital. When he is free to go home Father Ed comes in and drives him home. Randall had kindly kept his apartment available for him to return. By now almost everyone in the Gorge knows that Benjamin had attempted suicide but nobody has confronted him with it. Benjamin keeps insisting that he had no idea what had happened.

Benjamin hobbles into his Willow Creek office one morning as if it is no big deal. By the time he had returned to the Gorge he is walking with the use of a cane and speaking coherently, labored, but coherent, people can at least understand him.

"I'm b-back!" he announces.

He is able to drive, as it is only his left side that had been afflicted with a slight paralysis, but not really able to

320

The Suicide Note

think clearly or to speak without some difficulty. He visits both offices that first week he is home. He has some difficulty finding his office in Sunyton. In fact, he has some difficulty finding Sunyton, period. He travels ten miles past the three Sunyton exits before he realizes it and has to turn around. At times his mind will drift off and he will have to reset. The more he gets out and about, the more he makes people feel uncomfortable.

They all know that he had tried to commit suicide but nobody feels comfortable challenging him on it when he says things like: "Yeah, the cops are still looking for the guys who shot me."

He makes it very awkward and pretty soon all his agents, with the exception of Suzanne, abandon him. When the Willow Creek agents quit the receptionist refuses to be left alone in the office with Benjamin. She is afraid of him.

"He creeps me out," she confides in Suzanne.

The Sunyton office goes on strike and gives Benjamin an ultimatum; either sell the operation to them or they will all pack up and leave. He takes it well. He really doesn't understand what is happening but he takes it well. Bill Summerset draws up the paperwork and Suzanne helps with the transition. The only sales agent the Mathews Group has left now is Suzanne. The receptionist is hanging on because she needs a paycheck and Suzanne has promised her that she will be there everyday.

Most are afraid of Benjamin or at least weirded out by him. He isn't violent or crazy or anything, he's just weird. His speech is labored, he walks with a limp, his left hand is curled up and he, unintentionally of course, makes people

321

J. McGregor Colt

feel uncomfortable. Probably the oddest thing about him is that he always has a smile on his face and goes out of his way to say a hello to every person he passes on the sidewalk. It is awkward that he is in complete denial of his suicide attempt, it is uncomfortable that he has a speech impediment, and it is damn weird that he always has a crooked smile on his face with distant eyes in his head looking back at you. Most think him to be a complete crackpot compared to the pre-head-wound Benjamin.

Eventually it becomes apparent that Benjamin cannot continue operating as a real estate broker. He cannot concentrate on anything for a sustained period of time and his financial picture is deteriorating rapidly. Now that he only has but one office, Suzanne and the receptionist are able to keep the bills paid but there is no longer any commission coming in and eventually they have to close down. Benjamin puts the building up for sale and in a surprisingly short period of time it sells.

Benjamin is able to live on the proceeds from the sale of the office building for about a year. Over the months he doesn't seem to be getting any better and it is questionable if he is even capable of living by himself anymore. Ed and Suzanne will come by and make sure he has groceries. They only bring him microwaveable food as they do not trust him operating the stove. There were a couple of occasions when he had put something on the stove-top and forgotten about it. It wasn't until Randall smelled smoke upstairs that a fire was averted. Randall finally unplugs the stove and Benjamin is limited to the microwave.

One day when Benjamin is in River City just wobbling around he runs into Antonio and Giorgio coming toward

322

The Suicide Note

him on the sidewalk. As the two approach they start heckling him.

"Hey; look here, it's Benji. How you doing, Benji?" Giorgio asks insincerely.

"Benji, you wanna borrow my gun and try again?" Antonio gets right up in his face.

"Hi guys. Gee, I haven't seen you in a while." Benjamin isn't really sure who Giorgio and Antonio are but he pretends he does to be polite. The heckling stops once they both realize it.

"Listen to those birds. Isn't it b-beautiful?" he queries.

"Man, he is completely out of it," Antonio says to Giorgio as they walk off.

Benjamin doesn't really remember anybody except for the people he sees on a regular basis. He visits with Suzanne and Father Ed almost every day. They will meet in a coffee shop in River City and he will remember the people who work in the coffee shop. Of course Randall is always familiar to him but there are few others.

Eventually they move Benjamin into an assisted living facility and get him a job at Walmart as a greeter so he will have something to do, something for him to get up and look forward to. Benjamin makes a fabulous greeter at Walmart. He is genuinely friendly and welcoming to everyone who walks in the door. Once in a while there will be people who know him from prior days. They will stop and be friendly with him and he will try and act like he knows who they were.

Every Thursday he visits with a River City psychiatrist. The psychiatrist is never able to get Benjamin to admit that he had tried to take his own life. The evidence is presented and Benjamin will always deny it. He will say that he must have

323

J. McGregor Colt

been playing around with the gun and it went off accidentally. One time he even suggests that maybe someone tried to kill him and make it look like suicide.

Finally Father Ed Stead attends a session with him in an attempt to get him to come clean with the psychiatrist. They feel that the sooner he confronts the truth the sooner he can heal.

"Benjamin, the doctor and I feel that it is time for you to face the fact that you tried to kill yourself."

"Oh, come on, you guys, that's crazy," Benjamin proclaims.

"Okay, look, Benjamin. How do you explain this?"

Ed reaches in a bag he is carrying, pulls out the yellow pad and hands him the suicide note. Benjamin looks down at what is in Ed's hand and recoils. He wants nothing to do with it, he averts his eyes. In the distance he can hear a train coming and as it gets closer he imagines getting on the train and taking it to Chicago. He figures that they might have a pretty nice Walmart there and that they would probably hire him. He knows he's a really good greeter. He imagines what Chicago might be like. The bloodhounds are closing in. The howling is overwhelming.

THE END

The Suicide Note

J. McGregor Colt

Made in the USA
Middletown, DE
14 October 2023